"[Ross Macdonald] carried form and style about as far as they would go, writing classic family tragedies in the guise of private detective mysteries."

—*The Guardian*

* * *

"The most important successor to the Chandler/Hammett tradition, as well as the writer who elevated the hard-boiled private-eye novel to a new 'literary' form."

—**Marcia Muller**

* * *

"Ross Macdonald's work has consistently nourished me.... I have turned to it often to hear what I should like to call the justice of its voice and to be enlightened by its wisdom, delighted by its imagination, and, not incidentally, superbly entertained."

—**Thomas Berger**

* * *

"Without in the least abating my admiration for Dashiell Hammett and Raymond Chandler, I should like to venture the heretical suggestion that Ross Macdonald is a better novelist than either of them."

—**Anthony Boucher,**
New York Times Book Review

Also by Ross Macdonald

The Moving Target
The Chill
The Galton Case
The Blue Hammer
The Far Side of the Dollar

Published by
WARNER BOOKS

Praise for
THE WAY SOME PEOPLE DIE
and Ross Macdonald

"Macdonald's best to date...and automatically the top hard-boiled novel of the year."
—*New York Times*

* * *

"A subtle hard-boiled gem."
—**Kathleen Sproul**, *Saturday Review*

* * *

"Let's be honest: Ross Macdonald remains *the* grandmaster, taking the crime novel to new heights by imbuing it with psychological resonance, complexity of story, and richness of style that remain awe-inspiring. Those of us in his wake owe a debt that can never be paid."
—**Jonathan Kellerman**

* * *

"A more serious and complex writer than Chandler and Hammett ever were."
—**Eudora Welty**

more....

"Macdonald should not be limited in audience to connoisseurs of mystery fiction. He is one of a handful of writers in the genre whose worth and quality surpass the limitations of the form."
—**Robert Kirsch**, *Los Angeles Times*

* * *

"Ross Macdonald gives to the detective story that accent of class that the late Raymond Chandler did."
—**Seymour Korman**, *Chicago Tribune*

* * *

"It was not just that Ross Macdonald taught us how to write; he did something much more, he taught us how to read, and how to think about life, and maybe in some small, but mattering way, how to live....I owe him."
—**Robert B. Parker**

* * *

"Ross Macdonald is an important American novelist."
—**William Hogan**, *San Francisco Chronicle*

* * *

"Ross Macdonald must be ranked high amongst American thriller writers."
—*The Times Literary Supplement* (London)

ROSS MACDONALD

◆

THE WAY SOME PEOPLE DIE

A LEW ARCHER NOVEL

WARNER BOOKS

A Warner Communications Company

WARNER BOOKS EDITION

Copyright © 1951 by Alfred A. Knopf, Inc.
All rights reserved under International and Pan-American Copyright
Conventions. This book may not be reproduced in whole or in part, by
mimeograph or any other means, without permission.

This Warner Books Edition is published by arrangement with
Alfred A. Knopf, Inc., 201 East 50th Street, New York, New York 10022

Cover design by Jackie Merri Meyer
Cover illustration by Gary Kelley

Warner Books, Inc.
666 Fifth Avenue
New York, N.Y. 10103

 A Warner Communicatons Company

Printed in the United States of America

First Warner Books Printing: July, 1990

10 9 8 7 6 5 4 3 2 1

1

The house was in Santa Monica on a cross street between the boulevards, within earshot of the coast highway and rifleshot of the sea. The street was the kind that people had once been proud to live on, but in the last few years it had lost its claim to pride. The houses had too many stories, too few windows, not enough paint. Their history was easy to guess: they were one-family residences broken up into apartments and light-housekeeping rooms, or converted into tourist homes. Even the palms that lined the street looked as if they had seen their best days and were starting to lose their hair.

I parked in front of the number I had been given and leaned sideways in the seat to have a look at the house. The numerals, 1348, were made of rusted metal and tacked diagonally across one of the round porch pillars. A showcard above, printed black on white, offered ROOMS FOR TOURISTS. There were several rattan chairs and a faded green glider on the porch, which covered the width of the house. A second-story porch, with more rattan, was surrounded by a wooden railing that looked unsafe. The third story had Gothic-looking towers at each corner, fake battlements that time had taken and made ridiculous. The roller blinds were low over the windows on all three levels, so they stared at me sleepy-eyed.

The house didn't look as if it had money in it, or ever would have again. I went in anyway, because I'd liked the woman's voice on the telephone.

She came to the door in a hurry when I knocked. A tall woman in her fifties with worried vague dark eyes in a worried long face, a black crepe dress over a thick corseted body. A detective was an occasion in her life. Her iron-gray hair was set in a sharp new wave that smelt of the curling-iron, her nose and

1

cheeks and chin were stark with powder. The light fell through the purple glass in the fanlight over the door and made her complexion livid.

The woman's voice was her best feature, gentle and carefully modulated, in a low register: "I'm Mrs. Samuel Lawrence. You're Mr. Archer, of course? You got here in no time at all."

"The traffic's not so bad between nine and ten."

"Come in, Mr. Archer. Let me make you a cup of tea. I'm just having a midmorning snack myself. Since I've been doing all my own work, I find I need a bite between meals to sustain me."

I stepped inside, and the screen door swung to languidly behind me. The hall was still and cool and smelt of wax. The floor was old parquetry, and its polished patterns glowed like jewels. A carpeted stairway climbed to the high dim ceiling. An ancient oak hatstand with polished brass hangers stood at the foot of the stairs. The contrast with the traffic I'd been fighting gave me a queer feeling, as if I'd stepped backward in time, or out of it entirely.

She led me to an open door at the rear. "This is my own little sitting-room, if you please. I reserve the front parlor for guests, though I must say they haven't been using it lately. Of course it's the off-season, I only have the three just now, my regular, and a lovely young couple from Oregon, honeymooners! If only Galley had married a man like that—but sit down, Mr. Archer."

She pulled out a chair from the heavy refectory table in the middle of the room. It was a small room, and it was as crowded with coffee- and end-tables, chairs and hassocks and bookcases, as a second-hand furniture store. The horizontal surfaces were littered with gewgaws, shells and framed photographs, vases and pincushions and doilies. If the lady had come down in the world, she'd brought a lot down with her. My sensation of stepping into the past was getting too strong for comfort. The half-armed chair closed on me like a hand.

I took the present by the tail and dragged it into the room: "Galley," I said. "Is she the daughter you mentioned?"

The question struck her like an accusation, disorganizing her charm. She didn't like the look of the present at all. She faced it when she had to, with a face clouded by bewilderment and shame. "Yes. My daughter Galatea. It's why I phoned you, as

I said." Her gaze wandered, and lighted on the teapot that stood on the table. "You must let me pour you some tea before we get down to business. It's freshly made."

Her hand on the teapot was cracked and grained by dirty work, but she poured with an air. I said I took mine straight. The tea tasted like a clear dark dripping from the past. My grandmother came back with it, in crisp black funeral silks, and I looked out the window to dispel her. I could see the Santa Monica pier from where I sat, and beyond it the sea and the sky like the two curved halves of a blue Easter egg.

"Nice view you have from here."

She smiled over her teacup. "Yes. I bought it for the view. I shouldn't really say I've bought it. It's mortgaged, after all."

I finished my tea and set the thin white cup in the thin white saucer. "Well, Mrs. Lawrence, let's have it. What happened to your daughter?"

"I don't know," she said. "That's what upsets me so. She simply disappeared a couple of months ago—"

"From here?"

"No, not from here. Galley hasn't lived at home in recent years, though she always came to visit me at least once a month. She was working in Pacific Point, a special-duty nurse in the hospital there. I always hoped for something better for Galley—my husband Dr. Lawrence was a medical man, and a very well respected one, too—but she wanted to be a nurse and she seemed to be very happy in the work—"

She was veering away from the present fact again. "When did she disappear?"

"Last December, a few days before Christmas." This was the middle of March, which made it about three months. "Galley *always* came home for Christmas. We never failed to decorate a tree. Last Christmas for the first time I spent Christmas by myself. Even her card came a day late." And the vague eyes swam with self-pity.

"If you've heard from her, I wouldn't call it a disappearance. Can I have a look at the card?"

"Of course." She took a black leather volume of Swedenborg out of the bookcase, opened it, and drew out a large square envelope which she handed to me as if it contained a check. "But she *has* disappeared, Mr. Archer. I haven't seen her since early in December. None of her friends has seen her since the first of the year.''

"How old is she?''

"Twenty-four. She'll be twenty-five next month, April the 9th, if she's alive.'' She bowed her face in her hands, having brought herself to tears.

"She'll probably have many happy returns,'' I said. "A twenty-five-year-old registered nurse can look after herself.''

"You don't know Galley,'' the damp voice said from the hidden face. "She's always been so fascinating to men, and she's never realized how evil men can be. I've tried to unknow the error, but it does no good. I keep thinking of the Black Dahlia, all the young girls that have been stolen away and destroyed by evil men.'' The wide gold wedding band on the hand over her face gleamed dully like a despairing hope.

I took out the card, which was large and expensive, decorated with a sparkling mica snow scene. Inside it said:

> Though my boat has left the harbor
> In the sea of life so wide
> I think with cheer of Mother Dear
> Each joyous Christmastide.

It was subscribed in green ink by a bold and passionate hand: "Much love, Galley.'' The envelope had been mailed in San Francisco on December 24.

"Did—does your daughter have friends in San Francisco?''

"Not that I know of.'' The woman showed me her face, with tear-tracks in the powder. She blew her nose discreetly in a piece of pink Kleenex. "The last few years, since she graduated, I didn't really know her friends.''

"Do you think she's in San Francisco?''

"I don't know. She came back from there, you see. She didn't come to me, but the man who runs the apartments down there, a Mr. Raisch, saw her. She had a small furnished apartment in Pacific Point, and about the end of December she turned up there and moved out, took away all her things. There was a man with her.''

"What sort of a man?''

"Mr. Raisch didn't say. There seemed to be some kind of secret about the man—something sinister.''

"Is that a fact, or only your impression?"

"My impression. I suppose I've been too open to impression, lately. I can't tell you what my life has been these last few weeks. I've gone down to Pacific Point on the bus half a dozen times, whenever I could get away. I've talked to the nurses that knew her at the hospital. She hasn't been near the hospital since before Christmas, when she finished her last case. It was a man named Speed who had been shot in the stomach. The police came to question him, and he nearly died. The people at the hospital seemed to think that this Speed person was a gangster. That's one of the things that frightens me. I've hardly slept a wink for weeks and weeks." There were deep bluish hollows under her eyes, pitiable and ugly in the morning light from the window.

"Actually, though," I said, "you've got nothing concrete to be afraid about."

"My only daughter is gone—"

"Girls leave home all the time. It tears the hearts out of their mothers, but they don't know it. They don't find out till their own kids grow up and do it to them. She probably ran off and married this man that was with her at the apartment."

"That's what Mr. Raisch thought. Still Galley wouldn't marry without letting me know. Besides, I've checked the registrations in Pacific Point, and Los Angeles as well, and there is no record of a marriage."

"That doesn't prove a thing. You can fly to New York or Hawaii in a day." I took a cigarette from a pack in my pocket and automatically asked her: "Mind if I smoke?"

Her face froze, as if I had suggested an obscenity. "Smoke if you must, sir. I know what a hold the nicotine habit has on its victims. Dr. Lawrence was a smoker for years, until he finally broke free, with God's help."

I replaced the cigarette in my pocket and stood up to leave. Even with a million dollars, she wouldn't have been the kind of woman I wanted to work for. And she probably didn't have two nickels to rub against each other. As for the daughter, ten to one she'd simply decided to have a life of her own.

I put it less bluntly to her: "I think you should take it to Missing Persons, Mrs. Lawrence. I don't think you have anything to worry about, but if you have, they can do more for you than I can. It would be a waste of money to hire me. I charge fifty a day and expenses. The police do everything free.''

Her answer surprised me: "I expected to pay you well. And I am not going to go to the police.''

"Why not? Missing daughters are their specialty. They've got a national system set up to find them.''

Grim bony lines came out in her face, and her eyes weren't vague anymore. "If Galley is living in sin with some man, it's nobody's business but my own.''

"Aren't you jumping to conclusions?''

"I tell you you don't know Galley. Men have been after her since high school, like flies to honey. She's a good girl, Mr. Archer, I know how good. But I was a handsome girl myself when I was young, and I've seen the pitfalls of the flesh. I want to know what has happened to my daughter.''

I stood by the table and lit my cigarette and dropped the match on the tea tray. She didn't say a word. After a stretching moment of silence, she reached from her chair and took a framed photograph from the top of the bookcase. "Look at her, you'll understand what I mean.''

I took the picture from her hand. There was something slightly shady about the transaction, a faint implication that she was offering her daughter's beauty as part payment on my services. Or maybe I was having impressions. I had one when I looked at the girl's face. It was passionate and bold like her handwriting. Even in a white nurse's cap, and a high chaste collar she was a girl you saw once and never forgot.

"It was her graduation picture, taken three years ago, but she still looks exactly the same. Isn't she pretty?''

Pretty was hardly the word. With her fierce curled lips, black eyes and clean angry bones she must have stood out in her graduating class like a chicken hawk in a flock of pullets.

"If you want to spend fifty dollars,'' I said, "I'll go down to Pacific Point today and see what I can find out. Write down her last address and the name of whoever you talked to at the hospital.''

With the caution of a pheasant hen returning to her nest, she went to an old-fashioned sewing machine by the window, lifted the closed top and removed a worn black purse from its hiding place. Opening the tarnished clasp, she rummaged in the purse and counted five reluctant tens onto the table.

Dropping my ashes in my empty teacup, I noticed the arrangements of the leaves. My grandmother would have said it meant money and a dark stranger. The stranger could have been male or female, vertical or horizontal, depending on how you looked at the bottom of the cup.

2

I drove south through Long Beach to Pacific Point. Crossing the mesa that flanked it to the northwest, you could see the town spread out, from the natural harbor half-enclosed by the curving finger of land that gave the place its name, to the houses on the ridge above the fogline. It rose from sea level in a gentle slope, divided neatly into social tiers, like something a sociologist had built to prove a theory. Tourists and transients lived in hotels and motels along the waterfront. Behind them a belt of slums lay ten blocks deep, where the darker half of the population lived and died. On the other side of the tracks—the tracks were there—the business section wore its old Spanish façades like icing on a stale cake. The people who worked in the stores and offices inhabited the grid of fifty-foot lots that covered the next ten blocks. On the slopes above them the owners and managers enjoyed their patios and barbecue pits. And along the top of the ridge lived the really wealthy, who had bought their *pieds-à-terre* in Pacific Point because it reminded them of Juan-les-Pins.

The wife of a client of mine had taken an overdose of sleeping pills in a Pacific Point hotel, so I knew where the hospital was. I made a left turn off the highway and drove through empty afternoon streets to the hospital building. It was a rambling place of bilious yellow plaster, and the sight of it depressed me. My client's wife had died of the sleeping pills. All that he really wanted was a divorce.

After a good deal of palaver I found myself in the basement waiting-room of the hospital's X-ray department, talking to a plump young thing in white nylon. Her arms and shoulders glowed a pleasant pink through this progressive fabric, and her straw-blond hair was cut sleek and short. Her name was Audrey Graham, and she didn't mind talking at all. I told her the truth—that I was a detective looking for Galley Lawrence because her mother was worried—which was a refreshing change from my usual approach.

"I never did know Galley really well," she said. "Sure, we were in the same class at Los Angeles General and graduated together and all. But you know how some girls are, introverted like. I'm more of an extrovert myself. I like meeting people, in a nice way, you know what I mean. Are you really a detective? I never met a *private* detective before."

"Yeah," I said. "The introverted kind. Mrs. Lawrence said you were Galley's roommate."

"Just for a while, last year. She got a chance at this apartment and I went in on the rent, but after a couple of months I found a place of my own. We agreed to disagree, you know what I mean."

"Not exactly."

She perched on the edge of the receptionist's desk and swung one round silk leg. "Well, I mean we got along all right but we didn't live the same. She ran around a lot and came in all hours of the day and night and it wasn't so happy-making, me with a regular job, I mean, and a steady boy friend. When Galley was on a case she was spit-and-polish but in between she liked to break loose a bit, and she was crazy for men—I've never been myself. I mean, a girl has a right to her own life and she can do what she pleases as far as I'm concerned, only she shouldn't try to attract a boy that's going with somebody else."

She colored slowly, aware that she'd given herself away. The round eyes in the rosy face were ice-blue, cold with memory. If Audrey Graham was Galley's best friend, Galley had no friends.

"Where did you live with her, and when?"

"August and September, I guess it was—I had my vacation in July. Galley found this little place in Acacia Court, one bedroom. It had twin beds, but that didn't work out either."

She'd embarrassed herself again, and the flush rose higher, to the roots of the straw-colored hair.

"What kind of men did she run around with?"

"All kinds. She had no discrimination, you know what I mean." The refrain was getting on my nerves. "My boy friend is going to college under the G.I. and you'd think a girl who thinks she's something special because her father was a doctor, or so she claimed—you'd think she'd watch out who she went out with. Of course she had a couple of doctors on the string but that was married stuff and I never could see it myself. She had boys from the Safeway, a law clerk, a fellow that said he was a writer but I never heard of him, even one that looked like a Mexican once. Italian, anyway."

"Know any of their names?"

"I mostly knew them by their first names, when I knew them. I wouldn't want to tell you the doctors' names. If you want my honest opinion, Galley just got sick of this town and ran off with one of her men. Las Vegas or someplace. She was always talking about seeing the world. She set a high opinion on herself. She blew her money on clothes she couldn't afford and half the time she was eating off of me."

There were footsteps in the hall, and the girl slid off the desk. A tall man in a white tunic looked in at the door. His eyes were masked by wide red spectacles. "The pyelogram's on the table, Audrey, be ready in five minutes." He turned to me. "Are you the barium enema for tomorrow?" I told him that I wasn't, and he went away.

"You can be glad you're not," the girl said. "I'm afraid I have to go now."

"He said five minutes. What about this man Speed, the bullet in the stomach Galley nursed?"

"Oh, that was Herman Speed. He had peritonitis from lead poisoning or something, she didn't go out with him. He was on Ward C for three weeks last December, and then he left town. I heard he was run out of town. He promoted the wrestling down at the Arena and there was an editorial in the paper about how he was shot in a gang war or something. I wouldn't know. I didn't read it myself, one of the doctors told me."

"She didn't leave town with him?"

"No, she was still in town after he left. I saw her one night with this Mexican-looking guy, I forget his name. Turpentine or something. I think he worked for Speed. He came to see him a couple of times when he was on Ward C. Tarantula, or something?''

''That's a kind of spider.''

''Yeah. Well, Galley was no fly. Anybody she went with, she had a darn good reason. I'll say one thing for her, she knew how to have a good time. But what she saw in this guy that worked for Speed—I wouldn't trust a Mexican or Italian, they have no respect for women.''

I was getting a little tired of her opinions, and she was repeating herself. I got out of my chair and stood up. ''Thanks very much, Miss Graham.''

''Don't mention it. If you need any more information, I get off here at half past four.''

''I may see you then. By the way, did you tell Mrs. Lawrence what you told me?''

''No, of course I didn't. I wouldn't ruin a girl's reputation with her own mother. I don't mean that Galley had a *really* bad reputation or I wouldn't of lived with her. But you know what I mean.''

3

Acacia Court was within easy walking distance of the hospital, on a quiet middle-class street across from a schoolground. It probably wasn't so quiet when school was out. The court consisted of ten small stucco bungalows ranged five on each side of a gravel driveway that led to the garages at the rear. The first bungalow had a wooden office sign over the door, with a cardboard NO VACANCY sign attached to it. There were two acacia trees in the front yard, blanketed with yellow chenille-like blossoms.

When I got out of my car a mockingbird swooped from one

of the trees and dived for my head. I gave him a hard look and he flew up to a telephone wire and sat there swinging back and forth and laughing at me. The laughter actually came from a red-faced man in dungarees who was sitting in a deck-chair under the tree. His mirth brought on some sort of an attack, probably asthmatic. He coughed and choked and wheezed, and the chair creaked under his weight and his face got redder. When it was over he removed a dirty straw hat and wiped his bare red pate with a handkerchief.

"Excuse me. The little devil does it all the time. He's my aerial defense. I think it's your hair they want, to build a nest. He drives the nurses crazy."

I stepped in under the shade of the tree. "Are you Mr. Raisch?"

"That's my name. I told them they better wear hats but they never do. Back where I was brought up, in Little Egypt, a lady never went out without a hat, and some of these girls don't even own one. You wanted to see me? I got no vacancy." He jerked a large gray thumb at the sign over the door. "Anyway I just take mostly girls from the hospital and a few married couples."

I told him I wasn't a prospective tenant, but that was all I had a chance to tell him.

"I can afford to pick and choose," he said. "My place doesn't look like much from the outside, maybe, but she's in absolutely tiptop shape. Redecorated the whole thing with my own two hands last year, put in new linoleum, fixed up the plumbing. And I didn't raise the rents a red cent. No wonder they come to me. What did you want to see me about? I don't need a thing if you're selling."

"I'm looking for Galley Lawrence. Remember her?"

"I should say I do." His blue eyes had narrowed and were appraising me. "I'm not so old and dried up that I forget a pretty girl like that one. Even is she had a hump on her back and one glass eye I wouldn't disremember her. I don't get the chance; seems that every few days somebody comes around asking after Galley. What do you want with her?"

"I want to talk with her. What did the others want?"

"Well, her mother was here a couple of times. You'd think I was in the white-slave traffic the way that biddy talked to me, and all I did was rent her daughter a home. Then there was all her young men calling up—I practically had to have my phone disconnected back around the first of the year. You one of her young men?''

"No." But I was grateful for the adjective.

"Let's see, you're from L.A., ain't you?'' The eyes were still appraising me. "You got an L.A. license on your car. These other customers were from L.A., the one from the pinball company. You work for the pinball company?''

"Not me.''

"You're carrying a gun. Or maybe you got a tumor under your armpit.''

I told him I was a private detective, and why I was looking for Galley. "Do you carry a gun if you work for the pinball company?''

"These customers did, the thin one anyway. He let me know he had a gun, he thought he'd throw a scare into me. I didn't tell him I was handling firearms before his dam dropped him on the curb and kicked him into the gutter. He wanted to think he was smooth and sharp and I let him go on thinking it.''

"You're fairly sharp yourself.''

The flattery pleased him, and his big red face relaxed into smiles again. He felt the need to express himself some more. "I didn't get where I am by sitting on my rump waiting for the cash to grow on trees. No sir, I been in every one of the forty-eight states and I watered every one of them with my good sweat. I lost a fortune in Florida and that's the last time anybody put anything over on me.''

I sat down tentatively in the canvas camp-chair beside his, and offered him a cigarette.

He waved it away. "Not for me. Asthma and heart condition. But you go right ahead. The old biddy must be really anxious, hiring detectives and all.''

I was beginning to think she had reason to be anxious. "You said the pinball boys tried to scare you. Any particular reason?''

"They thought I might know where Galley Lawrence was. Her and this slob she went away with, some kind of a dago or wop. They said his name was Tarantine, and I told them it sounded like something you put on your hair. The lean one wanted to make something out of that, but the short one thought it was funny. He said this Tarantine was *in* his hair.''

"Did he explain what he meant?''

"He didn't say very much. Seems that this Tarantine ran off with the collection money, something like that. They wanted to know if Galley left a forwarding address, but she didn't. I told them try the police and that was another laugh for the little short one. The lean one said they'd handle it themselves. That's when he showed me the gun, a little black automatic. I told them maybe *I* should try the police, and the short one made him put it away again."

"Who were they?"

"Pinball merchants, they said. They looked like thugs to me. They didn't leave their calling cards but I wouldn't forget them if I saw them again. The one with the automatic, the one that worked for the other one, he was as thin as a rake. When he turned sideways he cast no shadow. Frontways he had his shoulders built out so his jacket hung on him like a scarecrow. He had a jail complexion, or a lunger's, and little pinhead eyes and he talked like he thought he was tough. Take his gun away and I could break him in two, even at my age. And I'm old enough to qualify for the pension, if I needed it."

"But you don't."

"No sir. I'm a product of individual enterprise. The other one, the boss, was really tough. He walked into my office like he owned it, only when he saw he couldn't push me around he tried to be friendly-like. I'd just as soon make friends with a scorpion. One of these poolroom cowboys that made his way in the rackets and was trying to dress like a gentleman. Panama hat, cream gabardine double-breasted suit, hand-painted tie, waxy yellow shoes, and he rode up here in a car as long as a fire truck. A black limousine, and I thought the undertaker was coming for me for sure."

"You expecting the undertaker?"

"Any day now, son." He started to laugh, and then decided against it. "But it'll take more than an L.A. thief with an innertube on his waistline to kiss me off, I can tell you. The little man was hard, though. He had his own shoulders and you could see on his face that he'd taken his share of beatings. He had a way of looking at you, soft and steady-like, that chilled you off some. And the way he talked about this Tarantine, the man was as good as dead."

"What about Galley Lawrence?"

He shrugged his heavy collapsing shoulders. "I don't know.

I guess the idea was if they found her this Tarantine would be tagging along. I didn't even tell them I knew him by sight.''

"You didn't tell Mrs. Lawrence either. Did you?''

"Sure I did. Twice. I didn't like the lady but she had a right to know. I told her when Galley moved out this Tarantine carted her stuff away in his automobile. That was on December the 30th. She was away for a week or ten days and when she came back she said she wanted out. I could have soaked her thirty days' notice but I thought what the hell, I had people waiting. She drove away with Tarantine and I haven't seen her since. Didn't even tell me where she was going——''

"Mrs. Lawrence didn't know Tarantine's name.''

"Neither did I, till the pinball merchants told me. They only came here two days ago, Saturday it was, and Mrs. Lawrence hasn't been here for weeks. I thought she gave up.''

"She didn't. Can you tell me anything else about Tarantine?''

"I can tell you his fortune, maybe, and I don't need a Ouija board. Folsom or San Quentin, if the long and the short of it don't catch him first. He's one of these pretty-boy wops, curly black hair that the women want to run their fingers through. Hollywood clothes, fast roadster, poolroom brains. You know the type. You'd think a girl like Galley would show better taste.''

"Think she married him?''

"How the hell would I know? I've seen pretty young girls like her take up with coyotes and live on carrion for the rest of their lives. I hope she didn't.''

"You said he drove a roadster.''

"That's right. Prewar Packard with bronze paint and white sidewalls. She hopped into the front seat and tooted away and that was the last of Galley Lawrence. If you find her, you let me know. I liked the girl.''

"Why?''

"She was full of vim and vigor. I like a girl with personality. I've got a lot of personality myself and when I see somebody else that has it my heart goes out to them.''

Thanking him, I retreated to the sidewalk. His loud optimistic voice followed me: "But you can't get by on personality alone, I learned that in the depression. They say there's another one coming but I don't worry. I'm sitting pretty, ready for anything.''

I called back: "You forgot the hydrogen bomb."

"The hell I did," he yelled triumphantly. "I got the bomb outwitted. The doctors says my heart won't last two years."

4

It took me half an hour to find the Point Arena, though I had a hazy notion where it was. It stood in the lower depths of town, near the railroad tracks. Beyond the tracks the packing-case shanties of a small hobo jungle leaned in the corner of a dusty field. One of the huts had a roof of beaten gas-tins which gleamed like fish scales in the sun. A man lay still as a lizard in its dooryard.

From the outside the arena looked like an old freight warehouse, except for a kind of box-office at the street entrance, the size of a telephone booth. A dingy yellow billboard over the closed box-office window announced: WRESTLING EVERY TUES., GENERAL .80, RESERVED 1.20, RINGSIDE 1.50, CHILDREN .25. A door to the right of the window was standing open, and I went in.

The corridor was so dark, after the bright sun, that I could barely see. The only light came from a window high in the left wall. At least it served as a window; it was a square hole cut in the unpainted boards and covered with heavy chicken-wire. Stretching up on my toes I could see into the cubicle on the other side. It contained two straight chairs, a scarred desk bare of everything but a telephone, and an heirloom brass spittoon. The walls were decorated with calendar nudes, telephone numbers scrawled in pencil, publicity photographs of Lord Albert Trompington-Whist the Pride of the British Empire, Basher Baron Flores from the Azores, and other scions of the European aristocracy.

Somewhere out of sight a punching-bag was rat-tat-tatting on a board. I stepped through a doorless aperture opposite the door

I'd come in by, and found myself in the main hall. It was comparatively small, with seats for maybe a thousand rising on four sides to the girders that held up the roof. An ingot of lead-gray light from a skylight fell through the moted air onto the empty roped square on the central platform. Still no people, but you could tell that people had been there. The same air had hung for months in the windowless building, absorbing the smells of human sweat and breath, roasted peanuts and beer, white and brown cigarettes, Ben Hur perfume and bay rum and hair oil and tired feet. A social researcher with a good nose could have written a Ph.D. thesis about that air.

The punching-bag kept up an underbeat to the symphony of odors, tum-tee-tum, tum-tee-tum, tum-tee-tum-tee-tum-tee-tum. I moved toward a door with a push-bar marked EXIT, and the beat sounded louder. The door opened into an alley that led to the rear of the building. A colored boy was working on a bag fastened to the corner of the wall. On the other side of the alley a Negro woman was watching him across a board fence. Her black arms rested on the top of the fence and her chin was laid on her arms. Her great dark eyes had swallowed the rest of her face, and looked as if they were ready to swallow the boy.

"Who runs this place?"

He went on beating the bag with his left, his back to me and the woman. He was naked to the waist; the rest of him was covered by a pair of faded khakis, and pitiful canvas sneakers that showed half his bare black toes. He switched to his right without breaking the drumming rhythm. The full sun was on him, and the sweat stood out on his back and made it glisten.

He was light-heavy, I guessed, but he didn't look more than eighteen, in spite of the G.I. pants. With his height and heavy bone-structure, he'd grow up into a heavy-weight. The woman looked as if she could hardly wait.

After a while she called to him: "The gentlemen asked something, Simmie." All gentlemen were white; all whites were gentlemen.

He dropped his arms and turned slowly. The taut muscles of his chest and stomach stood out in detailed relief like moulded iron sculpture. The head was narrow and long, with a slanting forehead, small eyes, broad nose, thick mouth. He breathed through the nose. "You want me?"

"I wondered who runs this place."

"I'm the janitor. You want something?"

"I'd like to talk to the boss. Is he around?"

"Not today. Mr. Tarantine is out of town."

"What about Mr. Speed? Isn't Herman Speed the boss around here?"

"Not any more he isn't. Mr. Tarantine been running things since the beginning of the year. Before that."

"What happened to Herman?" The surprise in my voice sounded hollow. "He leave town?"

"Yeah. Mr. Speed left town." He wasted no words.

"He got shot," the woman said. "Somebody riddled his guts. It broke his health. It was a crying shame, too, he was a fine big man."

"Shut up, Violet," the boy said. "You don't know nothing about it."

"Shut up yourself," she answered in ready rapartee.

"Who shot him?" I asked her.

"Nobody knows. Maybe he knows, but he wouldn't tell the police, he was real tight-mouthed."

"I said shut up," the boy repeated. "You're wasting the gentleman's time."

I said: "Where's Tarantine?"

"Nobody knows that either," the woman said. "He left town last week and nobody seen him since. Looks as if they left young Simmie here to put on the shows all by himself." She laughed throatily. "Maybe if you talked to Mrs. Tarantine, she might know where he is. She just lives down the road a few blocks from here."

The boy jumped for the fence on silent feet, but the woman was already out of his reach. "Stay on your own side, Simmie, I given you fair warning. Trim's in his room."

"You're trying to get me in trouble, been trying to get me in trouble all winter long. Ain't you? Why don't you get out of my sight and stay out of my sight?"

She wiggled her heavy body disdainfully, and disappeared around the corner of the buildings: warped plyboard cubicles laid end to end like miniature ten-foot boxcars and fronting on another alley. There were dark faces at some of the windows in the row and after a while the woman appeared at one of them.

The boy was talking by then. I'd broken through his reserve by praising his muscles and asking about his fights. He had beaten the local talent, he said, and was grooming himself for his professional debut. He called it that. Unfortunately they hadn't had fights in Pacific Point since he started to get his growth. Mr. Tarantine was going to try and get him on a card at San Diego one of these weeks. I suggested that Mr. Tarantine was a pretty good friend of his, and he agreed.

"I hear he married a beautiful wife."

"Mr. Tarantine got no wife."

"I thought Violet said something about a Mrs. Tarantine."

"That's the old lady. Violet don't know nothing." He cast a wicked glance across the fence at the woman in the window.

"What does she think about the trouble he's in?"

"There isn't any trouble," the boy said. "Mr. Tarantine is a smart man. He doesn't get into trouble."

"I heard there was some trouble about the pinball collections."

"That's crap. He doesn't collect on the pinball machines anymore. That was last year, when Mr. Speed was here. Are you a policeman, mister?" His face had closed up hard.

"I'm opening a place on the south side. I want a machine put in."

"Look it up in the phone book, mister. It's under Western Variety."

I thanked him. The drumming of the bag began again before I was out of earshot. After a while he'd be a fighting machine hired out for twenty or twenty-five dollars to take it and dish it out. If he was really good, he might be airborne for ten years, sleeping with yellower flesh than Violet, eating thick steaks for breakfast, dishing it out. Then drop back onto a ghetto street-corner with the brains scrambled in his skull.

5

I stopped for gas at a service station near the arena and looked up Tarantine in the phone book attached to its pay phone. There was only one entry under the name, a Mrs. Sylvia Tarantine of 1401 Sanedres Street. I tried the number on the telephone and got no answer.

Sanedres Street was the one I was on. It ran crosstown through the center of the Negro and Mexican district, a street of rundown cottages and crowded shacks interspersed with liquor stores and pawnshops, poolroom-bars and flyblown lunchrooms and storefront tabernacles. As the street approached the hills on the other side of the ball park, it gradually improved. The houses were larger and better kept. They had bigger yards, and the children playing in the yards were white under their dirt.

The house I was looking for stood on a corner at the foot of the slope. It was a one-story frame cottage with a flat roof, almost hidden behind a tangle of untended laurel and cypress. The front door was paned with glass and opened directly into a dingy living-room. I knocked on the door and again I got no answer.

There was a British racing motorcycle, almost new, under a tarpaulin at the side of the house. Moving over to look at it, I noticed a woman hanging sheets on a line in the yard next door. She took a couple of clothespins out of her mouth and called:

"You looking for something?"

"Mrs. Tarantine," I said. "Does she live here?"

"Sure thing, only she ain't at home just now. She went to see her boy in the hospital."

"Is he sick?"

"He got mugged down on the dock the other night. He was beat up something terrible. The doctor thought he might of fractured his skull." She disposed of the sheets in her arms and pushed the graying hair back from her face.

"What was Tarantine doing down at the dock at night?"

"He lives there. I thought you knew him."

I said I didn't know him.

"Well, if you stick around she should be back before long. They don't let visitors stay after four o'clock."

"I'll try the hospital, thanks." It was a quarter of four by my watch.

At five to four I was back where I had begun. The nurse at the information desk told me that Mr. Tarantine was in room

204, straight up the stairs and down the hall to the right, and warned me that I only had a minute.

The door of 204 was standing open. Inside the room a huge old woman in a black and red dotted dress stood with her back to me so that I couldn't see the occupant of the bed. She was arguing in a heavy Italian accent:

"No, you must not, Mario. You must stay in bed until the doctor says. Doctor knows best."

A grumbling masculine bass answered her: "To hell with the doctor." He had an incongruous lisp.

"Swear at your old mother if you want to, but you stay in bed now, Mario. Promise me."

"I'll stay in bed today," the man said. "I don't promise for tomorrow."

"Well, tomorrow we see what the doctor says." The woman leaned over the bed and made a loud smacking noise. "*Addio, figlio mio. Ci vediamo domàni.*"

"*Arrivederci.* Don't worry, Mama."

I stepped aside as she came out, and became interested in a framed list of regulations on the wall. If her hips had been six inches wider she'd have had to take the door sideways. She gave me a black look of suspicion, and bore her huge flesh away on slow waddling legs. Varicose veins crawled like fat blue worms under her stockings.

I went into the room and saw that it contained two beds. A sleeping man lay on the far one by the window, an ice-bag around his throat. On the near one the man I was looking for was sitting up against the raised end, with two pillows behind his head. Most of the head was hidden by a helmet of white bandage which came down under the chin. The visible part of it looked more like a smashed ripe eggplant than a face. It was swollen blue, with tints of green and yellow, and darker marks where the skin had been abraded. Someone who liked hurting people had used his face for a punching-bag or a football.

The puffed mouth lisped: "What do *you* want, bud?"

"What happened to you?"

"I'll tell you how it is," he said laboriously. "The other day I took a damn good look at my face in the mirror. I didn't like it. It didn't suit me. So I picked up a ball-peen hammer and gave it a working over. Is there anything else you want to know?"

9

My car was parked six blocks away, where I had begun my rounds. Dalling's was waiting at the curb. If I had been asked to guess what kind of car he had, I would have said a red or yellow convertible, Chrysler or Buick or De Soto. It was a yellow Buick with red leather seats.

As we drove out of town, slowing down occasionally for a stop sign, I asked him what he did. He had been and done a number of things, he said, chorus boy in musicals before he grew too big, photographic model for advertising agencies, car and yacht salesman, navigator on a PBY during the war. He was proud of that. After the war he had married a rich wife, but it hadn't lasted. More recently he had been a radio actor but that hadn't lasted either because he drank too much. Dalling was frank almost to the point of fruitiness. Starting with the assumption that no man could like him in any case, he said, he figured he might just as well be himself. He had nothing to lose.

When we got on the highway he accelerated to eighty or so and concentrated on his driving, which interrupted our one-sided conversation. After a while I asked him where we were going. "At this rate we'll be in Mexico before long."

He chuckled. Surely I'd heard that chuckle on the radio. People didn't chuckle in real life. "It's just a few miles from here," he said. "A place they call Oasis. I suppose it's not exactly a place yet, but it will be. This country is filling up. Don't you love it?"

I watched the dim arid tundra sweeping by, dotted with cactus and gray sage like the ghosts of vegetation. "It looks like a sea floor. I like a sea floor with water over it, it's more interesting."

"It's funny you should say that. The Gulf of California reached almost to here at one time."

We turned right off the highway and followed an asphalt road across the lightless desert. A dozen miles to our right the town lights sparkled, a handful of white and colored stones thrown down carelessly. A few lights gleamed ahead of us, lost and little in the great nocturnal spaces. Dalling said they were the lights of Oasis.

"The pinball merchants find you, Tarantine?"

He watched me in silence for a moment. His dark eyes looked melancholy in their puffed blue sockets. He rubbed a black-haired hand across the heavy black beard that was sprouting on his chin. There were scabs on his knuckles where they had been skinned. "Get out of my room."

"You'll wake up your friend."

"Beat it. If you're working for him, you can tell him I said so. If you're a friggin' cop you can beat it anyway. I don't have to talk, see."

"I'm not on anybody's payroll. I'm a private detective, not a cop. I'm looking for Galley Lawrence. Her mother thinks something happened to her."

"Let's see your license then."

I opened my wallet and showed him the photostat. "I heard you drove her away when she left her apartment in town."

"Me?" His surprise sounded genuine.

"You drive a bronze-colored Packard roadster?"

"Not me," he said. "You're looking for my brother. You're not the only one. My name's Mario. It's Joe you want."

"Where is Joe?"

"I wish I knew. He blew three days ago, the dirty bum. Left me holding—" The sentence was left unfinished. His mouth sagged open, showing broken teeth.

"Was Galley Lawrence with him?"

"Probably. They were shacked up. You want to find them, huh?"

I acknowledged that I did.

He sat up straight, clear of the pillows. Now that he was upright his face looked even worse. "I'll make a deal with you. I know where they lived in L.A. You let me know if you find them, is it a deal?"

"What do *you* want him for?"

"I'll tell Joe why I want him. When I tell him he won't forget it."

"All right," I said. "If I find him I pass you the word. Where does he live?"

"Casa Loma. It's a ritz joint off of Sunset in the Hills. You might be able to trace him from there."

"Where do you live?"

"On my boat. It's the *Aztec Queen*, moored down in the yacht basin."

"Who are the others that want him?"

"Don't ask me." He lay back in the pillows again.

A cool trained voice said behind me: "Visiting hours are over, sir. How are you feeling, Mr. Tarantine?"

"Dandy," he said. "How do I look?"

"Why, you look cute in your bandage, Mr. Tarantine." The nurse glanced at the other bed. "How's our tonsillectomy?"

"He feels dandy too, he thinks he's dying."

"He'll be up and around tomorrow." She laughed professionally and turned away.

I caught her up in the hall: "What happened to Mario's face? He wouldn't tell me."

She was a big-boned girl with a long earnest nose. "He wouldn't tell us, either. A friend of mine was on emergency when he came in. He walked in all by himself, in the middle of the night. He was in terrible shape, his face streaming blood, and he's got a slight concussion, you know. He said he fell down and hurt himself on his boat, but it was obvious that he'd taken a beating. She called the police, of course, but he wouldn't talk to them, either. He's very reticent, isn't he?"

"Very."

"Are you a friend of his?"

"Just an acquaintance."

"Some of the girls said it was gang trouble, that he was in a gang and fell out with the other members. You think there's anything in that?"

I said the hospitals were full of rumors.

6

I ate dinner at Musso's in Hollywood. While I was waiting for my steak, I phoned Joseph Tarantine's apartment and got my nickel back. The steak came the way I liked it, medium rare, garnished with mushrooms, with a pile of fried onion rings on the side. I had a pint of Black Horse ale for dessert, and when I was finished I felt good. So far I was getting nowhere, but I felt good. I had the kind of excitement, more prophetic than tea-leaves, that lifts you when anything may happen and probably will.

I switched on my headlights as I wheeled out of the parking lot. The gray dusk in the air was almost tangible. Under its film the city lay distinct but dimensionless, as transient as a cloud. The stores and theaters and office buildings had lost their daytime perspectives with the sun, and were waiting for night to give them bulk and meaning. The double stream of traffic into which I turned continued the theme of change. Half of the lemmings were rushing down to the sea and the other half had been there and decided not to get wet. The wild slopes of the mountains overshadowed the slanting streets to the northwest and reduced their neons and headlights to firefly sparks.

The Casa Loma was on a side street a block from Sunset where the boulevard rose towards the hills. It was a four-story white frame building with cheerful lights shining from nearly half of the windows. Not quite the ritz, as Mario Tarantine thought, but it would do. The cars in the parking lot behind the building were nearly all new, and a Pontiac 8 was the cheapest one I saw. The people who lived there spent their money on front.

No doorman, though, which suited me. No desk clerk or hall attendant. I crossed the small carpeted lobby to the brass mailboxes banked on the wall by the plate-glass inner door. Joseph Tarantine was the name on number 7. His card was handwritten in green ink, apparently by the girl who had left the harbor on the sea of life so wide. Most of the other cards were printed, and one or two were engraved. Number 8 was very beautifully engraved with the name of Keith Dalling, whoever he was. I pressed the electric-bell button under his name and got no answer.

Number 12, a Mrs. Kinglsey Soper, was more alert. Probably she was expecting company. When I heard her answering buzz I pushed the plate-glass door open and inserted a doubled-up matchbook in the crack. An ancient ruse, but it worked sometimes. I walked to the corner and back, and found my matchbook where I had left it.

There were fifteen apartments in the building, so that number 7 was on the second floor. I went up in the halting automatic elevator and found it easily, a locked door at the end of a narrow corridor. I stood and looked at the grain of the wood for a minute, but there wasn't much sense in that. I could break the door open, or I could go away. The door of number 8 was directly across the hall, but there was nobody in it. I took the heavy screwdriver from my car out of my inside breast pocket. Number 7 had a Yale-type spring lock, and they were easy.

This one was very easy. The door fell open when I leaned my shoulder against it. Someone had got there before me. There were jimmy marks on the door-jamb, and the socket was loose. I put my screwdriver away and took out my gun instead. The room beyond the door was full of darkness, cut by a thin shaft of light from the hallway.

Facing inward, I closed the door and found the wall switch beside it. Even in the dark there seemed to be something queer about the room. There was a faint light from the large window opposite me, enough to see the vague shapes of furniture which didn't look right. I switched the light on, and saw that nothing was right. The four plaster walls and ceiling were there, but everything inside of them had been destroyed.

The upholstered chairs and the davenport had been slashed and disemboweled. Their stuffing covered the floor in handfuls like dirty snow. The glass coffee-table had its legs unscrewed. Torn reproductions of paintings lay by their empty frames. The metal insides of the radio-phonograph had been ripped out and thrown on the floor. Even the window drapes had been torn down, and the lampshades removed from the lamps. The pottery bases of two table-lamps had been shattered.

The kitchen looked worse. Cans of food had been opened and dumped in the sink. The refrigerator had been literally torn apart, its insulating material scattered on the floor. The linoleum had been torn up in great jagged sheets. In the midst of this chaos, a half-eaten meal, steak and potatoes and asparagus tips, lay on the dinette table. It was the sort of thing you might expect to find in a house that had been struck by a natural disaster, cyclone or flood or earthquake.

I entered the bedroom. The mattress and covered springs of

the Hollywood bed lay in shreds, and even the skeleton of the bed had been taken apart. Men's jackets and women's dresses had been slashed and thrown in a heap on the closet floor. The rags of some white nurses' uniforms lay among them. The dresser drawers had been pulled out and dropped, and the mirror taken out of its frame. There was hardly a whole object left in the room, and nothing personal at all. No letter, no address-book, not even a book of matches. A gray fuzz of duck down from a ripped comforter lay over everything like mold.

The bathroom was off a tiny hallway between the bedroom and the living-room. I stood in the bathroom doorway for an instant, feeling the inside wall for the light. I pressed the switch but no light went on. A man's voice spoke instead:

"I got you lined up and you can't see me. Drop the gun."

I strained my eyes into the dark bathroom. There was glint of light on metal but it could have been the plumbing. Nothing moved. I let my revolver clatter on the floor.

"That's my boy," the voice said. "Now back up against the wall and keep your hands up high."

I did as I was told. A tall man in a wide-brimmed black hat emerged from the dark room. He was as thin as death. His face had a coffin look, skin drawn over high sharp cheekbones, blue down-dragging mouth. His pale glistening eyes were on me, and so was his black gun.

"What's the pitch?" He had yellow teeth.

"I should be asking you."

"Only you're doing the answering." The gun nodded in agreement.

"Joe asked me up for a drink. When I knocked on the door it flew open. Where is Joe, anyway?"

"Come on, boy, you can do better than that. Joe never asked anybody up for a drink. Joe's been gone three days. And you don't drop into a friend's place with iron showing." He kicked my gun towards me. "Don't pick it up."

"All right," I said in tones of boyish candor. "Tarantine ran out on me. He owes me money."

Interest flickered wanly in the pale eyes. "That's better. What kind of money?"

"I manage a young fighter in Pacific Point. Tarantine bought a piece of him. He didn't pay up."

"You're doing better, eh? But you'll have to do better yet. You come along with me."

To the land of shades, I thought, the other side of the river. "Where do you stay, the morgue?" His temples were clean and hollowed like a death's-head under the black hat. The paper-thin wings of his nose were snowbird white.

"Be still if you want to walk. I can have you carried." He stooped quickly, scooped up my gun and dropped it in his pocket. I had no chance to move on him.

He made me walk ahead through the living-room. "You did a nice thorough shakedown on it," I said. "You should apply for a job in an asylum tearing hemp."

"I've seen it done to people," he told me dryly. "People that talked too much." And he jabbed his automatic hard in my kidneys.

We went down in the upended casket of an elevator, as close as Siamese twins, across the deserted lobby, into the street. The buildings had grown thick into nighttime shapes, and the lights had lost their hominess. The man at my side and one pace to my rear had a car with a driver waiting halfway down the block.

7

The man behind the wheel was a run-of-the-mine thug with a carbuncular swelling on the back of his neck. He gave me one dull look as I stepped into the back seat and paid no more attention to me. When he switched on his lights I saw that the thick windshield had the greenish yellow tinge of bulletproof glass.

"Dowser's?" the driver grunted.

"You guessed it."

The long black car rode heavily and fast. My companion sat

in one corner of the back seat with his gun on his knee. I sat in the other corner and thought of a brigadier I'd known in Colón during the war. His hobby was hunting sharks in the open sea, with no equipment but a mask and a knife. I used to run his speedboat for him sometimes. Nobody on his staff could figure out why he did it. I asked him about it one day when he nearly got himself killed and I had to go in after him. He said that it gave him background for dealing with human beings. He was a very shy man for a general.

They took me to a hilltop between Santa Monica and Pacific Palisades. A one-car private road turned off the highway to the left and spiraled up the steep slope. At the top a green iron gate barred the entrance to the driveway. The driver honked his horn. As if in automatic response two arc-lights on telephone poles on either side of the gate came on and lit up the front of the house. It was a wide low ranch-style bungalow painted adobe gray. In spite of the red tile roof, it looked a little like a concrete strong point. The man who came out of the gatehouse completed the illusion by strolling sentry-like with a shotgun under his arm. He leaned it against the gatepost, opened the gate, waved us through.

The front door had a Judas window shaped like a mail slot, above a brass knocker that represented copulating horses for some reason. Judas himself opened the door. He was a curly-headed man with a kind of second-hand Irish good looks. He was wearing headwaiter black for the occasion, with a dingy black bowtie that could have been made of leather.

Paleface lagged behind me and Judas walked ahead, down a hallway decorated with red, black, and gold striped wallpaper. It looked as if the decorator had been influenced by the Fun House at a carnival. The hallway ended in a door that opened into a bright high-ceilinged room. Judas stood aside to let us pass.

"Watch your lip with Dowser," the man behind me said, and reminded my right kidney of his gun.

A man in a midnight-blue suit was standing with one foot on the brass rail of a twenty-foot bar that took up most of the other side of the room. He made a point of waiting and turning very slowly, as if he could easily take me or leave me alone. Behind the bar a great mirror with an old fashioned gold-scrolled frame hung on the oak wall. It repeated all the contents of the room:

the television set built into a grandfather's clock, the silver-dollar slot machines, the full-size snooker table, the illuminated juke box, the row of French windows in the left-hand wall and the swimming pool beyond them, everything a gentleman needed to entertain his friends if he had any friends. I could see myself, in sports clothes and hatless, with a gunman on either side of me, and the gunmen's boss approaching across the polished floor. It made me angry. A Channel Island boar's-head sneered from the wall above the Mauve Age mirror. I sneered back.

"Trouble, Blaney?"

"I picked him up in Tarantine's flat," Paleface said respectfully. "He claims Joe owes him money."

"Him and everybody else. Was it smart to bring him here?"

"I did what you told me, Mr. Dowser, if anybody showed."

"All right," Dowser answered softly.

We sized each other up. He was a head shorter than I was, almost as wide in the shoulders, wider in the hips. His double-breasted blue suit made him look almost cubical. His head was a smaller cube topped by straight sandy hair that was trimmed too short in a brush cut. He was forty, perhaps, trying to feel like thirty and almost succeeding. His skin was fresh and boyish, but there was something the matter with his eyes. They were brown and wet and protuberant, as if they had been dipped in muddy water and stuck on his face to dry.

"Who are you?" he said.

Having nothing to lose by telling it, I told the truth.

"That isn't what he said to me," Blaney complained. "He said he managed fighters in Pacific Point."

"You caught me with my veracity down. When you cock a gun at me it breaks up my conversation."

"Talkative," Dowser said. "You from Pacific Point?" He took a sip from a pewter mug he was holding in his right hand. The liquid it contained looked like buttermilk. He made a buttermilk face. "I'll have a look at your wallet."

I took it out, removed the currency from it to insult him, and handed him the limp sharkskin folder. His dirty-brown eyes bulged over my identification, and his lips moved silently. I noticed that one of his ears curled inward on itself like a misshaped mushroom.

"You want me to read it to you, Mr. Dowser?"

His fresh skin turned a shade darker, but he held his anger. He had an actor's dignity, controlled by some idea of his own importance. His face and body had an evil swollen look as if they had grown stout on rotten meat.

"So you're looking for Joey Tarantine. Who you working for, Archer? Or you working for yourself?" He tossed the wallet at me unexpectedly. His motions were fast and trained.

I caught it, tucked the bills back in, put it away in my pocket. "I'm working for a certain Mrs. Lawrence. Her daughter seems to be traveling with Joe. She's worried about her daughter."

Dowser laughed without showing his teeth. "Now why should she be worried about her daughter? Joe's a sweet kid. Everybody likes Joe."

"I like Joe," Blaney said. "I like Joe," Judas repeated. Dowser had made a joke, so they made the same joke over again.

"And what are you going to do with the girl if you find her?"

"Take her home to mother."

"That will be fun."

"What girl is that?" a woman's voice demanded.

I had been watching Dowser so closely that I hadn't noticed her. He had a quality of unacted violence that held the attention. Now I saw her through the mirror standing in a doorway to my right, like somebody's conception of a Greek goddess painted in a frame. Probably her own. She moved into the room with white silk evening pajamas tossing about her ankles, a girl so colorless in hair and skin that she might have been albino. Except for the dark blue eyes.

They passed me over coolly. "What girl, Danny?"

"Mind your own business."

I said: "Galley Lawrence. Know her?"

"Shut up, you."

The girl took up a cheesecake pose on the edge of the snooker table. "Cert'ny I know her." The voice was flat and rasping, as incongruous from those fine lips as a peacock's screech from a peacock. "I heard she was in Palm Springs. How come I never get to go to Palm Springs, Danny?"

He walked towards her quietly, speaking more softly than

before: "What was that, Irene? You heard about Galley Lawrence someplace, huh?"

"Sandra down at the Beach Club. She said she saw Galley in Palm Springs last night."

"Where?"

"Some bar, she didn't say."

"Who with?" His right arm was straight at his side, the fingers opening and closing at the end of it.

"Not Joey. I know you're looking for Joey so I asked her. Some other male, she thought it was some actor. Sandra said he was cute."

"Cute, huh? *You're* cute. Why didn't you tell me, 'Rene?" He reached up suddenly and took her chin in his hand, clenching it hard.

She struck his arm down. "Don't handle me, you monkey. I was minding my own business, like you said."

His fingers kept on working. "So you bust out with your business in front of this jerk."

"He's cute," she said in a bored deadly whine, and shifted her look to me. "Danny can't get away with rough stuff on account of he isn't cute."

"I think he's cute." I was getting bored myself.

The bulged eyes swiveled to me and back to the girl on the green table. She was hugging her knees as if she found them lovable. Her blue eyes met him levelly.

His left hand jerked up with the pewter mug, and the buttermilk spattered her face.

"All right," she said, dripping white from the point of her chin. "You'll buy me a whole new outfit, *two* new outfits. Tonight you take me to Ciro's. Tomorrow I go to Westmore's for the works."

"I'll give you the works," he said slowly. "I'll drop you off the Santa Monica pier."

But he stood back as she swung her legs down. Her high-heeled gilt slippers hammered across the room. He followed her at a distance, shorter and much older and not nearly so beautiful.

"We might as well sit down," Blaney said. "It goes on like this all the time." The girl had given us something in common, though I didn't know exactly what it was.

Judas went away. Blaney and I sat at the bar, one empty stool and the gun in the space between us. He wouldn't talk, so I amused myself reading the labels on the bottles in the racks. Dowser had everything, including Danziger Goldwasser and pre-World-War Green River.

He came back ten minutes later, wearing a different suit. His mouth was red and slightly swollen, as if somebody had been chewing on it.

"Nice-looking girl," I said, hoping to needle him.

He was feeling too good to be needled. "I got a proposition for you, Archer." He even laid an arm across my shoulders. "A business proposition."

I stood up, placing my shoulders out of his reach. "You have a very peculiar business approach."

"Forget it." As if I had apologized to him. "Put the gun away, Blaney. You're working for old lady Lawrence, you said. You do a job for me instead, what do you say."

"Churning buttermilk?"

He took it without a word. "Doing what you're doing. You want to contact Galley Lawrence. Go to Palm Springs and contact her. I'll pay you one grand for her, five for Joey."

"Why?"

"I like them so much. I want to invite them over to look at my television."

"Why don't you go yourself?"

He paused, then decided to tell me: "It's out of my territory. I don't like crossing over out of my territory. Anyway I got you to go for me, isn't that right?"

"If you say so." It was an easy out.

"That's the old esprit de corpse," he said surprisingly. "You bring me Joey and I'll slip you a quick five G's." He showed me a thick pad of bills in a gold clip shaped like a dollar sign.

"Joey alive or dead?"

"Alive if you can handle it. Dead, the deal's still on. What could be fairer?" He turned to Blaney: "You got our friend's gun here?"

"Yeah." Blaney stood up to answer the boss.

"Okay, give it to him outside." Dowser turned back to me, smiling with a kind of canine charm: "No hard feelings, old man. Everybody's got to look out for himself, that's my philosophy, isn't that right?"

"Speaking of looking out for yourself, I usually get a

retainer." I didn't want Dowser's money, but I had to ask him for it. The giving and receiving of money, its demand and its refusal, were Dowser's basic form of communication with other people. That and the threat, the blow, the infliction of fear and pain.

He grunted, and gave me a hundred-dollar bill. A piece of money takes its feeling from the people that have handled it. This money twisted in my hand like a fat green tomato-worm.

By ten I was in Palm Springs, making the rounds of the bars. I worked up one side of the main street, a miniature Wilshire with horsy trimmings, and down the other side. Old or young, fat or thin, the bartenders gave me the same cool pitying smile. They looked at me and down at the photograph and back at me again.—Nice little beast, eh, nope I never see her.—What's the matter bud your wife run out on you?—If she was here last night I'd know it but she wasn't.—She wouldn't be your daughter would she? That was the most unkindest cut of all.

I had spent about six dollars on drinks that I left untouched or anyway unfinished, when I finally got my lead. It was in a little side-street place called the Lariat. A knotty-pine box of a place with longhorns over the bar, seats and stools upholstered with riveted saddle-leather, a color-retouched photomural of Palm Springs in the days when it was a desert outpost, which weren't so long ago that I couldn't remember them. A great deal had been done to fill the Lariat with old western tradition, but it was so contemporary that it barely existed yet. A pair of fugitives from a Los Angeles wolfpack were playing shuffle-board in the rear. The bartender, who was watching the game, came forward when I took a seat at the bar. He was a youngish man in a Hopalong Cassidy shirt and a wide carved cowhide belt.

I asked for a Scotch and soda. When he brought it, I showed him the photograph and made my little speech. He looked at me and down at the photograph and back at me again, but without the pitying smile. His eyes were large and brown, and they slanted downward from the middle of his face, so that he looked like a cocker spaniel. They had the earnest look of one who sincerely wished to help.

"Yeah, I know the face," he said. "She was in here last night. The joint was jumping last night, you wouldn't believe it. It always slows down on Mondays, after the week-end and all."

"What was her name?" It seemed to have come too easily, or maybe too much bar Scotch was making me uneasy.

"I didn't catch the name. They weren't at the bar, they sat down in the back booth there, by the shuffleboard. I just took them their drinks. Daiquiris, they were drinking."

"Who was the other half of the they?"

"Some guy," he told me cautiously after a while.

"You know him?"

"I wouldn't say I know him. He's been in here a few times, off and on."

"Maybe you know his name."

"I should. I thought I did. I guess it slipped my mind, though." He lit a cigarette and tried to look inscrutable and failed.

My change from a ten-dollar bill was on the bar between us. I pushed it towards him. "You can tell me what he looks like."

"Maybe I can and maybe I can't." He squirmed in his cowboy shirt, eying the money wistfully. "I don't know what the setup is, mister. If this is a deevorce rap or something like that, I wouldn't want to shoot my mouth off too free."

"If divorce comes into it, it's news to me." I told him it was a prodigal daughter case. But with Dowser and Tarantine in it, it was growing much bigger than that. I left them out, and tried to forget them myself.

The bartender was still worried. The bills and silver lay untouched on the black Lucite, nearer him than me. "I got to think about it," he said in pain. "I mean I'll try and remember his name for you."

With a great appearance of casualness he went to the other end of the bar and took a telephone out from under it. Leaning over the bar and hunching his shoulders around the instrument so I couldn't see him dial, he made a call. It took him a long time to get his party. When he finally did, he spoke low and close to the mouthpiece.

He came back briskly and took my empty glass. "Something more to drink, sir?"

I looked at my wrist watch, nearly midnight. "All right."

He set the second glass on the bar beside the money. "Do I take it out of this, sir?"

"It's up to you. It's eating into your profits, isn't it?"

"I don't get you," he said. But he waited for me to produce another bill.

I handed him a single from my wallet. "What did your friend tell you on the phone?"

"My girl friend, you mean?" he asked brightly. "She's coming over to meet me when I close."

"What time do you close?"

"Two o'clock."

"I guess I'll stick around."

He seemed relieved. He flicked a dish towel out from under the bar and began to polish a row of cocktail glasses, humming *Red River Valley* to himself. I moved to the back booth. I sat and wondered if that was as close as I'd get to Galley Lawrence, and watched the coatless boys at the shuffleboard. Red beat blue, which meant that blue paid for the drinks. They were drinking vodka, and they were all of eighteen.

Shortly after midnight a pair of short fat men came in, ridiculous in ten-gallon hats and jeans. They were very very particular about their drinks, and filled the room with name-dropping accounts of their recent social triumphs, related in high loud tenors. They didn't interest me.

A few minutes later a man came in who did. He was tall and graceful in a light flannel suit and an off-white snap-brim hat. His face was incredible. A Greek sculptor could have used him as a model for a Hermes or Apollo. Standing at the door with one hand on the knob, he exchanged a quick glance with the bartender, and looked at me. The tenors at the bar gave him a long slow once-over.

He ordered a bottle of beer and carried it to my booth.

"Mind if I sit down? I know you from somewhere, don't I?"
His voice was beautiful, too, rich and soft and full with deep
manly overtones.

"I don't place you. But sit down."

He removed his hat and exhibited the wavy auburn hair that
went with the long dark eyelashes. Everything was so perfect,
it made me a little sick. He slid into the leather seat across the
table from me.

"On second thought, maybe I do," I said. "Haven't I seen
you in pictures?"

"Not unless you get to look at screen tests. I never got past
them."

"Why?"

"Women don't do the hiring. Men don't like me. Even the
pansies hate me because I won't give them a tumble. You don't
like me, do you?"

"Not very much. Handsome is as handsome does, I always
say. Does it matter if I like you?"

He came to the point then, though it cost him an effort. His
purple eyes were shadowed by anxiety. "You could be working
for Dowser."

"I could be, but I'm not. Whoever Dowser is."

He waited for me to say more, leaning gracefully in the
corner of the booth with one arm on the table. He was tense,
though. There were wet dark blotches under both arms of the
flannel jacket.

I said: "You're scared stiff, aren't you?"

He tried to smile. The effect reminded me of a device I read
about once for making insane people feel happy. It consisted of
a couple of hooks that raised the corners of the mouth into
smiling position. Its beneficiaries were forced to smile, and this
made them feel like smiling, at least that was the theory.

"Okay," he said. "I'm scared stiff."

"You want to tell me about it? I'm wearing my hearing aid
tonight."

"That won't be necessary," with the forced wry smile again.
"You might explain how you come into the picture, Mr.—"

"Archer. Lew Archer."

"My name's Keith Dalling."

"I'm a private detective," I said. "A Mrs. Lawrence employed
me to look for her daughter." I was getting pretty tired of that

pitch. It sounded too simple and corny to be true, especially in the Palm Springs atmosphere.

"Why?"

"Maternal anxiety, I guess. She hadn't heard from her for a couple of months. Nothing to be afraid of, Mr. Dalling."

"If I could be sure of that." There was a beaded row of sweat along his peaked hairline. He wiped it away with the back of his hand. "I heard from a friend in L.A. that Dowser was looking for Galley. It puts me in a spot—"

"Who's he?"

"You must have heard of Dowser." He watched me carefully. "He isn't the kind of person you want on your trail."

"You were saying, it puts you in a spot."

Once he had begun, he was eager to talk. Dalling was big and strong-looking but he wasn't built for strain. He had bad nerves, and admitted it. He hadn't slept the night before, and he was the kind of fellow who needed his sleep.

"What happened last night?"

"I'll tell you from the beginning." He took out a briar pipe and filled it, as he talked, with English-cut tobacco. He was such a perfect artistic example of his type that I began to like him, almost as if he were a creature of my own imagination. "I own this little place in the desert, you see. The place was standing empty, and I had a chance to rent it to Joe Tarantine. He approached me about it week before last, and his offer was good so I took it."

"How do you happen to know him?"

"He's a neighbor of mine. We live across the hall from each other in the Casa Loma apartments." I remembered the engraved card on the mailbox, with his name on it. "I'd told him about the house, and he knew I wasn't planning to use it myself. He said he and his wife wanted to get away for a while, someplace where the pressure would be off."

"Galley is married to him, then."

"So far as I know. They've been living in that apartment as man and wife since the first of the year. I think he mentioned they were married in Las Vegas."

"What does he do?"

He lit his pipe with a wooden match and puffed out a cloud of smoke. "I didn't know until yesterday, when this friend of mine phoned me. Tarantine is a mobster, or something pretty close to it. He handles Dowser's interests in Pacific Point. Dowser has half a dozen towns on the coast sewed up, from Long Beach on down. But that's not the worst of it. Tarantine has stolen something of Dowser's and skipped out. Apparently he planned it ahead of time, and he's using my place as a hideout. I *wondered* why he asked me not to tell anyone. He said if it leaked out the deal was off."

"This friend of yours," I said, "how does he know all this?"

"I don't exactly know. He's a radio producer and he does a crime show based on police files. I suppose he hears inside information."

"But he didn't hear what Tarantine lifted from Dowser?"

"No. Money, perhaps. He seems to have plenty of it. I rented my house to him in all innocence, and now it's made me look as if I'm an accomplice." He gulped the beer that had been growing stale in his glass.

I signaled for more drinks, but he refused another. "I've got to keep my wits about me."

"I don't think it's so bad," I said. "If you're afraid of Dowser, why don't you go and talk to him?"

"I daren't show myself. Besides, if I talked to Dowser, I'd have Tarantine to worry about."

"Not for long."

"I can't be sure of that, either. Frankly, I'm in a mess. I phoned up Galley, Mrs. Tarantine, yesterday after I talked to my friend. She agreed to meet me here. She didn't realize what a chance she was taking, until I told her about her husband. She was shocked. She said she was practically a prisoner out there. She had to slip away last night while he was sleeping, and God knows what he did to her when she got back."

"You like her pretty well."

"Frankly, I do. She's a lovely kid, and she's got herself mixed up with an awfully nasty crew." Not all of his anxiety was for himself.

"I'd like to meet her," I said. "I never have."

He stood up suddenly. "I was hoping you'd say that. I have a normal amount of physical courage, I think, but I'm not up to dealing with gangsters, all by myself, I mean."

I said that that was natural enough.

We entered a maze of gravel roads crisscrossing like city streets, but practically uninhabited. A handful of houses scattered here and there, street-lights at most of the corners, that was Oasis. It reminded me of an army camp I had seen at a staging point in the far west Pacific, after its division had left for bloodier pastures.

"What is this, a ghost town?" I asked him.

"It almost looks like one, doesn't it? Actually it's the opposite of a ghost town, a town waiting to be born. It's a fairly new development, you see. I got in at the beginning, and it's growing by leaps and bounds." But he didn't sound too happy about his real estate investment.

He took a series of turns on tires that screeched and skittered in the gravel. I kept my sense of direction straight by watching the high escarpment that blotted out the horizon to the southeast. On the far edge of the skeleton town he slowed to a crawl.

"That's my house up ahead."

There was only one house ahead, a white frame shoebox with projecting eaves, lengthened by the garage appended to the rear. As we passed it I saw light in the front windows, leaking faintly around the edges of closed Venetian blinds.

"I thought we were going to stop and pay a visit." The Buick had kept on rolling, on to the next intersection and beyond. He finally brought it to a stop at the side of the road.

"I've been thinking," he said uneasily. "Tarantine knows me, and he doesn't know you. Wouldn't it be more strategic if you went in alone? I'll stand by, of course. I'll keep the car here with the motor running." His voice, trying to be charming, was pretty dreary.

If Dalling had a normal amount of physical courage, he must have used it up on me when he first came into the Lariat. I pitied him a little. "Whatever you say, Dalling."

The pity, or the contempt that went with it, must have showed: "After all," and the deep manly overtones had departed, "you've been hired to find Galley Lawrence, haven't you? I'm doing what I can to help you, man. And if Joseph Tarantine knows I've given him away, you know what will happen to me."

He made sense, in a way. If I had had an equal amount of sense of a similar kind, I might have stayed in the car and gone to work on Dalling. Two would get you twenty there was a soft spot in his story to go with the soft spot in his spine. The one thing real and certain was his fear. It hung around him like a damp contagion. It was Dalling's fear, or my reaction against it, that made me foolhardy. That and the whisky I had drunk in line of business. Without its fading glow in my insides I might have reacted in a different way. I might even have saved a life or two if I'd gone to work on Dalling.

But I contented myself with a smiling threat: "Don't stand me up or you won't be pretty any more. *Or* popular."

The invisible hooks worked on his mouth. "Don't worry." He switched off his headlights. "I really appreciate this, your attitude, I mean—" He gave it up and settled down for a wait.

There were more stars over Oasis than I'd seen since I left that island in the Pacific. The unbuilt street was still and peaceful as the desert was supposed to be. But I felt a hot prickling at the nape of my neck as I approached the stucco house. I transferred my gun from shoulder holster to pocket, and leaned my moral weight on it.

I circled the house at a distance. There was no fence, and the house stood by itself on the bare ground. The doors were closed, including the garage doors at the back, and all the windows were blinded. A bronze-painted Packard roadster shone dimly in the starlight at the rear of the gravel driveway. I passed it close enough to make sure there was no one in it, and circled around to the front of the house again.

The lights were still on behind the two front windows. The blinds fitted too well to let me see past them. Holding the gun in my pocket with the safety off, I mounted the low concrete porch and knocked on the screen door. My knocking wasn't loud, but it sounded loud to me.

Quick footsteps crossed the room on the other side of the door. The porch light flashed on over my head. Somebody pulled aside the blind in the near window, and I caught the gleam of an eyeball in the opening. The blind fell back into place, and there was a waiting silence. I knocked again.

Someone flumbled the inside knob. The lock clicked. Slowly the door opened to the width of a brass chain that held it secure. I saw a four inch segment of a woman's face and the muzzle of an automatic gun.

"Go away," she said.

"I would if I knew how." The obvious story was the best I could think of. "My car broke down up the road, and I've lost my way."

"Oh." Her voice relaxed a little, but her gun was steady. "Where are you going?"

"Indio."

"You're way off the track."

"I know that well enough. I hope you've got the safety on that automatic."

"If it bothers you, you can go away," she said. "As I suggested." But something told me, probably my ego, that she was glad to see me. Me or anybody.

"I guess it makes people very inhospitable living all by themselves on the desert like this. Are you a spinster?"

"No. Why?"

"You're acting like one. I wish you'd call your husband if you can't help me out. He probably has a road map of this place."

"Be quiet. You'll wake him." It was a natural thing for her to say, but she said it much too vehemently.

I wondered where Tarantine was sleeping, but I wasn't interested enough to want to disturb him. I kept my voice down. "Why don't you put up the gun and let me relax? I'm completely harmless to women."

To my surprise, she lowered the gun. Then, to my greater surprise, she unchained the door and opened it.

"You might as well come in, but please be quiet. I'll see if I can find a map."

I couldn't understand it. It had been some years since my boyish charm had been able to work minor miracles. "Why the sudden reversal? Not that it isn't pleasant."

"You don't look much like a holdup man, I guess." She unhooked the screen door and held it open for me. "Come in if you like."

I had my first good chance to look at her face. She was the girl in the picture I was carrying, a few years older, no less striking, I thought. The straight nose, curled lips, round chin, were the same, the boldness enhanced by the short black hair molded to her head. She was wearing a blue skirt and white blouse. The gun hanging low in her left hand completed the costume, and didn't seem wholly out of place.

As I passed her in the doorway I reached fast for the gun and twisted it out of her hand. She backed away from me in the confined space until she was flat against the wall of the little hallway. "Give it back to me."

"After we have a talk."

"There's nothing to talk about. Get out of here." But all the time she kept her voice quite low.

I dropped her gun in my left-hand pocket, to balance the one in my right. A faint cool breeze from an air-conditioning system was blowing past me. I shut the door behind me, quietly. "Why don't you go home to your mother, Galley? Joe isn't going to live long, and neither are you if you stick."

"Who are you? How do you know my name?" In the half-light from the open door of the living-room her dark eyes shone with an amber gleam.

"The name is Archer. Your mother sent me to find you. She's been worried about you. With reason."

"You're a liar. My mother doesn't know about Joe. She never sent you here."

"She gave me your graduation picture, I have it here."

"You stole it from her."

"Nonsense. You're just trying to unknow the error, Galley."

She recognized the phrase. Slowly she straightened up clear of the wall. In high heels, she was almost as tall as I was. "Please go away. If mother sent you, tell her I'm all right. Tell her anything."

"I think you should come along."

"Be quiet," she whispered.

From somewhere at the back of the house, I heard a faint dull sound. It could have been a man's boot drawn softly across the floor.

"Please." She was almost whimpering. "You've wakened Joe. He'll kill me if he finds you."

I opened the door. "Come along with me. Dalling's waiting in his car."

"I can't. I daren't." She was breathing quickly, her sharp breasts rising and falling under the blouse.

"Will you be all right?"

"If you go now, please." She leaned towards me, one hand on my shoulder pressing me backwards.

I reached for the screen door behind me, but it was already open. Galley cried: "Look out!"

The warning came too late. I was a sitting duck for the soft explosion of the sandbag against the back of my head.

10

The argument began in my head before I was fully conscious. Had Galley tried to save me, or set me up for Tarantine? In any case, I'd been a pushover. I was ashamed to open my eyes. I lay in my own darkness, face down on something hard, and endured the thudding pain at the base of my skull. The odor of some heavy mantrap perfume invaded my nostrils. After a while I began to wonder where it was coming from.

Something furry or feathery tickled my ear. I lifted one hand to brush it away, and the furry or feathery thing let out a small female yelp. I rolled over and sat up. Through ripples of pain distorting my vision like heat waves, I saw a woman standing above me, dimly silhouetted against the starlight.

"You startled me," she said. "Thank heaven you've come to. Who are you, anyway?"

"Skip the questions, eh?" My head felt like an old tired baseball after batting practice. I braced one hand against the wall beside me, and got to my feet. The woman extended a gloved hand to help me, but I disregarded it. I felt for my gun, which was gone, and my wallet, which wasn't.

"I only asked you who you were," she said in a hurt tone. "What happened to you?"

"I was sapped." I leaned my back against the wall and tried to fix her faintly shimmering outline. After a while it came to rest. She was a large hippy woman in a dark suit. A dead fox crouched on her neck, its feathery tail hanging down.

"Sapped?" she repeated blankly.

"Sandbagged. Hit over the head." My voice sounded nasty even to me, thin and dry and querulous.

"Goodness gracious, should I call the police?"

"No. Leave them out of it."

"The hospital, then? Don't you need some kind of first aid? Was it a robber?"

I felt the swelling at the base of my skull. "Forget it. Just go away and forget it."

"Whoever you are, you're not very nice." She was a spoiled little girl, twenty years later. "I've a good mind to go away and leave you to your own devices."

"I'll try to bear up under it. Wait a minute, though. How did you get here?" There was no car in the road.

"I was driving past and I saw you lying here and I wasn't going to come back and then I thought I should. I left my car and walked back. Now I'm sorry I did, so there."

But she didn't mean it. Spoiled child or not, there was something I liked about the big dim woman. She had a nice warm prewar middle-western voice.

"I didn't mean to be rude."

"That's all right. I imagine you don't feel very good, poor man." She was starting to mother me.

I turned to the door. The screen door was unhooked but the inner door was locked. I wrenched at the knob and got nowhere with it.

"Nobody answers," she said behind me. "I tried knocking when you were unconscious. Did you lose your key?"

She seemed to think I lived there, and I let her go on thinking it. "I'll be all right now," I said. "I can get in the back door. Good night and thanks."

"You're welcome." But she was unwilling to go.

I left her lingering hippily on the porch and went to the back of the house. The Packard was gone from the driveway. There were no lights behind any of the windows. The back door was locked, but it was equipped with a half-length window. I took off one of my shoes and used it to punch a hole in the glass. I was pretty certain that Tarantine had gone. He wouldn't have left me lying on the threshold if he was still inside.

I turned the inside knob and let myself into the kitchen. Hoping the woman would take it as a signal to go away, I switched on the kitchen light. Monel metal and porcelain and brand-new off-white paint dazzled my eyes. The kitchen had everything: dishwasher, garbage disposal unit, electric range, even a big deep-freezer in the corner by the refrigerator. There was a little food in the refrigerator, milk and butter and ham and a head of lettuce, but nothing at all in the freezer. It looked as if Tarantine hadn't intended to stay long.

I went through the small dark dinette into the living-room and found a table-lamp, which I turned on. It cast a parchment-yellowed light on a couple of overstuffed chairs and a davenport to match, a white oak radio cabinet, a tan-colored rug of cheap frieze, a small brick fireplace. The room was so similar to a hundred thousand others that it might have been stamped out by a die. There was nothing there to give me a clue to the people who had used it, except for a *Daily Racing Form* crumpled on one of the chairs. Even the ashtrays were empty.

The bedroom was equally anonymous. It contained twin beds, one of which had been slept in, from the middle-income floor of a department store, a dressing-table, and a chest of drawers with nothing in the drawers. The only trace of Galley was a spilling of suntan powder on the dressing-table. Tarantine had left no trace at all, if you didn't count the bump on the back of my head.

Going back into the living-room, I heard the tapping on the front door. I went to the door and opened it. "What do you want?"

"Why, nothing. I only wondered, are you quite sure you're going to be all right here by yourself?"

She was overdoing her Good Samaritan act. I switched on the porch light above her and looked hard into her face. It wasn't a bad sort of face, though you might have called it moon-shaped. It had a fine mouth, wide and full and generous. The eyes were blue, slightly damaged by recent grief; the lids were puffed. She looked like a soft and easy-going woman who had come up against something hard and unexpected. Her carefully curled red hair was too bright to be natural. The fox was blue and expensive.

"What are you looking at me like that for? Have I got a smut on my nose?"

"I'm trying to figure out why you're so persistent."

She could have taken offense, but she decided to smile

instead. Her smile, complete with nose wrinkling, was in a nice old-fashioned idiom like her speech. "It isn't every night I stumble over unconscious men, you know."

"All right," I said. "I'll lie down and you can stumble over me again. Then will you go away?"

"I will not." She stuck out her lower lip in an impressive pout. "I want to talk to you. What's your name?"

"Archer."

"Then you don't really live here. It belongs to a man named Dalling. I made inquiries this afternoon."

I had forgotten the man with the memorable face. I pushed past her out the door and beyond the circle of light from the porch. The road was bare on the other side of the intersection, and as far as I could see. Dalling had run out long ago.

She followed me like an embarrassing bulky shadow. "You didn't answer my question." Her voice was sibilant with suspicion.

"Dalling's my landlord," I said.

"What's his first name?" Her cross-questioning technique reminded me of a grade-school teacher conducting a spelling bee.

"Keith."

"I guess you really do live here, Mr. Archer. Excuse me."

While we were standing there on the unseeded lawn, lighting up the sky with our repartee, a pair of headlights swept up out of nowhere and slid along the road in our direction. The car passed us without stopping or even slackening speed, but my overworked gland spurted adrenalin. If Tarantine came back to inquire after my health, I didn't want to be available.

"You better go home," I said. "Where do you live?"

"I'm staying at the Oasis Inn, with my husband."

"Can I get transportation to Palm Springs?"

"There's a taxi stand at the Inn. I'll be glad to drive you over."

"Good. I'll be with you in a minute."

I went through the house turning off the lights, closed the doors, and rejoined her in the road. Her car, a new Cadillac, was parked on the shoulder a couple of hundred yards from the house. She had to use a key to open it. Another thing that puzzled me was the fact that the Cadillac was turned towards the house.

"Let me get this straight," I said as she started the engine. "You were driving past the house when you saw me lying on the porch. So you backed up two hundred yards in the dark, locked your car, and then went back to investigate. Is that what you did?"

She sat behind the wheel letting the motor idle. Her answer when it came was another question, off at another tangent: "Do you know my husband, Mr. Archer?"

The question took me by surprise. "Your husband?"

"Henry Fellows. Colonel Henry Fellows."

"I don't know him."

She fed gas to the motor, and the heavy car moved on the crackling gravel. "I really don't know him myself very well. We were married only recently." She added after a moment's pause: "As a matter of fact, we're on our honeymoon."

"Why don't you go home and get acquainted with him? No time like the present."

"He wasn't at the Inn when I left. I came out looking for him. Are you sure you don't know him, Mr. Archer?"

"I know several thousand people, several dozen colonels. I don't know a Henry Fellows."

"Then it couldn't have been Henry who struck you and knocked you unconscious?"

I felt out of touch with reality, wherever it was. The big car rolling across the star-blanched desert might have been a spaceship just landed on the moon. "Where did you get that idea?"

"I just wondered."

"Did you see him?"

"No, I didn't." She sounded uncomfortable. "It was a silly idea. I shouldn't have put it into words."

"What does he look like?"

She answered reluctantly, then warmed to her work: "He's a large man, in his forties—a great tall powerful creature. I need a big man to set me off, you know. Henry's quite distinguished looking with his nice brown wavy hair, and the gray at his temples." A sharper note entered her voice: "He's very attractive to women."

I tried to dredge up an image of the man who had knocked me out, but nothing came. I had had no time to turn and look at him. Perhaps I had seen his shadow on the veranda floor. I couldn't even be sure of that.

"I'm pretty sure it wasn't Henry," I said. "You don't have any reason to think it was?"

"No. I shouldn't have said it."

"How do you spell the last name?"

She spelled it out for me. "I'm Marjorie Fellows. But if he thinks he can carry on like this, even before our honeymoon is over—I shan't be Marjorie Fellows for long!" Her mind was helplessly hung up between love for Henry and resentment of him. New tears glittered like rhinestones on her lashes.

I felt sorry for the big soft woman, driving her car along unpeopled streets in early-morning darkness—a poor sort of way to pass a honeymoon. She seemed out of place on the California desert.

"Where did you meet Colonel Fellows?"

"In Reno." But she had remembered her pride, and it stiffened her voice: "I don't care to discuss it. Please forget what I said."

At the next corner, she jerked the steering-wheel viciously, cutting the wheels so the tires ground in the stones. There was a little settlement of lights ahead, which became a scattering of buildings behind an adobe wall. A score of cars were parked with their noses to the wall, a single taxi at the end of the line. A blue neon sign, OASIS INN, hung over the entrance of the largest building, which fronted on the road.

She turned her car into an empty space between two others, switched off the engine and headlights. We got out together.

As we walked down the line of cars towards the entrance, a man emerged from the shadows under the stucco portico. He strode towards us, literally shouting: "Marjorie! Where have you been?"

She stood still, frightened stiff, unable to answer him. He stepped up close to her, tall and wide and angry. "Where have you been?"

I said: "Fortunately for me, your wife decided to go for a midnight drive. I was lost in the desert, my car broke down, and she gave me a lift to civilization." This was civilization. And I was back on the little-boy-lost routine again.

"What made you do that, Marjorie?" One of his hands

closed over one of her arms. The flesh bulged out on either side of it, and she winced.

I thought of hitting him. He was big enough to make it worth while, a powerful-looking heavyweight with a nose like a battering ram. It would give me a good deal of satisfaction, but on the other hand it wouldn't help Marjorie. Henry would have the rest of their life together to take it out on her, and he looked like the man to do just that.

"Why shouldn't I go for a ride by myself?" She jerked her arm free. "What do you care? You go away and neglect me all the time."

"Now, darling, that's not fair. You had me worried sick when you didn't come home."

"Were you really worried, Henry?"

"You know I was. I can't have my sweet girl wandering around the desert at all hours of the night." His pale eyes glared in my direction, as if I had kidnapped his bride.

Marjorie was doing fine, it seemed. I thanked her and said good night. She fluttered a hand at me, then tucked it possessively under the big man's arm.

11

It was nearly eight by my watch, and delivery trucks were honking their matins, when I got back to town. I was feeling accident-prone, and I drove within the speed limit. The twisted scrap of mind the night had left me was concentrated on Keith Dalling. He had escorted me gracefully into a very queer setup, and gracefully run out. I owed him an opportunity to explain. His yellow Buick was in the parking lot behind the Casa Loma. I eased my car in beside it and got out. The Buick was locked and empty.

An outside wooden staircase led up from the parking lot to a series of long porches across the rear wall of the building. Dalling's back door, if he had one, would be on the second floor at the far right end. A milkman ran down the stairs, a metal basket full of empty bottles clanking in each hand. "Morning," he cried. "Up early, eh?" He disappeared down the alley.

I climbed the stairs to the second floor and followed the veranda to the end. Dalling's apartment had a back door, with a black 8 stenciled on it. The door was an inch ajar, and it opened wider when I knocked. An alarm clock chirped on the other side of the wall, uneager feet shuffled across a floor. Neither my knocking nor the neighbor's alarm clock wakened Dalling.

I pushed the door wide open and entered his kitchen. It was a bachelor's kitchen done by an expressionist scene-designer, probably a Russian. The sink was brimming with dirty water in which a half-submerged pagoda of dirty dishes stood precariously. There were more dirty dishes and a bottle half full of sour milk on the folding table attached to the wall in the breakfast corner. What I could see of the linoleum floor was glazed with grime. But most of it was covered with empty whisky bottles in staggered rows, a sad little monument to Dalling's thirst. Many of the bottles were pints and some were half-pints, which meant that Dalling had sometimes had no more than a dollar between him and sobriety.

I picked my way across the floor to the open door of the living-room. Someone had smashed a bottle on the door frame. The jagged dried splash on the wall still smelled of bourbon, and the floor was littered with brown shards of glass which crunched under my feet.

The living-room was dim behind closed Venetian blinds. I jerked the cord to let the morning in, and looked around me. A scarred prewar radio-phonograph stood by the window, with piles of records on the floor beside it. There was a shallow fireplace in the inside wall, containing a cold gas heater unnecessarily protected by a brass fire-screen. On the wall above the fireplace Van Gogh's much reproduced sunflowers burned in a bamboo frame. The mantel held some old copies of *Daily Variety* and *Hollywood Reporter*, and a few books: cheap reprints of Thorne Smith, Erskine Caldwell, the poems of Joseph Moncure March, and *The Lost Weekend*. There was one handsome book, a copy of *Sonnets from the Portuguese* bound in green tooled leather. Its flyleaf was inscribed: "If thou must love me, let it be for naught except for love's sake only. —Jane." Jane wrote a precise small hand.

The most conspicuous piece of furniture was a Murphy bed standing on its hind legs in a doorway across the room. I had to push it aside before I could get through the door. I did this with my elbow, instead of my fingerprint surfaces. I suppose I smelled the blood before I was conscious of it.

There was a great deal of blood in the little hallway on the other side of the door. It covered the floor from wall to wall, a dark pool filming over now and beginning to cake at the edges. Dalling lay in the middle of it, prone on his back and finished. His waxen profile caught the light that shone through the bathroom door. At first glance I couldn't make out the hole through which the blood had wasted. Leaning over, I saw the puncture in the far slope of his neck and the powder burns on his collar. He was dressed as I had seen him in Palm Springs, and he made a handsome corpse. Any mortician would have been proud of Dalling.

A sheaf of envelopes and folded papers lay on the unbreathing chest halfway out of the jacket's inside pocket. Hugging the door frame with one crooked elbow, I leaned further out over the red pool and got them. It wasn't legal, but on the other hand paper seldom took usable fingerprints.

I went back to the window with the papers, and read through them quickly. A Third Street auto agency intended to repossess the Buick if Dalling didn't pay overdue installments of one hundred and sixty-five dollars and fifty cents. A note on the letterhead of a talent agency, signed by one of its partners, stated that things were tough all over in show biz, if that was any comfort, but TV might make a few more jobs in the fall. An overdraft notice from a downtown bank hinted at a threat of legal proceedings. A Beverly Hills tailor was turning over his account to a collection agency.

I returned to the door of the hallway and took a second look for a gun. There was none in sight, and it wasn't likely that Dalling had fallen on it in his position. Somebody else had done him the final favor.

There was only one personal letter, written on an interoffice memo form from a Hollywood radio station. It was handwritten in neat small calligraphy, and signed Jane:

> *Dear Keith, It may be difficult for you to believe, under the circumstances, that I was glad to hear from you, but, even under the circumstances, I truly was. I shall always be glad to hear from you, whatever the reason. I don't think, however, that it would be good for either of us to try to renew our relationship, as you suggest. What's past is past, though I think of you often and bear you no ill feeling. I do hope, Keith, that you are taking better care of yourself now. I enclose my personal check for one hundred dollars, and trust it will tide you over your current embarrassment.*
>
> > *Yours sincerely,*
> > *Jane*

Jane's full name was written above the station call-letters that were printed on the envelope. It was Jane Starr Hammond. The envelope had been postmarked early in March.

I found her name again in the small red leather address-book that was the last of the items from Dalling's breast pocket. There were a great many names in the book, nine out of ten of them female, and a great many telephone numbers. The only addresses and telephone numbers that interested me deeply were the ones on the last page: Mrs. Samuel Lawrence's and my own. I tore out that last page, and put the book and the bills and the letters back where I had got them.

Dalling had no more use for Malibu telephone numbers or hundred-dollar loans. He'd keep no more whisky vigils in the Murphy bed, with desperation and a dying bottle for bedmates. No one would ever send him another book of poems with love written small and neat on the flyleaf.

There were two men starting their cars in the parking lot, but they didn't pay any special attention to me. I got into my car and switched on the engine. The yellow Buick stood there waiting to be repossessed.

12

I called Jane Starr Hammond's number from a short-order restaurant on the boulevard. If I reached her beforen the body was discovered and the police visited her, I might learn something that I otherwise wouldn't. A maid with a Negro lilt in her voice answered the phone immediately. Miss Hammond had already left for the studio; she would be in her office there the rest of the morning. I went back to my seat at the counter and contemplated the ham and eggs I had ordered. The yolk of one of the eggs had leaked out onto the plate like a miniature pool of yellow blood. I had black coffee for breakfast.

Parking spaces in downtown Hollywood were as scarce as the cardinal virtues. I found a place on Cahuenga and walked back to the studio, which occupied the third and fourth floors of a stone-faced building on Sunset. When I asked for Miss Hammond's office, the blue-uniformed elevator attendant let me off on the third floor and pointed down the corridor. Her name was on the translucent glass pane of a door, with PRIVATE printed underneath. I knocked lightly and waited, undergoing a rare attack of embarrassment. It passed.

"Come in," a cool voice answered, "it isn't locked."

I stepped into a light and airy office and closed the door behind me. Its opposite wall was a giant studio window. A young woman sat with her back to the light, working at a bleached mahogany desk. She was as crisp and exact as the daffodils in the square white bowl at her elbow. She was shiny and trim in a navy blue faille suit and a flat blue sailor hat, too trim and shiny. She looked as if she was made of rustless alloys, synthetic rubber and dyes, powered by a chrome-plated engine clicking away inside her porcelain chest. She wore a fresh gardenia on her lapel.

She looked up from the typescript she was penciling, and caught me regarding the hat. "Pay no attention to the flying saucer." She showed her small even teeth in a practiced smile. "I have to interview a ladybird this morning. As a matter of fact, I thought you might be she."

"I'm usually compared to insects like the cockroach."

"I mean when you knocked. Don't you know what a ladybird is? A ladybird is a bird who thinks she's a lady. The hat helps me to dominate, you know? This particular ladybird has slain wild elephants with a wild elephant gun, so she'll take some dominating. Now tell me you're her husband." She smiled expertly again. If her nose had been a trifle less sharp, her eyes a few degrees warmer, she would have been a very pretty woman. I couldn't imagine her writing the inscription in the *Sonnets from the Portuguese*

I said: "My name is Archer. You *are* Miss Hammond?"

"You surprise and distress me, Mr. Archer. My fair pan was on the cover of *Radio Mirror* last month." I wondered if she worked this hard selling herself all day every day.

"What can I do for you?" she said. "I only have a minute."

"I'm looking for a woman named Galley Lawrence. Mrs. Joseph Tarantine. Do you know her?"

A shadow crossed her face. Her hardening blue gaze reminded me that I hadn't shaved or changed my shirt for over twenty-four hours. "I think I've heard the name. Are you a detective?"

I admitted that I was.

"You should shave more often; it puts people off. What has this Mrs. Tarantine been up to?"

0¼ "I'm trying to find out. What did she used to be up to?"

"I really don't know Mrs. Tarantine. She lives in the same apartment building as a friend of mine. I've seen her once or twice, I think, that's all."

"Under what conditions?"

"Normal conditions. She dropped into my friend's apartment for a cocktail one afternoon when I was there. I didn't like her, if that's what you mean. Her appeal is to the opposite sex. Frank sexuality is her forte. If I wanted to be catty I'd call it blatant." Her forte was the cutting word.

"Do you know her husband?"

"He was there, too. I didn't like him either. He was sleek and crawling with charm, like a tomcat, you know? They made a well-suited couple. Keith—my friend implied that Tarantine was some sort of gangster, if that's the sort of thing you're looking for." She took a cigarette from a silver box on the desk and broke it clean in half between her carmine-tipped fingers. "What *are* you looking for, anyway?"

I didn't know myself. "Just information. Is this friend of yours Keith Dalling?"

"Yes. Have you talked to Keith—Mr. Dalling?" She managed to get the second cigarette between her lips.

I leaned across the desk and held my lighter to it. "I'd like to. He doesn't answer his phone."

She puffed hungrily on the cigarette. "What did she do? I've always considered her capable of anything. I named her Ignoble Savage."

"Her husband seems to have committed a theft."

"From whom?"

"I daren't say."

"And you want to question Keith?"

"Yes."

"He isn't involved in it, is he?" Now she was really worried. And that was just as well, if she loved Dalling or ever had.

"He may be. If he's mixed up with Mrs. Tarantine."

"Oh no." She'd come close to the edge of candor but I had pushed her too fast. She drew away from it, her personality almost visibly receding. "They're just the merest acquaintances, apartment-house neighbors."

"You said they were friends."

"I certainly did not, because they aren't." The clicking machine was back in place, everything under control. "I'm afraid we've run out of time, Mr. Archer. Good morning and good luck." She crushed out her cigarette in a silver ashtray, and the last smoke puffed from her nostrils like a tiny exhaust.

"Something I almost forgot," I said. "There's a radio producer, a friend of Dalling's, who does a crime show based on police work. He wouldn't work for this station?"

"You are checking up on Mr. Dalling, then. Is he in some kind of trouble?" Her voice was tense, though she had regained her composure.

"I hope not."

"Of course you wouldn't tell me if he was. You probably mean Joshua Severn. Mr. Dalling used to work for him. He doesn't work for the studio, he owns his own show, but he has an office down the hall. Sometimes he's even in it."

"Thank you, Miss Hammond."

"Don't mention it, Mr. Archer."

There was a telephone booth in the first-floor lobby of the

building next door. The man behind the news counter wore the frosted glasses of the blind. I called police headquarters from the booth, and told the sergeant on duty that I was worried about a friend of mine. His name was Keith Dalling and he lived in the Casa Loma, Apartment 8. He didn't answer when I phoned or when I knocked on the door—

"And what is your name, sir?" he cut in sharply.

I deliberately misunderstood the question: "Keith Dalling. He lives at the Casa Loma."

"Just one minute, sir." His voice was soothing.

There was a buzzing silence on the line, terminated by a double click. It probably meant that the body had been found and they were tracing my call.

I hung up. I went back to the studio building and up in the elevator again to the third floor. I found the name Joshua Severn on a door at the rear of the building. It was standing slightly ajar; a continuous low murmur came from the other side. I knocked and was told to come in.

It was a working room, containing two desks piled with papers, a pair of metal filing-cabinets, a blackboard on one wall. At the moment the blackboard showed the odds on a half-dozen Derby candidates quoted from the winter book. A heavy middle-aged man switched off the dictating machine on the table beside him and straightened up in his chair.

"Mr. Severn?"

"That's what it says on the door." He said it cheerfully. He had a broad cheerful face surmounted by a brush of erect gray hair, like iron filings tempted by a magnet.

"My name is Archer."

"Wait a minute. Not Lew Archer?" He stood up and offered me a stubby hand. "I'm glad to meet you, Archer. Have a seat."

I said that I was glad to meet him, too, and sat in the chair he pushed up beside his desk. I added I hadn't been aware that my name was a byword in the upper echelons of the radio industry.

He grinned. Most of his features, nose and ears and chin, were a little larger than life-size and slightly squashed-looking, as if they'd outgrown their mold. "It's a darn funny thing, Archer. It happens to me all the time. The extra-sensory boys, the parapyschologists, have got me half convinced. I start thinking about somebody I haven't seen or heard of for maybe two years. Within twenty-four hours after I get the flash, I meet the guy on the street or he marches into my office, just like you." He glanced at the yachtman's chronometer on his wrist. "It took you thirty-six."

"I'm always a little slow. I take it you were thinking about me around nine thirty Sunday night. Why?"

"A fellow I know called in from Palm Springs. He wanted the name of a good private detective, one who works alone. I gave him yours. I have a beach house in Santa Teresa, and Miranda Sampson was singing your praises last year. Okay?"

"Miranda's a nice girl," I said. "Who was the fellow that called you Sunday night?"

"Keith Dalling. Did he get in touch with you?"

I made a quick adjustment. "Yes, he did. I talked to him on the phone, but I haven't seen him yet."

"Funny, he sounded in a hurry. What sort of job does he want you for, anyway?"

"He asked me to keep it confidential. I have my doubts about it. That's why I'm here."

"Hell, there goes my extra-sensory perception. Dalling mentioned *me* to *you*, eh?" He took a long black Havana out of a box on the desk and bit its end off. "Have a cigar."

"Not in the morning, thanks. Yes, Dalling mentioned you. He said you told him a little story about a man called Dowser."

"The mobster?" Unconsciously he began to eat the unlit cigar. "Dowser's name never came up between us."

"You didn't give him any information about Dowser?"

"I don't know anything about Dowser. I've heard he was in the dope racket but they're saying that about them all these days. You were the only name I mentioned. What kind of a line has Keith been feeding you?"

"Grade B movie stuff," I said. "Is he a pathological liar?"

"Not when he's sober. You've got to watch him when he's drunk, and it's hard to tell when he is. He's a terrible alcoholic." Severn removed the cigar from his mouth and looked at the wet mashed end without seeing it. "I hope our Keith hasn't gotten himself mixed up with a crew of thugs. I warned him about the girl he was running with."

"Galley Tarantine?"

His eyebrows moved. "She comes into the picture, too, eh? Did Dalling tell you who her husband is? I don't know

Tarantine, but he had a bad name with the police. I told Keith he better lay off her or he'd end up with a knife stuck under his ribs. Is he in trouble with Tarantine?''

"He may be. He didn't say very much. If you can fill me in on his background, it might help.'' I tried to sound as diffident as possible. Severn looked sharp.

Very sharp. The blue eyes under his heavy black brows were hard and bright as diamonds. "Are you working for Keith or against him? You're not very communicative yourself.''

"I'm for him a hundred percent.'' Which was true. I was a sucker for underdogs, and dead men were at the bottom of the heap.

"Good enough. I'll take Miranda's word for your honesty. I like the boy, you see, I've known him since he was a kid. He used to crew for me before the war when I had my Star boat, and we won the cup at Santa Monica one year. I didn't fire him until I was forced to; the sponsor was raising Cain.''

"He worked for you?''

"He worked on a lot of shows, he's a good actor. Trouble was, he couldn't lay off the liquor and they canned him one by one and finally blacklisted him. I was the last one that kept him on; he played my detective-lieutenant for over two years. It got pretty rough. He fluffed so many lines I was scissoring the tape every bloody week. One day he passed out in the middle of a show and I had to go out on the streets for an actor. I cut him off, though it broke my heart to do it. It played hell with his life, I guess. He was going to get married, and he was building himself a house. I guess he lost the house. I know he lost the girl.''

"Jane Hammond?''

"Yeah. I feel kind of sorry for Jane. She works here, you know. A lot of women have carried the torch for Keith—that's probably what ruined him—only Jane is different. He was the one big love in her life, but she was too successful for him. When I fired him, he ran out on her. I was afraid for a while she'd go crazy, though she keeps a stiff upper lip.''

"When was this?''

"Around the first of the year. I fired him the day after Christmas.'' He made a sour face, champing savagely on the cigar. "Nice timing, eh? Soon after that he started with Tarantine's wife. I see them in night spots now and then. As a

matter of fact, I slip him a few lakhs of rupees when I can."
He glanced at the dictating machine in polite impatience. "Will
that do? The things I know about Keith would take all day."

I rose and thanked him. He followed me to the door, massive
and quick-moving: "I've let down the old back hair, Dalling's
anyway. Do you care to tell me what it's all about?"

"He'll have to tell you himself."

He shrugged his shoulders, easily, as if his weight of integrity was no burden. "Okay, Archer."

"Give my love to Miranda."

"I never see her. She moved to Hawaii. See you around."

I had to pass Jane Hammond's door to get to the elevator.
The door was standing open. She was still behind her desk,
sitting erect and trim with a telephone receiver in her left hand.
Her right hand gripped her right breast, its carmine nails
digging into the soft flesh. Her eyes were dark and deep in her
head. They looked straight at me and failed to recognize me.

The police had found her name in the red leather address-book.

13

I crossed to Pico Boulevard and drove to Mrs. Lawrence's
house in Santa Monica. Tiredness was catching up with me.
The glittering late-morning traffic hurt my eyes and feelings. I
had a notion at the back of my mind that at worst Mrs.
Lawrence could rent me a room to sleep in, out of reach of
policemen's questions for a while. At best she might have
heard from her daughter.

Mrs. Lawrence had done better, and worse, than that. The
bronze Packard was parked at the curb in front of her house.
The sight of it acted on me like benzedrine. I took the veranda
steps in one stride, and leaned my weight on the doorbell. She
came to the door immediately:

"Mr. Archer! I've been trying to get you by phone."

"Is Galley here?"

"She was. It's why I called you. Where have you been?"

"Too far. I'd like to come in, if I may."

"Excuse me. I've been so dreadfully upset I don't know if I'm coming or going." She looked distraught. Her gray hair, which had been so carefully done the previous morning, was unkempt, almost as if she'd been tearing at it with her hands. A single day had drawn deeper lines in her face.

Still she was very courteous as she stood back to let me enter and led me down the hall to her hoard of old furniture. "You look quite worn out, Mr. Archer. May I make you some tea?"

I said: "No, thanks. Where's Galley?"

"I don't know where she went. A man came to get her about ten o'clock, when I was just giving her her breakfast. I was frying the bacon, crisp, as she's always liked it, when this man came to the door. She went away with him, without a single word of explanation." She sat down in a platform rocker just inside the door of the room, her clenched hands resting stiffly on her knees.

"Could he have been her husband? Did you see him?"

"Her husband?" Her voice sounded weary and bewildered. She had encountered too much life in too short a time. "Surely she isn't married."

"She seems to be, to a man called Tarantine. Didn't she tell you?"

"We barely had a chance to talk. She came home late last night—I don't know how to thank you, Mr. Archer, for what you've done—"

"Galley mentioned me, then."

"Oh yes. She came straight home after you found her. It was very late, after dawn in fact, and she was too tired to want to talk very much. This morning I let her sleep in. It was so grand to have my girl back in her own bed. Now she's gone away again." She sat gazing at the fact, drearily blinking her eyes.

"This man," I nudged her to attention. "Did you see the man she went with?"

"Certainly. I answered the door myself. I didn't like his looks at all. He was a very thin man, a walking skeleton. I thought when I looked at him he must have tuberculosis.

Galley wouldn't marry a man like that." But her statement curled at the edges into a question.

"That isn't her husband. Did he threaten you, or her?"

"Heavens, no. He simply asked for Galley, very quietly. She came to the door and they talked together for a minute. I didn't hear what was said. Galley closed the door and stepped outside. Then she came back in and put on her coat and left."

"Without a word?"

"She said good-bye. She said she would be back soon. I tried to get her to eat her breakfast first, but she was in too great a hurry."

"Was she frightened?"

"I don't know. I've never seen my daughter show fear. She is a very courageous girl, Mr. Archer, she always has been. Her father and I tried to teach her to face the world with fortitude."

I was standing above her, resting part of my weight on the edge of the refectory table. I noticed that she was looking at me with growing disapproval.

"Is something the matter?"

"Please sit down in a *chair*, Mr. Archer. That table was one of the doctor's favorite pieces."

"Sorry." I sat down.

Her past-encumbered mind came back to the present again: "You've implied several times that Galley is in danger."

"I got the idea from you."

"Don't you believe she will come back soon, as she promised? Has something happened to my girl, Mr. Archer?" One of her fists was steadily pounding one of her bony knees.

"I don't know. All you can do is wait and see."

"Can't *you* do something? I'll give you anything I have. If only nothing dreadful happens to Galley."

"I'll do what I can. I'm in this case to stay."

"You're a good man." The fist stopped pounding.

"Hardly." She lived in a world where people did this or that because they were good or evil. In my world people acted because they had to. I gave her a little bulletin from my world: "Last night your daughter's husband knocked me out with a sandbag and left me lying. I make a point of paying back things like that."

"Goodness gracious! What kind of a man is Galley married to?"

"Not a good man." Perhaps our worlds were the same after all, depending on how you looked at them. The things you had to do in my world made you good or evil in hers. "You'll probably be hearing from the police some time today."

"The police? Is Galley in wrong with the police?" It was the final affront to Dr. Lawrence's memory and the furniture. Her hands rose to her head and lifted her hair in two gray tangled wings.

"Not necessarily. They'll want to ask some questions. Tell them the truth. Tell them I told you to tell them the truth." I moved to the door.

"Where are you going?"

"I think I know where Galley is. Did she go away in a car?"

"Yes, a big black car. There was a second man driving."

"I'll bring her back if I can."

"Wait a minute." She followed me down the dim hallway and detained me at the front door. "There's something I must tell you."

"About Galley? If it isn't you'd better save it."

Her roughened hand moved on my sleeve. "Yes, about Galley. I haven't been entirely candid, Mr. Archer. Now you tell me the police are coming here—"

"Nothing to worry about. They'll want to do some checking."

"A policeman was here Sunday night," she said. "He warned me not to divulge the fact to anyone, not even you."

"How did I come into the conversation? I entered this case on Monday."

"Lieutenant Dahl urged me to employ you. He's a detective in the Vice Squad, he said, a very lovely young man. He said my girl was living with a criminal whom he was shortly going to have to arrest. But he knew that Galley was an innocent good girl, and he didn't want to involve her if he could help it. So he gave me your name and telephone number. He said that you were honest and discreet, but even so I wasn't to tell you about his conversation with me." She bit her lip. "It's terribly wrong of me to violate his confidence like this."

"When did he come here?"

"Sunday night, after midnight. He got me up out of bed."

"What did he look like?"

"He was in civilian clothes—an extremely handsome young fellow."

"Tall, wavy reddish hair, purple eyes, movie-actor's profile, radio-actor's voice?"

"Do you know Lieutenant Dahl?"

"Very slightly," I said. "Our friendship never had a chance to come to its full flower."

14

I went up the looping road in second and stopped at the green iron gate. The sentry was already out of the gatehouse with the shotgun. The sun burned on the oiled and polished barrels.

"How's the hunting?" I asked him.

He had a bulldog face whose only expression was a frozen ferocity intended to scare off trespassers. "You better beat it. This is private property."

"Dowser is expecting me. I'm Archer."

"You stay in your car and I'll check." He retired to the gatehouse, from which a telephone wire ran to the main building. When he came out he opened the gate for me. "You can park over here by the fence."

He moved up close to me as I got out of the car. I stood still and let his hands run down me. They paused at my empty holster. "Where's the gun?"

"I ditched it."

"Trouble?"

"Trouble."

Blaney met me at the front door, still wearing the wide black hat. "I didn't expect you back."

I took a long look at the mushroom-colored face, the ground glass eyes. They told me nothing. If Blaney had shot Dalling he'd done it without a second thought.

"I can't resist your charming hospitality," I said. "Where's the boss?"

"Eating lunch in the patio. You're to come on out, he says."

Dowser was sitting alone at a wrought-iron table by the swimming pool, a crabmeat salad with mayonnaise in front of him. His short hair was wet, and he was wrapped to the chin in a white terrycloth robe. With his bulging eyes and munching jaws he looked like an overgrown gopher masquerading as a man.

He went on eating for a while, to remind me of his importance in the world. He ate pieces of crabmeat and lettuce with his fingers, and then he licked his fingers. Blaney stood and watched him like an envious ghost. I looked around at the oval pool still stirred and winking with the memory of Dowser's bathe, the spectrum of flowers that fringed the patio, all the fine things that Dowser had pushed and cheated and killed for. And I wondered what I could do to take them away from Dowser.

He pushed the demolished salad away and lit a cigarette. "You can go in, Blaney." The thin man vanished from my side.

"Did you get my special delivery?"

"Come again. Sit down if you want to."

I took a chair across the table from him. "I flushed the girl for you. Tarantine was too quick for me, or I'd have brought him in too."

"*You* flushed her! We had to find her ourselves. Some dame called in this morning that she was at her old lady's. That wasn't you on the phone, was it, doing a female impersonation?"

"I don't have the figure for it," I said, looking him up and down.

"So where do you come in?"

"I brought her from Palm Springs for you. You said it was worth a thousand."

"The way I understand it, she came by herself. I pay for value received."

"You've got her, haven't you? You wouldn't have her if I hadn't sent her home to mother. I talked her into it."

"That's not her story."

"What is her story?"

"She isn't talking much." He looked uncomfortable, and changed the subject: "Did you see Tarantine?"

"I didn't see him. He sapped me from behind. The girl tried to stop it, I think. There's a possibility she isn't in this with him. Whatever *this* is."

He laughed his unenjoyable laugh. "You'd like to know, huh?"

"When I get beaten over the head, I'm interested in the reason."

"I'll tell you the reason. Tarantine has something of mine, you maybe guessed it, huh? I'm going to get it back. The girl says she don't know nothing about it."

"What does it look like?"

"That doesn't matter. He won't be toting it around with him. When I get him, then I get *it* afterwards."

"Junk," I said under my breath. If he heard me he paid no attention.

"You working for me, Archer?"

"Not for love."

"I offered you five grand for Tarantine. I'll raise it five."

"You offered me one for Galley. You're full of offers." I was watching his face closely, to see how far I could go in that direction.

"Be reasonable," he said. "You brought her in, I'd of slipped you the cash just like an expressman at the door. You didn't bring her. Blaney had to go and get her himself. I can't afford to throw money away on good will. My expenses are a friggin' crime these days. I got a payroll that would break your heart and now the lawyers tell me I got to pay back income-tax to clear myself with the feds." His voice was throbbing with the injustice of it all. "Not to mention the politicians," he added. "The God-damn politicians bleed me white."

"Five hundred, then," I said. "We'll split the difference."

"Five hundred dollars for nothing?" But he was just haggling now, trying to convert a bargain to a steal.

"Last night it was a thousand. Only last night you didn't have the girl."

"The girl is no good to me. If she knows where Joe Tarantine is, she isn't telling."

"Let me talk to her?" Which was the point I had been aiming at from the beginning.

"She'll talk for me. It takes a little time." He stood up, tightening the sash around his flabby waist. There was something womanish about the gesture, though the muscles bulged like angry veins in his sleeves.

On his feet he looked smaller. His legs were proportionately shorter than his body. I stayed in my chair. Dowser would be more likely to do what I wanted him to do if he could look down at the top of my head. There were two-inch heels on the sandals that clasped his feet.

"A little time," I repeated. "Isn't that what Tarantine needs to get lost in Mexico? Or wherever he's gone."

"I can extradite him," he said with his canine grin. "All I need to know is where he is."

"And if she doesn't know?"

"She knows. She'll remember. A man don't leave behind a piece like her. Not Joey. He loves his flesh."

"Speaking of flesh, what have you been doing to the girl?"

"Nothing much." He shrugged his heavy shoulders. "Blaney pushed her around a little bit. I guess now I got my strength up I'll push her around a little bit myself." He punched himself in the abdomen, not very hard.

"I wish you'd let me talk to her," I said.

"Why all the eager interest, baby?"

"Tarantine sapped me."

"He didn't sap you in the moneybags, baby. That's where you get the real agony."

"No doubt. But here's my idea. The girl has a notion I might be on her side." If Galley had that notion, she was right. "If you muss my hair and shove me in alongside her, it should convince her. I suppose you've got her locked in some dungeon?"

"You want to stool for me, is that the pitch?"

"Call it that. When do I get my five hundred?"

He dug deep into the pocket of his robe, slipped a bill from the gold money-clip and tossed it on the table. "There's your money."

I rose and picked it up against my will, telling myself it was justified under the circumstances. Taking his money was the only way I knew to make Dowser trust me. I folded the bill and tucked it into my watch pocket, separate from the other money, promising myself at the earliest opportunity I'd bet it on the horses.

"It might be a good idea," he said. "You have a talk with the girl before we rough her up too much. I kind of like her looks the way she is. Maybe you do too, huh?'' The bulging eyes shone with a lewd cunning.

"She's a lovely piece," I said.

"Well, don't start getting any ideas. I'll put you in where she is, see, and all you do is talk to her. Along the lines we discussed. I got a mike in there, and a one-way window. I put the one-way window in for the politicians. They come to visit me sometimes, see. I take my own sex straight."

So does a coyote, I thought, and did not say.

15

After the sunswept patio, the room was very dim behind three-quarters-drawn drapes. A thin partition of light fell through it from the uncovered strip of window, dividing it into two unequal sections. The section to my right held a dressing-table and a long chair upholstered in dark red satin. I saw myself in the mirror above the dressing-table. I looked disheveled enough without even trying. The heavy door slammed shut and a key turned in the lock.

In the section to my left there were more chairs, a wide bed with a red silk padded head, a portable cellarette beside the bed in lieu of a bedside table. Galley Tarantine crouched on the bed like a living piece of the dimness and the stillness. Only the amber discs of her eyes showed life. Then the point of her tongue made a slow circuit of her lips at the pace of a second hand:

"This is an unexpected pleasure. I didn't know I was going to have a cellmate. The right sex, too." There was some irony here. Her voice, low and intense, was well adapted to it.

"You're very observant." I went to the window and found that it was a casement, but bolted top and bottom on the outside.

"It isn't much use," she said. "Even if you smashed it, the place is too well guarded to get away from. Dowser plays with gunmen the way other spoiled little boys play with lead soldiers. He thinks he's Napoleon Bonaparte and he probably suffers from the same anatomical deficiency. I wouldn't know myself. I wouldn't let him touch me with a ten-foot pole." She spoke quietly but clearly, apparently taking pleasure in the sound of her own voice, though it had growling overtones. I hoped that Dowser was hearing all of this, and wondered where the mike was.

Perhaps in the cellarette. I turned from the window to look at it, and the light fell on my face. The woman sat up higher on her heels and let out a little gasp of recognition. "You're Archer! How did you get here?"

"It all goes back about thirty-seven years ago." She was too bright for a Lochinvar approach. "A few months before I was born, my mother was frightened by a tall dark stranger with a sandbag. It had a queer effect on my infant brain. Whenever anybody hits me with a sandbag, I fall down and get up angry."

"You touch me deeply," she said. "How did you know it was a sandbag?"

"I've been sandbagged before." I sat down on the front of the bed and fingered the back of my head. The swelling there was as sore as a boil.

"I'm sorry. I tried to stop it, but Joe was too fast. He sneaked out the back of the house and around the porch in his stocking feet. You're lucky he didn't shoot you." She shuffled towards me on her knees, her hips rotating with a clumsy kind of grace. "Let me look at it."

I bent my head. Her fingers moved cool and gentle on the swelling. "It doesn't look too bad. I don't think there's any concussion, not much anyway." Her fingers slid down the nape of my neck.

I looked up into the narrow face poised over me. The full red lips were parted and the black eyes dreamed downward heavily. Her hair was uncombed. She had sleepless hollows under her eyes, a dark bruise on her temple. She still was the fieriest thing I'd seen up close for years.

"Thanks, nurse."

"Don't mention it." The dark hawk face came down and

kissed my mouth. For an instant her breast came hard against my shoulder, then she withdrew to the other end of the bed.

It made the blood run round in my veins too fast. But she was calm and cool, as if it were a thing she did for all her patients.

"What did Joe do after that?" I said.

"You haven't told me how you got here.—Have you a comb?"

I tossed her my pocket comb. Her hair crackled and ran smooth like black water through her hands. I looked around the room for Dowser's one-way window. There was a double band of black glass along the edges of the panel heater near the door.

"You wouldn't be one of Dowser's lead soldiers, would you?" She was still combing her hair, her bosom rising and falling with the movement of her arms.

"That bum? I wouldn't be here if I was. I told you your mother hired me."

"Ah yes, you're Mother's helper. Did you see her?"

"No more than an hour ago. Stop combing your hair, it disturbs me."

A white grin lit her face. "Poor mans, did I excite hims?"

"That was the idea, wasn't it?"

"Was it?" The tossed comb would have hit me in the face if I hadn't palmed it. "What did Mother say?"

"She said she'd give whatever she has if I could bring you back."

"Really?" For the first time she sounded and looked dead serious. "Did she mean it?"

"She meant it all right. I said I'd do what I can."

"So you came up here and got yourself locked up. It took you less than an hour. You move fast, Archer."

I assumed an angry tone which turned out to be half real: "If I had my gun, it wouldn't have happened. Your husband took my gun last night."

"He took mine, too," she said.

"Where did he go?"

"You'll never catch him now."

"You know where he is, then?"

"I can guess. He didn't tell me anything himself. He never did."

"Don't kid me."

"I wouldn't if I could," she said. "It's true. When I went to Las Vegas with him—we were married at Gretna Green—I thought he was a wrestling promoter. I knew he worked as a pinball machine collector before that, but that seemed fairly innocent. He didn't tell me different."

"How did you meet him?'"

"In the line of duty, I suppose you'd call it. I had a patient by the name of Speed who used to be Joe's boss. Joe came to see this Speed in the hospital. Joe is a good-looking man, and I guess I fell." She was leaning against the padded headboard with her knees turned sideways under her. On the other side of the red chenille desert that lay between us, her thighs rose under the blue skirt like the slopes of blue mountain foothills.

"This Speed," I said. "What was the matter with him?"

"You probably know, or you wouldn't ask." The reclining slopes of her body shifted, and my nerves recorded the seismic vibrations. "Mr. Speed had a bullet wound in the stomach."

"But that didn't give you any ideas about Mr. Speed's employee?"

"I hate to admit I must have been naïve. Mr. Speed said it was an accident. He shot himself cleaning a gun, at least that was his story."

"So you married Joe, who probably shot Speed himself." I made the suggestion at random, fishing for facts.

Her eyes widened, black and depthless beneath their amber surfaces. "Oh. Joe and Herman Speed were always good friends. When Joe took over, Mr. Speed gave him pointers about the business—"

"What business?"

"The pinball machines and the wrestling contracts and various other things."

"All Dowser's things?"

"I guess so. I didn't know Joe's business. He kept me up here in L.A., you see, and Joe and I weren't very good friends after the first week. Joe had a pleasant trick of slapping people. That's why I bought my gun. It cooled him off but I was still afraid of him, and he knew it. It didn't make for marital confidences."

"But you know what Dowser wants him for?"

"I have a rough idea. He absconded with something valuable of Dowser's. But Dowser won't catch him either." She looked at the watch on her slim brown wrist. "He's probably in Mexico by now. Over the hills and far away."

"You think he went to Mexico?"

"That's what it looks like to me. I'll never see him again," she added bitterly.

"Is that going to ruin your life?"

She sat up straight, her face set in angry planes. "Look what he did. Married me under false pretences, took me for a ride, and now he's stood me up. Left me to take a beating from Dowser and his dirty rotten crew. The dirty rotten coward."

"Tell me where he went last night?"

"Why do you want to know?"

"I want to have the pleasure of hitting him over the head with a blackjack. If I bring him in, that will clear you with Dowser, won't it?"

"It will if you're man enough to do it. You weren't last night."

There was no answer to that. "Tell me about last night. I'd like to get it straight. I met your boy friend Dalling in a bar—I think he was expecting me—and he drove me out to Oasis—"

"Dalling is not my boy friend."

"All right, he likes you, though." I was careful about the tense. "He was worried about you."

"Keith is a terrible worrier. What next?"

"He parked down the road and stayed in his car. Joe slipped out of the house while I was talking to you at the door, and sapped me. Now it's your turn."

"To sap you?"

"To say what happened after that. Did he see Dalling's car?"

"Yes. He went after it, but Keith got away. Joe came back in a rage and told me to pack, we were leaving. We were off in fifteen minutes. You were still unconscious, and I think that saved your life. He made me drive him into Los Angeles though I didn't want to do it. I suspected he was after Keith for giving away his hideout. I could tell he blamed me for it, because Keith was my friend. *Not* my boy friend.

"He was so blind mad he went back to the Casa Loma, that's where we had our apartment. I told him Dowser's men would be watching it, but he shut me up. Keith's car was in the parking lot. Joe told me to stay down there and he went up the back way himself.''

''What time was this?''

''Around three, I think.''

''You got there in a hurry.''

''Yes, I was hitting ninety and ninety-five. I kind of hoped we'd have a blowout and put an end to the business, but no such luck.'' She stroked the side of her face with one hand, her eyes unfocused. ''Anyway, Joe came down in a couple of minutes and said Keith wasn't at home. He made me drive him to Pacific Point and let him out near the yacht basin. That was the last I saw of him. He didn't even say good-bye to me.'' She smiled narrowly. ''It might have been smart of him to say good-bye.''

''Why don't you tell Dowser about all this? He'll turn you loose.''

''I'll tell you why: Dowser let his gorilla put his paws on me. I wouldn't tell him which direction was up.''

I sat and looked at her, waiting for the key to turn in the lock. The more I looked at her proud body and head, the more I liked her, and the more I liked her, the more I felt like a heel.

I had to remind myself that a man was dead, that all was for the best in the best of all possible worlds, and that anything was fair in love and war and murder. I leaned sideways on one elbow, and sleep came over my head like a gunny sack. Just before I dozed off, I heard a car engine start with a roar somewhere outside the house.

16

When I awoke the strip of sunlight had moved to the foot of the bed. It drew a broad bright band diagonally across my body, like the sash of yellow satin that went with a South American decoration. I sat up, feeling my legs constricted, and saw that Galley had pulled the spread across me.

She stirred sleepily at her end of the bed. "You've been dead to the world for two hours. It isn't very flattering. Besides, you snore."

"Sorry. I missed my sleep last night."

"I didn't mind, really. You sounded like my father. My father was quite a guy. He died when I was eight."

"And you remember what his snoring sounded like?"

"I have an excellent memory." She stretched and yawned. "Do you suppose they'll ever let us out of here?"

"Your guess is as good as mine." I threw aside the spread and stood up. "Nice of you to tuck me in."

"Professional training. Which reminds me, now that Joe is gone, I suppose I'll have to get myself a job. He didn't leave me anything but my clothes."

I remembered the condition of the clothes in the Casa Loma apartment, and kept quiet on the subject. "You're giving him up pretty easily, aren't you?"

"He won't be back," she said flatly. "If he does come back, he won't survive. And even if he did, I wouldn't take him back. Not after what he said to me last night."

I looked my question.

"We won't go into it," she said.

She flung herself off the bed and walked to the other end of the room, soft-footed in her stockings. Her narrow high-heeled shoes stood together neatly on the floor. She leaned toward the dressing-table mirror, lifting her hair to examine the bruise on her temple.

"God damn it, I can't stand waiting. I think I'll smash something." She swung around fiercely.

"Go ahead."

There was a perfume atomizer on the table. She picked it up and hurled it at the door. The perfume splattered, and bits of glass rained down.

"You've made the place smell like a hothouse."

"I feel better, anyway. Why don't *you* break something?"

"It takes a skull to satisfy me. Is Joe long-headed or round-headed? Better put on your shoes or you'll cut your feet."

"Round-headed, I guess." Standing first on one leg and then

on the other, she slipped the narrow shoes on. Her legs were beautiful.

"I like the round-headed ones especially. They're like cracking walnuts, one of the happiest memories of my childhood."

She stood and faced me with her hands on her hips. "You talk a good fight, Archer. Joe can be rough, you know that."

"Tell me more."

But there were hustling footsteps in the corridor. They key turned in the lock. It was Dowser himself, in beige slacks and a chocolate jacket.

He jerked his thumb at me. "Out. I want to talk to you."

"What about me?" the girl said.

"Calm down. You can go home as far as I'm concerned. Only don't try to skip out, I want you around." He turned to Blaney behind him. "Take her home."

Blaney looked disappointed. She called out "Good luck, Archer" as he marched her away.

I followed Dowser into the big room with the bar. The curly-headed Irishman was shooting practice shots on the snooker table. He straightened up as the boss came in, presenting arms with his cue.

"I got a job for you, Sullivan," Dowser said. "You're going to Ensenada and see Torres. I talked to him on the telephone, so he knows you're coming. You stick with Torres until Joe shows up."

"Is Joe in Ensenada?"

"There's a chance he'll turn up there. The *Aztec Queen* is gone, and it looks as if he took it. You can have the Lincoln, and make it fast, huh?"

Sullivan started out and paused, fingering his black bowtie: "What do I do with Joe?"

"Give him my best regards. You take orders from Torres."

Dowser turned to me the big executive with more responsibility on his shoulders than one man should rightly have to bear. But always a genial host: "Want a drink?"

"Not on an empty stomach."

"Something to eat?"

"Most jails provide board for the prisoners."

He gave me a hurt look, and beat on the floor with the butt of the abandoned cue. "You're not my prisoner, baby, you're my guest. You can leave whenever you want."

"How about now?"

"Don't be in such a hurry." He hammered the floor still harder, and raised his voice: "Where the hell is everybody around here? I pay them double wages so they leave me stranded in the middle of the day. Hey! Fenton!"

"You should have a bell to ring."

An old man answered the summons at a limping run. "I was lying down, Mr. Dowser. You want something?" His eyes were bleared with sleep.

"Get Archer here something to eat. A couple of ham sandwiches, and some buttermilk for me. Hurry."

The old man ran out of the room, his shirtsleeved elbows flapping, the long white hair on his head ruffled by his own wind.

"He's the butler," Dowser said with satisfaction. "He's English, he used to work for a producer in Bel-Air. I should of made him talk for you, you ought to hear him talk. I'll make him talk when he comes back, huh? Ten-dollar words!"

"I'm afraid I have to leave," I said.

"Stick around, baby. I might have plenty of use for a man like you. That was the straight dope you got from the girl. I went to the Point and checked it personally. The bastard lammed in his brother's boat all right."

"Did you have to keep me locked up until you checked?"

"Come on, boy, I was doing you a favor. Don't tell me you didn't make out?" He leaned over the green table and sank a long shot in one of the far pockets. "How about a game of snooker, huh? A dollar a point, and I'll spot you twenty. You'll make money off me."

I was getting restless. The friendlier Dowser grew, the less I liked him. On the other hand, I didn't want to offend him. An idea for taking care of Dowser was forming at the back of my head, where it hurt, and I wanted to be able to come back to his house. I said that he was probably a shark and that I hadn't played the game for years. But I took a cue from the rack at the end of the bar.

I hardly got a chance to use my cue. Dowser made a series of brilliant runs, and took me for thirty dollars in ten minutes.

"You know," he said reminiscently, chalking his cue, "I made my living at this game for three years when I was a kid. I was going to be another Willie Hoppe. Then I found out I could fight: there's quicker money in fighting. I come up the hard way." He touched his rosebud ear with chalk-greened fingers. "How about another?"

"No, thanks. I'll have to be shoving off."

But then the butler came back with the sandwiches. He was wearing a black coat now, and had brushed his hair. "Do you wish to eat at the bar, sir?"

"Yeah. Fenton, say a ten-dollar word for Archer here."

The old man answered him with a straight face: "Antidisestablishmentarianism. Will that do, sir? It was one of Mr. Gladstone's coinages, I believe."

"How about that?" Dowser said to me. "This Gladstone was one of those English big shots, a lord or something."

"He was Prime Minister, sir."

"Prime Minister, that's it. You can go now, Fenton."

Dowser insisted that I share the buttermilk, on the grounds that it was good for the digestion. We sat side by side at the bar and drank it from chilled metal mugs. He became vivacious over his. He could tell that I was an honest man, and he liked me for it. He wanted to do things for me. Before he finished, he had offered me a job at four hundred dollars a week, and showed me the money-clip twice. I told him I liked working for myself.

"You can't make twenty thousand a year working for yourself."

"I do all right. Besides, I have a future."

I had touched a sore spot. "What do you mean by that?" His eyes seemed to swell like leeches sucking blood from his face.

"You don't last so long in the rackets. If you're lucky, you last as long as a pitcher or a fighter—"

"I run a legitimate business," he said with intensity. "I used to handle bets, sure, but that's over and done. I hardly ever break a law any more."

"Not even the murder laws?" I was getting very impatient, and it made me indiscreet.

But the question appealed to his vanity in some way. "I never even been indicted," he said.

"How many men have you lost in the last five years?"

"How the hell should I know? I got a rapid turnover, sure, it's the nature of the business. I got to protect myself from competition, I got to protect my friends." He slid off his stool and began to pace the floor: "I'll tell you one thing, Archer,

I'm going to live a long time. I come from a long-lived family. My grandfather's still living, believe it or not, he's over ninety years old. I keep myself in shape, by God, and I'm going to live to be a hundred. What do you think of that?" He punched himself in the stomach, easily.

I thought that Dowser was afraid to die, and I realized why he couldn't bear to be left alone. I didn't answer him.

"I'm going to live to be a hundred," he repeated, like a man talking in his sleep.

I heard the front door open and close. Blaney appeared in the hallway.

"Did you take her home?" Dowser asked him.

"I dropped her off at the corner. There was a patrol car in front of the house."

"Cops? What do cops want with her?"

"A man named Dalling was killed this morning," I said, looking from one to the other.

Apparently the name meant nothing to Dowser. "Who's he?"

"A friend of Galley's. The cops will be asking her a lot of questions."

"She better not answer too many." He sounded unworried. "What happened to the guy?"

"I wouldn't know. Good-bye."

"Gimme a rumble if you hear anything." And he gave me his private number.

Now that Blaney was back, Dowser lost interest in me. I walked to the door unescorted and let myself out. But I didn't entirely relax until I was back on the highway.

17

I had questions I wanted to ask Galley Lawrence in private, but the police had got to her first. I always believed in giving the police an official priority, when they got there first. So I stayed on the highway and drove south through Santa Monica.

It was after four o'clock when I reached the Pacific Point Hospital. I passed up the information desk and went straight upstairs to Room 204. Mario Tarantine's bed was empty. The other bed in the room was occupied by a small boy reading a comic book.

I checked on the room number again, and went down the corridor to the nurses' station. A gimlet-eyed head nurse looked up from a chart: "Visiting hours are over. We can't run a hospital if visitors don't obey regulations."

"You're absolutely right," I said. "Did Mr. Tarantine go home?"

"Mr. who?"

"Tarantine, in 204. Where is he?"

Her sharp little angled face expressed stern disapproval. "Yes, he did go home. Against his doctor's orders and his own best interests, he put on his clothes last night and walked out of the hospital. I suppose you're a friend of his?"

"I know him."

"Well, you can tell him that if he has a relapse, on his own head be it. We can't run a hospital if patients won't cooperate." The waspish buzzing followed me down the corridor.

I drove across town to the end of Sanedres Street, and parked in front of Mrs. Tarantine's cottage. The late afternoon sun shining through the laurels in the front yard made gold filigree patterns on the worn lawn. I tapped on the glass door and a man's voice called: "Come in."

I turned the knob and stepped directly into a small dim living-room. The air in the room smelled of spices and scrubbed floors and rotting flowers. The plaster wall opposite the door was almost covered with a crude painting of a four-masted schooner in full sail. Above the warped mantelpiece a tarnished gold Christ writhed on a dark wood cross.

In front of the dead fireplace, Mario Tarantine was sitting with his legs up on a time-eaten mohair davenport, a white pillow behind his bandaged head. "You again," was all he said when he saw me.

"Me again. I tried the hospital first. Are you all right?"

"Now that I'm getting some decent food I'm all right. You

know what they tried to feed me in that hospital? Chicken broth. Fruit salad. Cottage cheese." His swollen mouth spat out the words as if he could taste their flavor. "How can I get my strength back on cottage cheese? I just sent Mama down to the butcher shop for the biggest steak she can find." He smiled painfully, showing his broken front teeth. "What's the word?"

"About your brother? He's been getting around. Your boat is gone, but I suppose you know that."

"The *Aztec Queen*?" He leaned toward me, heavy-shouldered, the old davenport creaking under his weight. "Gone where?"

"To Mexico, perhaps. Wherever Joe's gone."

"For Christ's sake!" His dark eyes, peering distracted from the ruined face, glanced around the room. His gaze rested on the gilt Christ above the mantel, and dropped. He stood up and moved towards me. "How long has the boat been gone? How do you know Joe took it?"

"I talked to Galley. She dropped him near the yacht basin early this morning, four or five o'clock. Does Joe have a key to the boat?"

"The bastard has *my* keys. You got a car with you? I got to get down there."

"I'll drive you if you're feeling up to it."

"I'm feeling up to it. Wait, I'll get my shoes on." He shuffled out of the room in stocking feet, and stamped back wearing boots and a leather jacket. "Let's go."

He noticed that I was looking at the painted schooner on the wall. It wasn't a lithograph, as I'd thought at first glance, but a mural painted directly on the plaster, with a black frame painted around it. The colors were garish, made worse by an impossible sunset raying the stiff water, and the draftsmanship was wobbly. Still, the leaning ship looked as if it was moving, and that was something.

"How do you like the picture?" Mario said from the open door. "Joe did it when he was a kid. He wanted to be an artist. Too bad he had to grow up into an all-round heel."

I saw then that the painting had a signature, carefully painted in script: Joseph Tarantine, 1934. It had a title, too, probably copied from a calendar: *When My Ship Comes In*.

I drove downhill to the palm-lined boulevard that skirted the seashore, and along it to the dock. Mario directed me to a lot at the base of the breakwater, where I parked beside a weatherbeaten Star boat perched on a trailer. A brisk offshore wind was blowing the sand, and tossing puffs of spray across the concrete breakwater. It its lee a hundred boats lay at their moorings, ranging from waterlogged skiffs to seventy-foot sailing yachts with masts like telephone poles.

Mario looked across the bright water of the basin and groaned out loud. "It's gone all right. He took my boat." He sounded ready to cry.

I followed him up the sand-drifted steps to a gray one-room building marked HARBORMASTER. Its door was locked. We could see through the window that the office was empty.

An old man in a dinghy with an outboard chugged up to the landing platform below. Mario hailed him. "Where's the Chief?"

The old man's answer was blown away by the wind. We went down the slanting gangway to the platform, which rose and dropped with the swells. "Where's Chief Schreiber?"

"He went out on the Coast Guard cutter," the old man said. "They got a radio call from a San Pedro tuna boat." He lifted the outboard motor clear of the stern and heaved it onto the dock. "There's a boat on the rocks at Sanctuary. They said it looks as if it's breaking up. What happened to your face, chum?"

"Never mind that." Mario's hand closed on the old man's arm. "Did you catch the name of the boat?"

The old man pulled away. "Don't get excited, friend. Just take it easy. The tuna boat didn't get close enough to read the name. You lose a boat?"

"You guessed it."

"It's a sport-fishing boat with aluminum outriggers."

Mario turned to me urgently: "Drive me out to Sanctuary, how about it?" The ugly bruises around his eyes were livid against his pallor.

"Don't you think you better take it easy?"

"When my boat's breaking up on the rocks? You don't want to drive me, I'll take my motorcycle."

"I'll drive you," I said. "How far is it?"

"Less than ten miles. Come on."

"Is it your boat?" The old man's question blew after us like a seagull's cry, and blew away unanswered.

We drove down the coast highway in silence. Mario sat glum

beside me, glaring down at his skinned knuckles, which he rapped together fiercely time after time. With his bandage-helmeted head and damaged Latin features, he looked like a wounded gladiator. I hoped he wasn't going to pass out on my hands.

"Who beat you up, Mario?" I asked him after a while.

It was some time before he answered. When he did, his voice was thick with remembered anger. "There were three of them. Two of them held me while the other one sloughed me. Who they were is my own business. I'll take care of them personally, one at a time."

He dug into the pocket of his jacket and brought out a dully gleaming object. I took my eyes from the road to glance at it. It was a curved metal bar of aluminum, about five inches long, with four round fingerholes and a taped grip. Mario slipped it over his fingers and smacked his armed right hand in the open palm of his left. "I'll take care of them personally," he growled to himself.

"Put it away," I said. "It's a felony to carry knuckles like that. Where did you get it?"

"Took it away from a customer one time. I used to be a bartender in town." He kissed the cruel edge of the metal and dropped it back in his pocket. "I thought it might come in handy. I'm glad I kept it."

"You'll get yourself in worse trouble. Why did they beat you, Mario?"

"It was my lousy brother's fault," he said. "He skipped on Friday night and left me holding the bag. They thought I was in it with him. He didn't even warn me ahead of time. They came aboard the *Queen* in the middle of the night and dragged me out of my bunk. I couldn't handle three."

"Is that the night you and Joe got back from Ensenada?"

He looked at me suspiciously. "What about Ensenada? Joe and me went fishing off Catalina Thursday and Friday. We anchored off the island overnight."

"Catch anything?"

"Not a damn thing. What's this about Ensenada, anyway?"

"I heard that Dowser has a Mexican branch. Your loyalty to Dowser is very moving, especially after what he did to your face."

"I don't know any Dowser," he answered unconvincingly. "You wouldn't be Treasury, would you?"

"I would not. I told you I'm a private detective."

"What's your angle. You said you talked to Galley, you must of found her."

"Your brother slugged me last night. It bothers me, for some reason." But it was the dead man who lay heavy on my mind.

"I'll lend you my knucks when I finish with them," he said. "Turn down the next side road."

It was a rutted lane, meandering across a high meadow to the lip of a sea-cliff. Near the cliff's edge a grove of eucalyptus, with smooth pink trunks like naked flesh, huddled raggedly in the wind. There were weathered redwood tables for picnickers scattered among the trees. Mario ran down a path toward the edge of the cliff, and I followed him. I could see the moving water through the trees, as bright as mercury, and then the gray Coast Guard cutter a half-mile out from shore. It was headed north, back to Pacific Point.

The path ended in a sagging wooden barrier beyond which the cliff dropped sheer. A hundred feet below, which looked like a hundred yards, the running surges burst on its rocky base. Mario leaned on the barrier, looking down.

Where the surf boiled whitest on the jutting black basalt, the boat lay half-capsized. Wave after wave struck it and almost submerged it, pouring in foam-streaked sheets down its slanting deck. The boat rolled with their punches, and its smashed hull groaned on the rocks. The outriggers flopped loose like broken wings. It was a total loss.

Mario's body was swaying in sympathy with the boat. I didn't have to ask if it was his. He groaned when the surf went over it, and his face was wetter than the spray accounted for.

"I wonder what happened to Joe," I said.

"The bastard wrecked my boat. I hope he drowned."

A cormorant flew over the water from north to south like a sharp black soul hell-bent. Mario watched it out of sight.

18 _____

We were waiting at the yacht basin when the Coast Guard cutter docked. As the gray hull nudged the truck-tire buffers along the edge of the dock, two men jumped ashore. One was a tanned young Coast Guard lieutenant in working uniform, apparently the commander of the cutter. The other was a gray-bearded man in ancient suntans without insignia. He had the sea-scoured faded eyes, the air of quiet obstinacy and the occupational pot of an old Navy petty officer.

"The *Aztec Queen*'s on the rocks at Sanctuary," he said to Mario.

"I know it. We just got back from there."

"No chance to salvage it," the Coast Guard lieutenant said. "Even if we could get in close enough, it wouldn't be worth it now. It's breaking up."

"I know it."

"Let's get inside." The harbormaster hugged himself. "That's a cold wind."

We followed him to his office on the breakwater at the foot of the dock. I sat in on a conference in the barren cubicle, or stood in on it, because there were only three chairs. They had seen nobody aboard the wreck. The skipper of the tuna boat who had reported it in the first place had seen nobody, either. The question was: how did the *Aztec Queen* get out of the yacht basin and nine miles down the coast?

In official company, Mario wasn't outspoken. He said he had no idea. But he looked at me as if he expected me to do the talking.

"It's your boat, isn't it?" the harbormaster said.

"Sure it's my boat. I bought it secondhand from Rassi in January."

"Insured?" the lieutenant asked him.

He shook his head. "I couldn't afford the premiums."

"Tough tiddy. What were you using it for?"

"Fishing parties, off and on. Mostly off, in this season. *You* know that, Chief." He turned to Schreiber, who was leaning back in his chair against the wall. The coastal-waters chart behind his head showed a round grease spot where he had leaned before.

"Let's get back on the beam," he said heavily. "The boat didn't slip her moorings and steer herself onto the rocks. There must have been *some*body aboard her."

"*I* know that," Mario stirred uneasily in his chair. If talking had to be done, he wanted somebody else to do it for him.

"Well, it wasn't Captain Kidd. Didn't the engine have a lock on it?"

"Yeah. My brother had the keys, my brother Joe."

"Why didn't you say so? Now we're getting somewhere. Your boat was gone this morning when I come on duty. I thought you took it."

"I been laid up," Mario said. "I was in an accident."

"Yeah, I can see. Looks as if your brother got himself in a worse accident. Did you give him permission to take the boat?"

"He didn't need permission. He owned an interest in it."

"Well, it ain't worth much now," Schreiber said sententiously. "About two red cents. Are you sure it was your brother took her out?"

"How can I be sure? I was home in bed."

"Joe was here this morning," I said. "His wife drove him down before dawn."

"Did he say he was going out in the boat?" the lieutenant asked.

"He didn't say anything so far as I know."

"Where's his wife now?"

"She's staying in Santa Monica with her mother. Mrs. Samuel Lawrence."

Schreiber made a note of the name. "I guess we better get in touch with her. It looks as if her husband's lost at sea."

The lieutenant stood up and pulled his visored cap down over his forehead. "I'll call the sheriff's office. We'll have to make a search for him." He peered through the window across the yacht basin; red sunset streamers were unraveling on the horizon. "It's getting pretty late to do anything tonight. We can't get to the boat until low tide."

"Better try, though. There's an off chance he's still inside the cabin." Schreiber turned to Mario: "Your brother have heart attacks or anything like that?"

"Joe isn't aboard," Mario answered flatly.

"How do you know?"

"I got a feeling."

Schreiber rose, shrugging his thick shoulders. "You better go home, boy, and crawl back into the sack. I don't know how you feel, but you look God-awful."

We went back to my car and turned toward the city. It lay serene on its terraced slopes in the last of the sunset, a few lights winking on like early stars. The white African buildings lay in the red air like something seen through rose-colored glasses in memory. Everything was still except the sea, which drummed and groaned behind us to the slow blues-beat of time.

I was glad enough for once to get out of hearing of the sea. But I didn't get far. Mario wouldn't go home.

He stopped me at a waterfront bar and said he could use a drink. I parked the car and got out. I could use one, too. Below the sea-wall that lined the other side of the boulevard, the surf complained and pounded like a tired heart. The heavy closing door shut out the sound.

A fat old waiter came to the door, shook hands with Mario, lamented like a mother over his face. He seated us in a booth at the back of the room and lit a bottled red candle on our table. The bottle was thickly crusted with the meltings of other candles, like clotted blood. I thought of Dalling in his blood on the floor. He'd be on a mortuary slab by now, or under white light on an autopsy table, with a butterfly incision in his torso. Dalling seemed very distant and long ago.

The waiter finished dabbing at the table with the end of a soiled napkin. "Something to eat, gentlemen? Or you want drinks?"

I ordered a steak and a bottle of beer. Mario wanted a double whisky, straight.

"Aren't you going to eat? You'll knock yourself out."

"We got minestrone tonight, Mario," the waiter said. "It's pooty good for a change."

"I got to save my appetite," he explained. "Mama is waiting dinner for me."

"You want to phone your mama?"

"Naw, I don't want to talk to her."

The waiter padded away on flat feet.

"What am I going to tell her?" Mario asked no one in particular. "I lost the boat, that's bad enough, she never wanted me to buy the boat. I was a damn fool, I let Joe talk me into it. I put up all my cash, and now what have I got? Nothing. I'm on the rocks. And I could of bought an interest in this place, you know that? I tended bar here all last fall and I got on fine with the customers. I got on fine with George, the old guy. He's getting ready to retire and I could of been sitting pretty instead of on my uppers the way I am."

He was falling into the singsong of a man with a grievance, as if the whisky he ordered had hit him in the emotions before he drank it. George brought our drinks, silencing Mario. I looked around the room he might have bought a piece of. It had more decorations than a briefcase general: strings of colored bulbs above the bar, deer heads and stuffed swordfish, photographs of old baseball teams, paintings of cardboard mountains, German beer-mugs. On a platform over the kitchen door, an eagle with glaring glass eyes was attacking a stuffed mountain-lion. All the group needed to complete it was a stuffed taxidermist.

"The boat is bad enough," Mario repeated dismally. "What am I going to tell her about Joe? Joe's always been her favorite, she'll go nuts if she thinks he's drowned. She used to drive us crazy when we were kids, worrying about the old man when he was out. It was kind of a relief when the old man died in bed—"

"You said you had a feeling Joe isn't aboard. Where do you get that feeling?"

He drained his double shot-glass and rapped on the table for another. "Joe's awful smart. Joe would never get caught. He was shoplifting in the stores before he was out of grade school, and he never got caught. He was the bright young brother, see, he had that innocent look. I tried it once and they hauled me off to Juvenile and Mama said I was disgracing the family. Not Joe."

The waiter brought his whisky, and told me that my steak would soon be ready.

"Besides," Mario said, "the bastard can swim like a seal. He used to be a lifeguard on the beach. He's been a lot of things, most of them lousy. I got a pretty good inkling where Joe is. He isn't on the *Queen* and he isn't on the bottom of the sea. He skipped again and left me holding the bag."

"How could he skip at sea?"

"He abandoned the *Queen*, if you want my opinion. He had

five hundred in it, I had fifteen. What did it matter to him, he makes big money. The bastard took her out and ditched her, so it would look as if he drowned himself. He probably made a rendezvous with the guy that has the cabin cruiser in Ensenada—" He cut himself off short, peered anxiously into my face.

"Torres?" I said as casually as I could.

His bruises served as a mask for whatever feelings he had. Deliberately, he emptied his second shot-glass, and sipped with fumbling lips at a glass of water. "I don't know anything about any Torres. I was making it up as I went along, trying to figure how he ditched the boat."

"Why would he go to all that trouble?"

"Take a look at my face and figure it out for yourself. They did this to me because I'm Joey's brother, that's all the reason they had. What would they do to him?" He answered his own question in pantomime, twisting his doubled fists in opposing directions, the way you behead a chicken.

The steak came, and I washed down what I could eat of it with the remnant of my beer. Mario had his third double. He was showing signs of wear, and I decided not to let him have any more. But it turned out that I didn't have to interfere.

Customers had been drifting in by ones and twos, most of them heading for the bar at the front, where they perched like roosting chickens in a row. I was trying to catch the waiter's eye, to signal for my check, when a man opened the front door. He stood with his hand on the knob, scanning the bar-flies, a big man with a ten-gallon hat who looked like a rancher in his Saturday suit. Then his glance caught the back of Mario's bandaged head, and he strode toward us.

Mario half-turned in his seat and saw him coming. "Dammit," he muttered. "It's the deputy sheriff."

The big man laid a hand on his shoulder. "I thought you might be in here. What's this about your brother? Move over, eh?"

Mario slid reluctantly into the corner. "Your guess is as good as mine. Joe doesn't tell me his plans."

The deputy sat down heavily beside him. Mario leaned away as if contact with the law might be contagious.

"You had some trouble with Joe, I hear."

"Trouble? What kind of trouble?"

"Take a look in a mirror, it might stir up your memory."

"I haven't seen Joe since last Friday night."

"Friday night, eh? Was that before or after you got your face ploughed under?"

Mario touched his cheekbone with an oil-grained finger. "Hell, that wasn't Joe."

"Who was it?"

"A friend of mine. It was a friendly fight."

"You got nice friends," the deputy said with sarcasm. A downward smile drew his sun-wrinkles deeper. "What about Joe?"

"I told you I didn't see him since Friday night. We got in from a fishing trip and he beat it back to L.A. He lives in L.A. with his wife."

"If he doesn't live in Davy Jones's locker with a mermaid. I heard he dropped out of sight last Friday, hasn't been back here since."

"He came back this morning," I said. "His wife drove him down."

"Yeah, I mean until this morning. I got in touch with the wife, she's on her way. She didn't see the other one, though."

"What other one?"

"That's what I'm trying to find out," he snapped, and turned his flat red face on Mario: "Were you down here this morning? Aboard your boat?"

"I was home in bed. The old lady knows I was home in bed." Mario looked bewildered, and his words were whisky-slurred.

"Yeah? I was talking to her on the telephone. She didn't wake up until seven. Your boat went out around four."

"How do you know that?"

"Trick Curley, he's a lobsterman, he just got in from the island. You know him?"

"Seen him around."

"He was up early this morning, and he saw the skiff go out in the *Aztec Queen*. The skiff is still there, by the way, tied to the moorings. There were two men in it when it passed Trick's boat."

"Joe?"

"He couldn't tell, it was dark. He hailed them but they didn't answer him. He heard them go aboard, and then the boat went out past the end of the breakwater." He turned on Mario suddenly, and rasped: "Why didn't you answer him?"

"Me? Answer who?"

"Trick, when he hailed you in the skiff."

"For Christ's sake!" The appalling face looked genuinely appalled. "I was home in bed. I didn't get up till nine. Mama gave me breakfast in bed, you ask her."

"I already did. That wouldn't stop you from sneaking out in the middle of the night and coming down here."

"Why would I do a crazy thing like that?" His upturned hands moved eloquently in the air.

"There was bad blood between you and Joe," the deputy said dramatically. "That's common knowledge. Last week in this very bar you threatened to kill him, in front of witnesses. You told him it would be a public service. If you killed him, it would be the only public service you ever did, Tarantine."

"I was drunk when I said that," Mario whined. "I don't know what happened to him, sheriff, honest to God. He took my boat and wrecked it and now you're blaming me. It isn't fair."

"Aw, shut your yap."

"Okay, arrest me!" Mario cried. "I'm a sick man, so go ahead and arrest me."

"Take it easy, Tarantine." The deputy rose ponderously, his wavering shadow climbing the opposite wall as high as the ceiling. "We haven't even got a *corpus delicti* yet. When we do we'll come and see you. Stick around."

"I'm not going any place."

He sat slack and miserable in the corner. The only life in his face came from the small jumping reflections of the candle in the black centers of his eyes. I waited until the deputy was out of sight, and steered him out to my car. Mario cursed steadily under his breath in a mixture of English, *bracero* Spanish, and Italian.

19

We drove down Sanedres Street on the way to Mario's house. From a distance I could see a small crowd gathering in front of the arena, clotting in groups of two and four and six. A string of naked bulbs above the entrance threw a one-sided light on their faces. There were many kinds of faces: the fat rubber faces of old sports wearing cigar butts in their lower middle, boys' Indian faces under ducktail haircuts, experienced and hopeful faces of old tarts, the faces of girls, bright-eyed and heavy-mouthed, gleaming with youth and interest in the kill. And the black slant face of Simmie, who was taking tickets at the door.

Mario clutched my right forearm with both hands and cried out: "Stop!"

I swerved and almost crashed into a parked car, then braked to a stop. "That wasn't very smart."

He was halfway out of the car, and didn't hear me. He crossed the road in a loose-kneed run. The faces turned toward him as he floundered into the crowd. He moved among them violently, like a killer dog in a flock of sheep. His hand came out of his pocket wearing metal. There was going to be trouble.

I could have driven away: he wasn't my baby. But a light jab to the head might easily kill him. I looked for a parking place, found none. Both sides of the road were lined with cars. I backed and turned up the alley beside the arena. The faces were regrouping. Most of the mouths were open. All of the eyes were turned toward the door where Mario and Simmie had disappeared.

I started to get out of my car. The exit door in the wall in front of my headlights burst open with sudden force, as if a rectangular piece of the wall had been kicked out. Simmie, in a yellow shirt, came out of the door head down and crossed the alley in three strides. Mario came after him, running clumsily with his striking arm upraised. Simmie had one knee hooked over the top of the fence when Mario overtook him. The glaring whites of his eyes rolled backward in terror. The metal fist came down across his face. The black boy fell in slow motion to the gravel.

I took hold of Mario from behind. His metal knuckles flailed my thigh and left it numb. I shifted my grip and held him more securely.

"Calm down, boy."

"I'll kill him," he cried out hoarsely between laboring breaths. "Let me go!" His shoulders heaved and almost took me off my feet.

"Take it easy, Mario. You'll kill yourself."

Simmie got onto his knees. The blood was running free from a cut on his brow. He rose to his feet, swaying against the fence. The blood splashed his shirt.

"Mr. Blaney will shoot you dead for this, Mr. Tarantine." He spat on the gravel.

Mario cried out loudly, making no words. His muscles jerked iron-hard and broke my grip. His striking arm swung up again. Simmie flung himself over the fence. I pinned Mario against it and wrenched his metal knuckles off. His knee tried for my groin, and I had to stamp the instep of his other foot. He sat down against the fence and held the foot in both hands.

The Negro woman I had seen the day before came around the corner of the building on the other side of the fence. She was the first of a line of Negro men and women who stood at the end of their row of hutches and watched us silently. One of the men had the black-taped stock of a sawed-off shotgun in his hands. Simmie moved to his side and turned:

"Come on over here and try it."

"Yeah," the man beside him said. "Come on over the fence, why don't you?"

The woman touched the bloody side of the boy's face, moaning. I looked around and saw that the faces were dense in the alley around my car. One of the fat rubber faces opened and called out:

"Attaboy, Tarantine. Go and get the black bastard. Let him have it." The face's owner stayed where he was, in the second line of spectators.

I pulled Mario to his feet and walked him toward the car.

"Did the dirty nigger hit him?" a woman said.

"He's drunk. He knocked himself out. You might as well break it up."

I got in first, pulled Mario after me, and backed slowly through the crowd.

"I got one of them," Mario said to himself. "Christ! did you see him bleed? I'll get the others."

"You'll get yourself a case of sudden death." But he paid no attention.

One of the bright-eyed girls followed the car to the sidewalk and hooked one arm over the door on Mario's side. "Wait!"

I stopped the car. She had short fair hair that clasped her head like a cap made out of gold leaf. Her young red-sweatered breasts leaned at the open window, urgently. "Where's Joey, Mario? I'm awful hard up."

"Beat it. Leave me alone." He tried to push her away.

"Please, Mario." Her red-shining mouth curved in some kind of anguish. "Fix me, will you?"

"I said beat it." He struck at her with the back of his open hand. She held on to it with both of hers.

"I heard you lost your boat. I can tell you something about it. Honest, Mario—"

"Liar." He jerked his hand free and turned the window up. "Let's get out of here, I'm feeling lousy."

I took him home. When he stepped out of the car, he staggered and fell to his knees on the edge of the curb.

I helped him to the door. "You better call the doctor and let him look at your head."

"To hell with the doctor." He said it without energy. "I just need a little rest, that's all."

His mother opened the door. "Mario, where you been, what you been doing?" Her voice was thin and piping with anxiety, as if a frightened small girl were sunk in the inflation of her flesh.

"Nothing," he said. "Nothing to worry, Mama. I went out for some fresh air, that's all."

20

There was no sign of Simmie when I got back to the arena. The man in the box office who sold me my ticket tore it in half himself and told me to go on in. The crowd was gone, except for a few small boys waiting around the door for a chance to duck in free. They watched me with great dark eyes full of silent envy, as if Achilles was fighting Hector inside, or Jacob was wrestling with the angel.

Inside, a match was under way. A thousand or more people were watching the weekly battle between right and wrong. Right was represented by a pigeon-chested young Mediterranean type, covered back and front with a heavy coat of black hair. Wrong was an elderly Slav with a round bald spot like a tonsure and a bushy red beard by way of compensation. His belly was large and pendulous, shaped like a tear about to fall. The belly and the beard made him a villain.

I found my seat, three rows back from ringside, and watched the contest for a minute or two. Redbeard took a tuft of hair on the other's chest between the thumb and forefinger of his right hand and tugged at it delicately, like someone plucking lilies of the valley. Pigeon Chest howled with pain and terror, and cast a pleading look at the referee. The referee, a small round man in a sweat-shirt, rebuked Redbeard severely for thus maltreating his colleague. Redbeard wiggled his beard disdainfully. The crowd roared with anger.

Redbeard waddled across the ring to the corner where Pigeon Chest was gamely enduring his anguish, and smote the young hero lightly on the shoulder with his forearm. Pigeon Chest sank to his knees, pitifully shaken by the blow. Wrong beat its breast with both fists and looked around with arrogance at the crowd.

"Kill him, Gino," a grandmotherly lady said beside me. "Get up and kill the dirty Russian coward." She looked as if she meant it, stark and staring. The rest of the crowd was making similar suggestions.

Warmed by their encouragement, Gino struggled manfully to his feet. Redbeard swung again, with the speed and violence of a feather falling, but this time Gino ducked the blow and hit back. The crowd went mad with delight. "Murder him, Gino." Wrong cowered and skulked away; all bullies were cowards. Wrong had a yellow streak down its back a yard wide, as the old lady said beside me. She could probably see the yellow streak through her bifocal glasses.

Since Right was triumphing, I could afford to take my eyes off the ring for a little while. The girl I was looking for was easy to find. Her bright hair gleamed from a ringside seat on the other side of the platform. She was sitting very close to a middle-aged man in a gabardine suit a little too light for the season and a Panama hat with a red-blue-yellow band. He had a convention badge on his lapel. She was practically sitting in his lap. With a kind of calculated excitement, her fingers moved up and down his arm, and played with his vest-buttons and tie. His face was red and loose, as if he'd been drinking. Hers was on her work.

Now Redbeard was on his hands and knees on the canvas beside the ropes. Gino was begging the referee to make him get up and fight. The referee grasped the evil Russian by the beard and raised him to his feet. Gino went into swift and murderous action. He threw himself into the air feet first and brushed the jutting red beard with the toe of one wrestling shoe. Redbeard, felled by the breeze or the idea of the kick, went down heavily on his back. Right landed neatly on the back of its neck and sprang to its feet in triumph like a tumbler. Wrong lay prostrate while the referee counted it out and declared Right the winner. The crowd cheered. Then Wrong opened its eyes and got up and disputed the decision, its red beard wagging energetically. "Oh, you dirty cheater," the old lady cried. "Throw him out!"

The gilt-haired girl and the man in the Panama hat got up and started to move toward the entrance. I waited until they were out of sight and followed them. The rest of the crowd, heartened by their moral victory, were laughing and chattering, buying peanuts and beer and coke from the white-capped boys in the aisles. Right and Wrong had left the ring together.

When I went out the man and the girl were standing by the box-office, and the ticket man inside was phoning a taxi for them. She was clinging to the man like lichen to a rock. What I could see of her face looked sick and desperate. The fat gabardine arm was hugging her small waist.

By the time the taxi came, I was waiting in my car with the

motor idling, a hundred feet short of the entrance. The taxi paused to pick them up and headed for downtown. It was easy to follow in the light evening traffic, six straight blocks to a stop sign, left on Main Street past Mexican movies and rumdum-haunted bars, down to the ocean boulevard again. Another leftward jog along the shore. The taxi paused and let them out.

Their destination was a small motel standing between a dog hospital and a dark and immobile merry-go-round. A sign over the entrance inscribed its name, THE COVE, in blue neon on the night. As I went by, the girl's face, drawn and hollowed by the glare, was intent on the open wallet in the man's hands. Her lean and sweatered body cast a jagged shadow beside the man's squat open-handed one.

I parked my car at the curb on the other side of the boulevard. Beyond a row of dwarf palms the sea was snoring and complaining like a drunk in a doorway. I spat in its direction and walked back to the motel. This was a long narrow building at right angles to the street, with a row of single rooms reached by a gallery on each side, and open carports below, most of them empty. A light went on toward the rear of the gallery on my side, and for an instant I saw the ill-assorted couple framed in the doorway. Then a T-shirted boy came out, closing the door solicitously behind him. He heel-and-toed along the gallery towards the open stairway at the front. I kept on walking.

When I heard the door of the front office close, I turned and sauntered back. There was a pickup truck in the driveway beside the dog hospital. I went and sat on its running board in the shadow, and watched the lighted window. In no time at all the light in the room went out.

I noticed then that the boy in the T-shirt shared my interest in it. He had mounted the steps without my seeing him, and was walking very lightly toward the closed door. When he reached it, he flattened himself against the wall, tense and still like a figure in a frieze. I sat and watched him. He looked as if he were waiting for a signal to move. I heard it when it came: the girl's voice calling softly behind the door. I couldn't make out the words; perhaps the call was wordless.

The boy unlocked the door and stepped inside and closed it. The curtained window lit up again. I decided to move in closer.

There was another set of stairs at the rear of the building, where the gallery widened into an open sunporch. I stepped across a scrubby eugenia hedge and climbed the stairs; moved softly along the gallery to the lighted window, staying close to the wall where the boards were less likely to creak. I could hear the voices before I reached the window: the boy's voice speaking with quiet intensity: "How can she be your wife? You're registered from Oregon, and she lives here. I thought I recognized her, and now I know it." And the man's, strained and subdued by anxiety: "We just got married today, didn't we? Didn't we?"

The boy was scornful: "I bet she doesn't even know your name."

"I don't," the girl admitted. "What are you going to do?"

"You didn't have to tell him that!" Hysteria threatened the man, but it was still controlled by the fear of being heard. "You didn't have to bring me here in the first place. You said it was safe, that you had an understanding with the management."

"I guess I was wrong," the girl said wearily.

"I guess you were! Now look at the mess I'm in. How old are you anyway?"

"Fifteen, nearly sixteen."

"God." The word came out with a rush of air, as if he'd been rammed in the stomach by a piledriver. I leaned at the edge of the window trying to see him, but the window was covered completely with curtains of rough tan cloth.

"That makes it worse," the boy said virtuously. He sounded very virtuous for a night clerk in a waterfront motel. "Contributing to the delinquency of a minor. Statutory rape, even."

The man said without inflection: "I got a daughter at home as old as her. What am I going to do? I got a wife."

The virtuous youth said: "You're remembering a little late. I tell you what I have to do. I have to call the police."

"No! You don't have to call the *police*. She doesn't want you to call them, do you? Do you? I paid her money, she won't testify. Will you?"

"They'll make me," she said glumly. "They'll send me away. You, too."

"This isn't a call-house, mister," the boy said. "The manager says if this sort of thing comes up, I got to call the police. *I* didn't invite you here."

"*She* did! It's all her fault. I'm a stranger in town, son. I didn't realize the situation. I came down here from Portland for the ad convention. I didn't realize the situation."

"Now you do. We let this sort of thing go on, they take away our license. The manager hears about it, I lose my job. And I'm not your son."

"You don't have to get nasty." The older man's voice was querulous. "Maybe what you need is a punch in the nose."

"Try it on, you old goat. Only button yourself up first."

The girl's voice cut in shrilly: "Talk to him. You won't get anywhere like that. He'll tag you for assault along with the rest."

"I'm sorry," the older man said.

"You've got plenty to be sorry about."

The girl began to sob mechanically. "They'll send me away, and you too. Can't you do anything, mister?"

"Maybe I could talk to the manager? It isn't good business if you call the police—"

"He's out of town," the boy said. "Anyway, I can handle this myself."

After a pause, the man asked haltingly: "How much money do you make a week?"

"Forty a week. Why?"

"I'll pay you to forget this business. I haven't got much ready cash—"

"You've got some twenties in your wallet," the girl said. She had given over sobbing as suddenly as she'd started. "I saw them."

"You shut up," the boy said. "I couldn't take a bribe, mister. It would mean my job."

"I have about eighty-five in cash here. You can have it."

The boy laughed flatly. "For contributing to statutory rape? That would be cheap now, wouldn't it? Jobs are scarce around here."

"I have a hundred-dollar traveler's check." The man's voice was brightening. "I'll give you a hundred and fifty. I got to keep a little to pay my hotel."

"I'll take it," the boy said. "I don't like to do it, but I'll take it."

"Thank God."

"Come on down in the office, mister. You can use the fountain pen in the office."

"Gee, thanks, mister," the girl said softly. "You saved my life for sure."

"Get away from me, you dirty little tart." His voice was furious.

"Quiet," the boy said. "Quiet. Let's get out of here."

I moved back to the sun-porch, and watched them around the corner as they came out. The boy moved briskly ahead, swinging his arms. The older man slouched behind with his hat in his hand. His untied shoelaces dragged on the floor of the gallery.

21

I tapped on the door.

"Who is it?" the girl whispered.

I tapped on the door again.

"Is that you, Ronnie?"

I answered yes. Her bare feet padded across the floor, and the door opened. "He was easy—" she started to say. Then her hand flew up to her mouth, and her eyes darkened at the sight of me. "Augh?"

She tried to shut the door in my face. I pushed through past her and leaned on the door, closing it behind me. She backed away, the fingers of both hands spread across her red-smeared mouth. She had nothing on but a skirt, and after a moment she remembered this. Her hands slid down to cover her breasts. They were young and small, easy to cover. The bones in her shoulders stood out, puny as a chicken's. A part of her left arm was pitted like ancient marble by hypo marks.

"Yours is a keen racket, sister. Can't you think of anything better to do with your body?"

She retreated further, as far as the unmade bed in the corner of the room. It was an ugly little room, walled and ceiled with sick green plaster that reminded me of public locker rooms, furnished with one bed, one chair, one peeling veneer dresser and a rug the moths had been at. It was a hutch for quick rabbit-matings, a cell where lonely men could beat themselves to sleep with a dark brown bottle. The girl looked too good for the room, though I knew she wasn't.

She picked her sweater off the floor and pulled it over her head. "What business of yours is it, what I do with my body?" Her red-eyed breast looked dully at me for an instant before she covered it. "You get out of here or I'll call the key-boy."

"Good. I want to talk to him."

Her eyes widened. "You're a policeman." There was something peculiar about her eyes.

"A private cop," I said. "Does that make you feel any better?"

"Get out of my room and leave me alone, then I'll feel better."

I moved toward her instead. Her face was pinched thin and white by an internal chill. The peculiar thing about her eyes was that they had no centers. I looked through them into darkness, cold darkness inside her. A tremor started in her hands, moved up her arms to her shoulders and down her body. She sat down on the edge of the bed and gripped her knees with both hands, bracing her limbs against each other to keep them from flying apart. A shadow crossed her face as dark and final as the shadow of death. She looked like a little old woman in a gold wig.

"How long has it been?" I said.

"Three days. I'm going crazy." Her teeth began to chatter. She closed them hard over her lower lip.

"The bad stuff, kid?"

"Uh-huh."

"I'm sorry for you."

"A lot of good that does me. I haven't slept for three nights."

"Since Tarantine went away."

She straightened up, having repressed the tremor. "Do you know where Joey is? Can you get me some? I've got the money to pay for it—"

"I'm not in the business, kid. What's your name, anyway?"

"Ruth. Do you know where he is? Do you work for him?"

"Not me. So far as Joey's concerned, you'll have to sweat it out."

"I can't. I'll die." And maybe she was right.

"How long have you been on the kick?"

"Since last fall. Ronnie started me."

"How often?"

"Once a week, about. Then twice a week. Every day the last couple of months."

"How much?"

"I don't know. They cut it. It was costing me fifty dollars a day."

"Is that why you started shaking down the tourists?"

"It's a living." She raised her heavy eyes. "How do you know so much about me?"

"I don't. But I know one thing. You should see a doctor."

"What's the use? They'll send me away to a Federal hospital, and then I'll die for certain."

"They'll taper you off."

"How do you know, have you had it?"

"No."

"Then you don't know what you're talking about. It turns you inside out. I was down on the beach last night and every time a wave slapped the sand it hit me like an earthquake, the end of the world. I lay back and looked straight up and there wasn't any sky. Nothing but yellow specks in my eyes, and the black. I felt the beach slanting down under me and I slid off in the black. It's funny, it felt as if I was falling into myself, I was hollow like a well and falling down me." She touched her stomach. "It's funny I'm still alive. It was like dying."

She lay back on the rumpled bed and looked at the ceiling with her arms under her head, her breasts pulled almost flat, her nose and mouth and chin carved stark by strain. Sweat was darkening her narrow golden temples. The sick-green ceiling was her only sky. "I guess I'll have to go through it again, though, before I really die."

"You're not going to die, Ruth." That was my statement. But I felt like a prosecutor cross-questioning a dead girl in the lower courts of hell. "What were you doing on the beach last night?"

"Nothing." Her answer was like a memory of an earlier, happier life: "We used to go down to the beach all the time before Dad went away. We had a dog then, a little golden cocker, and he used to chase the birds and we used to take our lunch down to the beach and have a picnic and light a fire and have a lot of fun. Dad always collected seashells for me: we made a real collection.'' She propped herself up on her elbows, wrinkling her blank young brow. ''I wonder where my seashells are, I don't know what happened to them.''

''What happened to your father?''

''I hardly ever see him anymore. He went away when my mother left him: they ran a photographer's studio in town. He got a job as radio operator on a ship, and he's always way off somewhere, India or Japan. He sends my grandmother money for me, though.'' Her tone was defensive. ''He writes me letters.''

''You live with your grandmother, do you?''

She dropped back flat on the bed. ''More or less. She's a waitress in a truck-stop down the line. She isn't home at night and she sleeps in the daytime. That was the trouble last night. The house began to breathe around me, in and out, and I got scared and I was all alone. I thought if I went down the beach, maybe I'd feel better. It always used to make me feel good when I smelled the ocean. It didn't work. It was worse in the open. I told you about the stars, how they were like holes in my head, and falling into the black. When I woke up from that, I saw the man come out of the sea and I guess I blew my top. I thought he was a merman like the poem we had in English last year. I still don't know for sure if he was real.''

''Tell me about the man. Where did you see him?''

''Mackerel Beach, where they have the barbecue pits: that's where we always used to have our picnics.'' She raised one hand and gestured vaguely southward. ''It's about a mile down the boulevard. I was lying behind one of the windshelters on the sand, and I was awful cold.'' The recollection made her shiver a little. ''The black was gone, though, and I wasn't falling. I thought the worst was over. There was a little light on the water, and I always feel better in daylight when I can see things. Then this man stood up in the surf and walked out of the water up on the beach. It scared me stiff. I had a crazy idea that he belonged to the sea and was coming to get me. It was still pretty dark, though, and I lay still and he didn't even see me. He walked into the bushes behind the barbecue pits. I think he had a car parked in the lane back there. I heard a motor starting after a while. He was real enough, I guess. Do you think he was real?"

"He was a real man, sure. Did he have a bandage on his head?"

"No, I don't think so. It wasn't Mario. Ronnie told me about Mario's boat getting wrecked, and I thought it might have something to do with Mario's boat—"

"Did you see the boat?"

"No. Maybe I heard it, I don't know. Half the time if a seagull screams it blasts my ears like a steam whistle and half the time I'm deaf, I can't hear a thing." Like most dope addicts she was hypochondriac, more interested in her symptoms than anything else and talented in describing them.

I said: "What did he look like?"

"There wasn't much light. I couldn't see his face. He was mother-naked, or else he was wearing a light-colored bathing suit. I think he had a bundle around his neck."

"Was it anybody you know?"

"I don't think so."

"Not Joe Tarantine?"

"It couldn't have been Joey. I wish it was. I'd have known Joey, mother-naked or not."

"He's your source of supply, I take it."

"I've got no source of supply," she said to the ceiling. "For three days now like three years. What would you do in my place, mister? Ronnie's got weed, but that just makes me sicker. What would you do?"

"Go to a doctor and taper off."

"I can't do that, I told you. I can't. You're from L.A., aren't you? You know where I can get it in L.A.? I made two hundred dollars the last three nights."

I thought of Dowser, who liked blondes. She'd be better sweating it out than going to Dowser, even if Dowser had the stuff to give her. "No, I don't know."

"Ronnie knows a man in San Francisco. Ronnie was a runner for Herman Speed, before old Speed got shot. Do you think I could get some if I went to Frisco? I've been waiting for Joey to come back. He doesn't come. Do you think he'll ever come?"

"Joey's either dead or out of the country now. He won't come back."

"I was afraid he wouldn't. To hell with waiting for Joey any more. I'm going to Frisco." She sat up suddenly and began to comb her hair.

"Who's the man there Ronnie told you about?"

"I don't know his name, they don't use names. He calls himself Mosquito. He pushed the stuff for Speed last year. Now he's doing it in Frisco." She leaned over to pull on her shoes.

"That's a big city."

"I know where to go, Ronnie told me." She covered her mouth with her hand in a schoolgirl's gesture. "I'm talking too much, aren't I? I always talk too much when people are nice to me. You've been awful nice to me, and I thought you were a policeman."

"I used to be," I said, "but I won't spoil your chance."

She was looking much better, now that she'd made up her mind to travel that night. There was some blood moving under her skin, some meaning in her eyes. But she still looked old enough to be her own mother.

22

The door sprang open without warning, as doors were always opening in my life. The boy Ronnie came in. A big nineteen or twenty, he had the face of a juvenile lead instead of a juvenile delinquent, keen and dark with a black brush of hair, a heavy single eyebrow barring his brow. His arms below the T-shirt were tanned and heavy-looking. The right one held a tire-iron.

I saw this in the instant before he swung at my head. I ducked and moved in on him before he could swing again. The girl was silent behind me. My fingers found the wrist that held the tire-iron. I twisted it away with my other hand and tossed it clanking in a corner of the room. Then I pushed him away, looped an obvious left at his head, to bring up his guard, and put my weight behind a straight right to his center. It was a sucker punch, not on the side of the angels. A single futile blow for the damned.

He fell turning on his face, and writhed on the floor for air. The girl joined him there, kneeling across him with little cries of love. He'd started her on heroin, given her yellow fever and white death, so she was crazy about him.

His paralyzed diaphragm began to work again. He drew deep sighing breaths. I stood and watched him sit up, and thought I should have hit him harder.

The girl's white face slanted up towards me. "You big bully."

"You wait outside, Ruth. I want to talk to Ronnie."

"Who are you?" The boy's words came hard between gulps of air. "What goes on?"

"He says he's a private cop." Her arms were around his shoulders; one of her hands was gently stroking his flank.

He pushed her away and rose unsteadily. "What do you think you want?" His voice was higher than it had been, as if my blow had reversed his adolescence.

"Sit down." I glanced at the single chair standing under the ceiling light. "I want some information."

"Not from me you don't." But he sat down. A nerve was twitching in his cheek, so that he seemed to be winking at me gaily again and again.

"Close the door," I said to the girl. "Behind you."

"I'm staying. I'm not going to let you hurt him any more."

The boy's face screwed up in sudden fury. "Get out of here, God damn you. Sell yourself for dog meat, only get out." He was talking to the girl, taking out his humiliation on her.

She answered him soberly: "If you say so, Ronnie," and went out, dragging her feet.

"You were a runner for Speed," I said to the boy.

Fury took hold of his face again and pulled it sharp and ratty. His ears were unnaturally small and close to his head. "Ruth's been flapping at the mouth, eh? She's a real fun person, Ruth is. I'll have to talk to Ruth."

"You'll lay off her entirely. I've got some more punches that you haven't seen. No girl would look twice at your face again."

His light eyes flicked towards the tire-iron in the corner, and quickly away from it. He groped for a boyish and dutiful expression and presented it to me. "I can't stay here, mister, honest. I got to get out in the office."

"There won't be any more easy marks tonight."

He managed to show me crooked teeth in a crooked little smile. "I guess maybe I'm stupid, mister. I don't get you at all."

"A century and a half is a lot of money to earn for five minutes' fast talking."

The cheek twitched, and he winked again. He was the least charming boy I had ever talked to. "You'd never get him to testify," he said.

"Don't kid yourself. He'll wake up mad tomorrow morning. I can easily find him."

"The old goat was asking for it, wasn't he?"

"You're the one that's asking for it, boy. They don't like badger games in a tourist town."

"I get it. You want a split." He smiled and winked again.

"I wouldn't touch it. Information is what I want."

"What kind of information? I got no information."

"About Herman Speed. I want to know what happened to him, and why."

Without moving his body, he gave the impression of squirming. He ran his hand nervously over his dark brush of hair. "You a State agent, mister? Federal?"

"Relax. It's not you I want. Though I'll turn you in for extortion if I have to."

"If I don't talk, you mean?"

"I'm getting impatient."

"I don't know what you want me to say. I—"

"You worked for Speed. You don't any more. Why not?"

"Speed isn't in business any more."

"Who do you work for?"

"Myself. Tarantine doesn't like me."

"I can't understand that," I said. "You've got looks, brains, integrity, everything. What more could Tarantine ask?"

That nicked his vanity and he showed a little shame. Only a

little. "I was a runner for Speed, so Tarantine doesn't like me."

"He worked for Speed himself."

"Yeah, but he double-crossed him. When the corporation moved in, he changed sides. He saw an independent like Speed couldn't hold out against them."

"So he shot Speed and took over the business for the corporation."

"Not exactly. Tarantine's too smart to do any shooting himself. Maybe he fingered Speed. I heard he did."

"How did it happen?"

"I wasn't there, I only know what I heard." He did some more of his motionless squirming. Under the single eyebrow his eyes looked very small and close together. Transparent pimples of sweat dotted his forehead. "I shouldn't be talking like this, mister. It could get me blasted. How do I know I can trust you?"

"You'll have to take the chance."

"You couldn't use me for witness, I only know what I heard."

"Tell me."

"I'll tell you the best I can, mister. Speed was driving up from Tijuana that night. He had some packages of white in his tires; his system was pockets vulcanized on the inside of the tubes. Tarantine was riding with him and I guess he tipped off the mob. They hijacked Speed on the highway this side of Delmar, blocked him off the road with an old truck or something. Speed objected so they shot him down, drove his car away and left him for dead. Tarantine brought him in, he was Speed's palsy-walsy. That's what Speed thought. When Speed got out of the hospital, he left town. He almost died, I guess that scared him off. He couldn't stand a shooting war, he was a gentleman."

"I can see that. Where's the gentleman now?"

"I wouldn't know. He blew, that's all. He sold the Arena lease to Tarantine and blew."

"Describe the gentleman, Ronnie."

"Speed? He's a sharp dresser. Two-hundred-dollar suits and custom shirts and ties with his own monogram. A big stout guy, but sharp. He talks like a college graduate, the genuine class."

"Does he have a face?"

"Yeah, he's pretty good-looking for an older guy. He's still got most of his hair—light brown hair. A little fair mustache." He drew a finger across his upper lip. "Pretty good features, except for his nose. He has a bump on his nose where he had it broken."

"About how old?"

"Middle-aged, forty or so. About your age, maybe a little older. Speed hasn't got your looks, though, mister." He tried to look earnest and appealing.

He was the kind of puppy who would lick any hand that he was afraid to bite. It was depressing not to be able to hit him again because he was younger and softer and too easy. If I really hurt him, he'd pass it on to somebody weaker, like Ruth. There was really nothing to be done about Ronnie, at least that I could do. He would go on turning a dollar in one way or another until he ended up in Folsom or a mortuary or a house with a swimming pool on top of a hill. There were thousands like him in my ten-thousand-square-mile beat: boys who had lost their futures, their parents and themselves in the shallow jerry-built streets of the coastal cities; boys with hot-rod bowels, comic-book imaginations, daring that grew up too late for one war, too early for another.

He said: "What's the matter, mister? I told you the truth so far as I know the truth." His cheek twitched, and I realized that I had been gazing down sightlessly into his empty hazel eyes.

"Maybe you have at that. You didn't make it all up, you haven't the brains. What was Tarantine's system?"

"I wouldn't know about that." He ran his uneasy fingers through his short black hair again.

"Sorry, I forgot. You're a respectable citizen. You don't have truck with crooks like Tarantine."

"Him and his brother bought this boat," he said. "The boat that got wrecked today. How would I know what they used it for? They went on a couple of fishing trips, maybe they went to Mexico. That's where Speed got the stuff when he was here, from a guy in Mexico City that manufactured it out of opium." He leaned forward toward me, without leaving the security of the chair. "Mister, let me go out to the office now, I told you all I know. What do you say?"

"Don't be such an eager beaver, Ronnie. There's another

friend of yours I want to hear about. Where do I get in touch with Mosquito, in case I ever have the urge?''

''Mosquito?''

''He's selling in San Francisco now, Ruth says. He used to sell for Speed here.''

''I don't know any Mosquito,'' he said without conviction, ''only the ones that bite me.''

I clenched my fist and held it for him to look at, telling myself that I was a great hand at frightening boys.

The hazel eyes crossed slightly looking at it. ''I'll tell you, mister, promise you won't use my name. They wouldn't appreciate me talking around. He wrote me I might get a job up there this summer—''

''I'm not making any promises, Ronnie. I'm getting impatient again.''

''You want to know where to find him, is that it?''

''That will do.''

''I contacted him through a musician plays the piano in a basement bar, a place called The Den. It's right off Union Square, it's easy enough to find.''

''When was this?''

''About a month ago. I flew up for a week-end last month. I get a buzz out of Frisco. It suits my personality, not like this one-horse town—''

''Yeah. Did you see Mosquito to talk to?''

''Sure, he's a big shot now, but he's a good friend of mine. I knew him in high school.'' Ronnie expanded in the thought. He knew Mosquito when.

''What's his real name?''

''You won't tell him I told you, mister, will you? Gilbert Moreno.''

''And the musician?''

''I don't know his name. You'll find him in The Den, he plays piano every night in The Den. He's a snowbird, you can't miss him.''

''Does Mosquito know where Speed is?''

''He said Speed was up there Christmas trying to raise a stake. Then he went to Reno, I think he said Reno. Can I go now, mister?''

The pattern was starting to form on the map at the back of my mind. It was an abstract pattern, a high thin triangle drawn in red. Its base was the short straight line between Palm Springs and Pacific Point. Its apex was San Francisco. Another, shadowier triangle on the same base pointed its apex at Reno. But when I tried to merge the two into a single picture, the entire pattern blurred.

I said: "All right, get."

When we went out, the girl had disappeared. I felt relieved. She was a bigger responsibility than I wanted.

23

The lighted clock on the tower of the county courthouse said that it was only five minutes after eleven. I didn't believe it. I had a post-midnight feeling. My tongue was already furred with the dregs of a long bad evening. A criminal catechism ran on like a screechy record in my head. What? Blood. Where? There. When? Then. Why? Who knows. Who? Him. They. She. It. Us. Especially us.

I parked in front of the wing of the courthouse that held the county jail. The windows of the second and third floors were barred with ornamental ironwork, to appeal to the aesthetic sense of the thieves and muggers and prostitutes behind them. Part of the first floor of this wing was occupied by the sheriff's office, whose windows showed the only lights in the building below the tower clock.

The tall black oak door stood open, and I walked in under white fluorescent light. Behind the counter that divided the anteroom in two, a fat young man was talking into a telephone. No, he said, the chief wasn't there. He couldn't give out his private number. Anyway, he was probably in bed. Is that right, he was very sorry to hear it. He'd bring it to the chief deputy's attention in the morning.

He set the receiver down and sighed with relief. "A nut," he said to me. "We hear from her every day or two. She thinks she can receive radio waves, and foreign agents are bombarding her nervous system with propaganda. Next time I'm going to tell her to get her tubes adjusted so she can receive television."

He left his desk and lumbered to the counter: "What can I do for you, sir?" He had the friendly manner of a corner grocer, dispensing justice instead of bread and potatoes.

"I don't suppose the chief *is* here?"

"Not since supper. Anything I can do?"

"One of the deputies is working on a disappearance case: Joe Tarantine."

"One of the deputies, hell. There's three or four working on it." He buried his eyes in a smile.

"Let me talk to one of them."

"They're pretty busy. You a reporter?"

I showed him my photostat. "The one I was talking to is a big man in a ten-gallon hat, or do they all wear ten-gallon hats?"

"Just Callahan. He's in there with Mrs. Tarantine just now." He jerked his thumb towards an inner door. "You want to wait?"

"Which Mrs. Tarantine, mother or wife?"

"The young one. If I was Tarantine, I wouldn't run out on a bundle of goodies like that one." A leer started in his eyes and moved across his face in sluggish ripples.

I swallowed my irritation. "Is that the official view, that Tarantine ran out? Maybe you've got some inside dope that he can walk on water, or maybe a Russian sub was waiting to pick him up."

"Maybe." He fanned his face with his hand. "You and the old lady should get together. She says the voices in her head talk with a Russian accent. Matter of fact, there ain't no official view, won't be until we complete our investigation."

"Did they get aboard the *Aztec Queen*?"

"Yeah, it's all broken up on the rocks. Nobody in the cabin. What's your interest, if I may ask, Mister—?"

"Archer. I have some information for Callahan."

"He should be out any minute. They been in there nearly an hour." Casting an envious glance at the inner door, he meandered back to his desk and inserted his hips between the arms of the swivel chair.

I had time to smoke a cigarette, almost my first of the day. I sat on a hard bench against the wall. The minute hand of the electric clock on the opposite wall inched round in little nervous jumps to eleven thirty. The deputy on duty was yawning over a news magazine.

The latch of the inner door clicked finally, and Callahan appeared in the doorway. His big hat was in his hand, exposing a sun-freckled pate to the inclement light. He stood back awkwardly to let Galley precede him, smiling down at her as if he owned her.

She looked as trim and vital as she had in the afternoon. She was wearing a dark brown suit and a dark hat, their suggestion of widow's weeds denied by a lime-green blouse under her jacket. Only the bluish crescents under her eyes gave me an idea of what she had been through.

I stood up and she paused, one knee forward and bent in an uncompleted step. "Why, Mr. Archer! I didn't expect to run into you tonight." She completed the step and gave me her gloved hand. Even through the leather, it felt cold.

"I thought I might run into you. If you don't mind waiting a minute, I want to see Callahan."

"Of course I'll wait."

She sat down on the bench. Callahan hung over her and thanked her profusely for her aid. Her smile was a little strained. The fat young man leaned across the counter, his fleshbound eyes regarding her hungrily.

The big man put on his hat as he turned to me. "What's the story, mac? Let's see, you were with Mario down on the waterfront. You a friend of his?"

"A private detective, looking for Joe Tarantine. The name is Archer."

"For her?" He cocked his head towards Galley.

"Her mother." I walked him to the other end of the counter. "A girl I've been talking to saw something this morning that ought to interest you. She was lying behind a wind-shelter on Mackerel Beach at dawn, all by herself."

"All by herself?" Perplexity or amusement corrugated the skin around his eyes.

"She says all by herself. A man swam in to shore with a bundle around his neck, probably clothes because he had nothing on. She saw him cross the beach and then she heard a car start up in the grove of trees behind the barbecue pits."

"So that's what happened to Tarantine," he drawled.

"It wasn't Joe, according to her, and it wasn't Mario either. She knows both of them—"

"Who is this girl? Where is she?"

"I met her at the wrestling match. I tried to bring her in but she ran out on me."

"What does she look like?"

"Blonde and thin."

"Hell, half the girls in town are blondies nowadays. When did you say she saw this guy?"

"Shortly before dawn. It was still too dark to see him very clearly."

"She wouldn't be having delusions?" he muttered. "Any girl that was lying on the beach by herself at that time."

"I don't think so." But perhaps he had something. There were better witnesses than Ruth, a hundred and fifty million of them, roughly.

He turned to Galley, removing his hat again. Even his voice changed when he spoke to her, as if he had a separate personality for each sex: "Oh, Mrs. Tarantine. What time did you say you drove your husband down here?"

She rose and came toward us, walking with precision. "I don't know the time exactly. About four a.m., I think it was."

"Before dawn, though?"

"At least an hour before dawn. It wasn't fully daylight when I got back to Santa Monica."

"That's what I thought you told me."

"Is it important?"

He answered her with solemnity: "Everything is important in a murder case."

"You think he was murdered?" I said.

"Tarantine? No telling what happened to him. We'll start dragging operations in the morning."

"But you mentioned murder."

"Tarantine is wanted for murder," he said. "L.A. has an all-points out for him. Didn't you hear about the Dalling killing?"

I glanced at Galley. Her head moved in a barely perceptible negative. I said: "Oh, that."

"I'm horribly tired," she said. "I'm going to ask Mr. Archer to drive me home."

I said I'd be glad to.

24

She took my arm on the courthouse steps, her fingers gripping me hard but not unpleasantly. "I'm grateful you showed up, Archer. I've been answering policemen's questions for hours and hours, and I feel quite unreal, like a character in a movie. You're something solid to hold on to, aren't you?"

"Solid enough. I weigh a hundred and eighty-five."

"That's not what I mean, and you know it. All those official faces are like death masks. You have a human face, you're made of flesh and blood."

"Flesh and blood and all things nice," I said. "I used to be a policeman. And I think you're walking on eggs."

Her grip on my arm tightened. "Walking on eggs?"

"You heard me. I can't understand why the L.A. cops haven't locked you up as a material witness."

"Why should they put me in jail? I'm perfectly innocent."

"Maybe you are in deed. Not in the mind. You're much too smart to be taken in by Tarantine. You couldn't live with him for over two months without knowing what he was up to."

She dropped my arm, and hung back when I opened the door of the car for her.

"Get in, Mrs. Tarantine. You asked me to drive you home. Where's your own car, by the way?"

"I didn't trust myself to drive tonight. I had a terrible day, and now you're cross-questioning me." Her voice broke, whether artificially or naturally I couldn't tell.

"Get in. I want to hear the story you told the cops."

"You've got no right to speak to me like this. A woman

can't be forced to accuse her husband.'' But she got in.

I said: "She can if she's accessory.'' And slammed the door to punctuate the sentence.

She stayed in the far corner of the seat while I started the engine. "I didn't even know that Joe was wanted for murder until Mr. Callahan told me. Actually there is no warrant for him. He's simply wanted for questioning. They found his fingerprints in Keith's apartment.'' Her voice was thin.

"You must have known.'' I turned left towards the main street. "As soon as they told you Dalling had been shot, you must have thought about Joe's visit to Dalling this morning. What did you give Homicide on that?''

"Nothing. I left it out entirely. I said I drove him straight to Pacific Point.''

"And you don't know what I mean by walking on eggs?''

"I couldn't tell them,'' she whispered. "They'd use it to put him in the gas chamber, if they ever find him.''

I stopped for a flashing red light, and crossed the main street in the direction of the highway. "This afternoon you were strongly anti-Tarantine. What transformed you into the loyal wife?''

"You can save your sarcasm, Archer.'' Her spirit was flickering up again. "Joe isn't a very nice person, but he's incapable of killing anyone. Besides, I'm married to him.''

"I know it. It didn't make him incapable of peddling heroin.''

"How did you find that out?''

"The hard way. The point is that I didn't find out from you.''

"I only knew the last few weeks. I hated it. I'd have left him if I hadn't been afraid to. Does that make me a criminal?''

"Afraid of what, Galley? Joe wouldn't hurt a fly, the way you tell it.''

"He didn't kill Keith,'' she cried. "I'm certain he didn't. He had no reason to.''

"Come off it, you know he had. You won't admit it, because you're afraid of getting involved yourself. As if you weren't up to your neck already.''

"What reason did he have?''

"You gave me one reason this afternoon: Joe was blind mad, you said, because Dalling brought me to the hideout in Oasis. You've changed your story, now that the thing's come real.''

"Keith wasn't in his apartment. There was no shot. I would have heard the shot."

"Nobody else heard it, either, but there was one. You want more motives? Joe must have known that you and Dalling were having an affair. Everybody else did."

"You're a liar!"

"About what, the fact, or the public knowledge of it?"

"It isn't a fact. Keith was a friend, and that's all. What do you think I am?"

"A woman who hated her husband. Call the thing platonic if you want to. Joe isn't the kind to split hairs. You won't deny that Dalling was crazy about you."

"Certainly I deny it. I gave him no encouragement."

"He didn't need encouragement. He was a romantic kid. He would have died for you, and perhaps he did. He brought me into the case, you know."

"I thought you said my mother—"

"Keith persuaded her. He paid a visit to her Sunday night and talked her into hiring me."

"Did she tell you that?"

"She did. And it's the truth."

"She didn't know Keith."

"She met him Sunday."

"How can you be sure?"

"The whole thing was a setup, when I met him in Palm Springs. He wanted me to find him there. Keith was afraid to come to me openly on his own, on account of Joe and Dowser. He felt caught in the middle between them. Still, he had guts enough to take me out there. It must have been hard to do, for a tender personality like Keith. And it really meant something."

"Yes, it meant something." I thought she added under her breath: "Poor fool." She was quiet then.

We were on the open highway, headed north toward Long Beach. A strong wind was blowing across it, and I reduced my speed to keep the car from weaving. I caught occasional glimpses of the sea, white-capped and desolate under a driving sky. The unsteady wind whined in the corners of the cut-banks and fell off in unexpected silences. In one of the silences, under the drive of the motor, I heard Galley crying to herself.

The lights of Long Beach angered the moving sky ahead of us. The wind rose and fell and rose, and the woman's crying continued through strata of peace and violence. She moved against me gently and leaned her head on my shoulder. I drove left-handed so as not to disturb her.

"Did you love him, Galley?"

"I don't know, he was sweet to me." She sighed in the corners of her grief; her breath tickled my neck. "It was too late when I met him. I was married to Joe, and Keith was going to marry another woman. I took him away from her, but it couldn't work out. He wasn't quite a man, except when he was loaded. Then he was worse than a man."

"He's finished now."

"Everything's finished," she said. "Everything's on its last legs. I wish I had had a blowout when I was driving Joe in from Oasis. There wouldn't be all these loose ends to gather up and live with, would there?"

"You didn't strike me as the kind of a girl who wants an easy out."

"There are no easy outs, I guess. I thought I was taking an easy out when I married Joe. I was sick of taking hospital orders, fighting off interns in the linen room, waiting for something good to happen to me. Joe looked like something good for a little while. He wasn't."

"How did you meet him?"

"I told you that, this afternoon. It seems like years ago, doesn't it?"

"Tell me again."

"There are things I'd rather not talk about, but I will if you insist. I was on twenty-four-hour duty with Mr. Speed for over two weeks. Joe came to see him nearly every day. He was running the Arena for him."

"Who shot Speed?"

"One of Dowser's men, Blaney I think. I didn't dare speak out this afternoon. They might have been listening."

"Did Speed tell you that?"

"No, he never admitted anything about the shooting. When the police questioned him in the hospital, he claimed he shot himself by accident. I suppose he was afraid they'd finish him off if he talked. It was Joe told me, after we were married. I promised him I'd never tell a soul, but I guess my promises to Joe are canceled now. He's gone away without caring what happens to me."

"Gone where? Surely he gave you a hint."

"I only know what I told you," she said. "I believe he took Mario's boat."

"The *Aztec Queen* didn't get very far."

"Joe might have been covering his tracks. He could have had another boat waiting at sea for him."

"His brother had the same idea."

"Mario? Mario would know, better than I. Joe has friends in Ensenada—"

"I wonder. He may have business connections, but they really belong to Dowser. If Joe's as sharp as he sounds, he'll be running in the opposite direction.—Did anybody meet him at the yacht basin?"

"I didn't see anyone, no. I heard what you told Mr. Callahan about the man on the beach. It might have been Joe, mightn't it, in spite of what the girl said?"

"It might. I think it was somebody else."

"Who?"

"I haven't any idea."

"What do you think happened to Joe?"

"God knows. He may be in Los Angeles or San Francisco. He may have flown to Cleveland or New York. He may be at the bottom of the sea."

"I almost hope he is."

"What was he carrying, Galley?"

"He didn't tell me, but I can guess that it was heroin. It's what he deals in."

"Does he take it himself?"

"Not Joe. I've seen some of his customers, and that's when I started to hate him. I didn't even like his money after that."

"He ran out with Dowser's shipment, is that it?"

"Evidently. I didn't dare to ask him."

"How much?"

"I couldn't even guess."

"Where did he keep it?"

"I don't know that, either." Her body turned inward to me, and she sighed. "Please stop talking like a policeman. I really can't stand it any longer."

The traffic was still fairly heavy in the Long Beach area, and I concentrated on my driving. On both sides of the road, the oilfield derricks marched like platoons of iron men across the suburban wilderness. I felt as if I were passing through dream country, trying to remember the dream that went along with the landscape and not being able to. Galley removed her hat and lay heavy and still against me until I stopped the car in front of her mother's house.

"Wake up," I said. "You're home."

25

It was nearly two o'clock when I reached my section of the city. I lived in a five-room bungalow on a middle-class residential street between Hollywood and Los Angeles. The house and the mortgage on it were mementos of my one and only marriage. Since the divorce I never went home till sleep was overdue. It was overdue now. The last few miles down the night-humming boulevard I drove by muscle memory, half-asleep. My consciousness didn't take over until I was in my driveway. I saw the garage door white in my headlights, a blank wall at the end of a journey from nowhere to nowhere.

Leaving the motor idling, I got out of the car to open the garage. Two men walking abreast emerged from the shadows on the porch beside me. I waited in the narrow passage between the house and the open door of the car. They were big young men, dressed in dark suits and hats. In the half-light reflected from the garage door, their wide shoulders and square faces looked almost identical. A pair of heavenly twins, I guessed, from the Los Angeles police. The thought of Dalling in his blood had followed me all day. Now Dalling was catching up.

"Archer?" one of them said. "Mr. Lew Archer?"

"You have me. Hearthstone of the Death Squad, I presume." I was running short of élan. "Accompanied by Deathstone of the Hearth Squad. Where's Squadstone of the Death Hearth?"

"I'm Sergeant Fern," said First Policeman. "This is Sergeant Tolliver."

"Pronounced Taliaferro, no doubt."

Second Policeman said: "It's pretty late to be making corny jokes, isn't it, Mr. Archer?"

"Bloody late. Can't this wait until morning?"

"Lieutenant Gary said to bring you in whenever you showed. He wants to talk to you now."

"About the Dalling killing?"

The plain-clothes sergeants looked at each other as if I had said something significant. The first one said: "Lieutenant Gary will be glad to explain."

"I suppose there's no way out of it." I switched off the headlights and slammed the car door shut. "Let's go."

The patrol car was waiting around the corner. Lieutenant Gary was waiting in his Homicide Division cubicle.

It was a small square room dismally equipped with gray-painted steel furniture: a filing-cabinet, a desk with a squawkbox and In and Out baskets piled with reports, a water-cooler in a corner. A street map of the city nearly covered one wall. The single window opened on the windowless side of an adjacent building. A ceiling fixture filled the room with bright and ugly light.

Gary stood up behind his desk. He was a man in his forties with prematurely white hair. It stuck up all over his head in thistly spikes, as if his fingers had been busy at it. Gary had the shoulders of a football guard, but there was nothing beef-trust about his face. He had quarterback's eyes, alert and shifting, a thin inquiring nose, a mobile mouth.

"Lew Archer, eh?" he said, not unpleasantly. His shirt was open and his tie hung askew. He tugged at it half-heartedly and forgot it. "Okay, Fern, thanks."

The sergeant who had escorted me into the station closed the glass door behind him. Gary sat down at his desk and studied me. There was a green cloth board on the wall beside him, with several pictures of wanted men, full-face and profile, pinned to it. I had a fellow-feeling with the black-and-white smudged faces.

"You'll always remember me, Lieutenant."

"I do remember you. I've been checking your record, as a matter of fact. A pretty good record, as records go, in your job, in this town. I can't say you've ever co-operated very freely, but you've never tried to cheat us, and that's something. Also, I've talked to Colton on the D.A.'s staff about you. He's in your corner, one hundred percent."

"I served under him in Intelligence during the war. What are you working up to, Lieutenant? You didn't haul me in at two in the morning to compliment me on my record."

"No. I mention the record because if it wasn't for that you'd be under arrest."

It took me a little while to swallow that. He watched me, his nervous mouth chewing on itself.

I decided to come up smiling. "As it is I'm paying you a social call. Charming occasion, isn't it?"

His eyes narrowed and brightened. They were like rifle slits in his walled face, with blue steel glinting behind them. "The warrant's drawn," he said softly. "If I decided to execute it, you wouldn't think it was funny."

"What's it for? Spitting on the sidewalk?"

I got no rise out of him. He answered me with a question: "What have you been doing with yourself all day?"

"Eating. Working. Drinking. Having laughs."

He answered his own question: "Looking for Joe Tarantine. Tell me why."

"I have a client."

"Name him."

"My memory for names is very lousy."

He shifted in his chair, his blue gaze circling the room as if he wanted out. "I have several questions to ask you, Archer. I hope this isn't going to be typical of your answers."

"You seem to know the answers."

"Hell, let's get down to cases. Soft-pedal the repartee."

"I'm afraid when you wave a warrant at me it brings out the comedian."

"Forget the warrant. It wasn't my idea." Against all the odds, he sounded like a fair man. "Sit down and tell me why in God's name you should start running errands for Dowser at this late date."

"What have you got against Dowser?" I sat in the one straight chair in front of the desk. "Dowser's a solid citizen. He's got a swimming pool and a private bar to prove it. He entertains politicians in his charming ranch-type home on an exclusive hilltop. He even supports a butler and a blonde.''

''I don't get it, Archer.'' He sounded disappointed. ''You're working for him?''

''Why not? He must be on good terms with the law or he wouldn't be running loose. I wonder how many cops he has on his payroll. I'm just an ex-cop with a living to hustle.''

His eyes shut tight. For an instant the long gray face looked dead. ''Don't tell me about Dowser's payoff. I know. I also know why you left the Long Beach force. You wouldn't take Sam Schneider's monthly cut, and he forced you out.''

''Colton's been talking too much,'' I said. ''If you know all about Dowser, go out and bring him in and put him in Alcatraz where he belongs. Don't take out your official frustrations on me.''

''He isn't my department.'' Gary was masticating his lip again. ''The boys knock off his peddlers two and three a month, but that's as far as it goes. Tarantine's one of his right-hand men, you know that?''

''He was. Not any more.''

''Where is Tarantine now?''

''Nobody knows.''

''We found his fingerprints in Dalling's apartment.'' He changed the subject suddenly: ''What were you doing in Dalling's apartment this morning?''

I let it go by, trying not to show that he had startled me.

He went on: ''A driver for Western Dairy gave us your description this afternoon. He also described your car. You or your twin went in the Casa Loma the back way some time around eight o'clock this morning.'' He sat back and waited for me to have a reaction.

I had a number of them. This meant that his questions about Dowser were by-play. He'd told me to forget the warrant, but he remembered it.

There was nothing in being cagey. ''At eight o'clock Dalling had been dead for hours. The autopsist will tell you that, if he hasn't already.''

''You admit you were there? You admit that Dalling was dead.''

''I was there. He was dead.''

''You didn't report it to us. We had to wait until the blood soaked through the floor and made a spot on the ceiling of the apartment underneath and somebody finally got around to noticing it. That wasn't smart of you, Archer, it wasn't co-operative, it wasn't even legal. It's the kind of thing that makes for license trouble." He leaned forward across the desk, his eyes jumping like blue Bunsen flames, and tossed me a change-of-pace: "Of course license trouble is the least of your worries."

"Go on."

"You rushed straight from the Casa Loma to interview a couple of witnesses, Severn and the Hammond woman. God knows what you thought you were trying to do. The kindest interpretation is that you suddenly remembered you were an aging boy-wonder and decided to cut us out entirely and run a murder investigation as a one-man show. Have you been seeing a lot of movies lately? Reading *The Rover Boys at Hollywood and Vine*?"

"Maybe I have. What's the unkindest interpretation?"

"It's possible you were covering up for yourself." He dropped it very casually. "We found the gun, you see. A member of my detail picked it out of a storm drain on the street behind the Casa Loma parking lot."

Gary opened the drawer in front of him and set a squat black .38 automatic on the desk. "Recognize it?"

I recognized it. It was my own gun.

"You should," he said. "It's registered to you. Our ballistics man just completed some firing tests with this gun a couple of hours ago. It's his opinion, based on examination with a comparison microscope, that this gun fired the slug that was dug out of Dalling's cortex. It severed the jugular vein and imbedded itself in the cortex. Dalling bled to death. How do you like that, Archer?"

"Not very much. Go on. You haven't warned me that anything I say may be used against me yet."

"I'll give it to you now. Have you got anything to say?"

"I'm very smart," I said, "and very devious. I saw Dalling for the first time last night and decided that he was too pretty to live, a fit subject for the perfect crime. So I committed it. I shot him with a gun that could easily be identified as mine and carefully deposited it in the nearest drain, where any cop would be sure to look for it. Four or five hours later I returned to the scene of the crime, as murderers must, in order to admire my handiwork. Also to let a milkman spot me for you. I wanted to make things difficult for myself—"

"You have." Gary was using his gentle voice once more. "This isn't very funny. It doesn't make me laugh."

"It isn't funny. It has some funny elements, though—"

He cut me off again: "You've acted like a damn fool, and you know it. I could probably get an indictment and possibly make it stick—"

"The hell you could. I was just going to tell you the funniest thing of all. I shot Dalling at a range of one hundred and twenty miles. Pretty good for a .38 automatic that normally can't hit a barn door at fifty paces."

"Failing a murder indictment," he went on imperturbably, "I could be very nasty about your failure to report discovery of the corpse. It happens I don't want to be nasty. Colton doesn't want me to be nasty, and I value his judgment. But you're going to force me to be nasty if you go on talking like a damn fool on top of acting like one." He chewed his upper lip. "Now what was that about an alibi?"

It struck me that vaudeville was dead. "At the time Dalling was shot, I was fifteen or twenty miles on the other side of Palm Springs, talking to a woman by the name of Marjorie Fellows. Why don't you get in touch with her? She's staying at the inn there."

"Perhaps I will. What time was that?"

"Around three in the morning."

"If you know that Dalling was shot at three, you know more than we do. Our doctor places it around four, give or take an hour." He spread his hands disarmingly, as if to underline the fact of his candor. "There's no way to determine how long he lived after he was shot, or exactly when he was shot. It's evident from the blood that he lived for some time, though he was almost certainly unconscious from the slug in his cortex. Anyway, you can see how that plays hell with any possible alibi. Unless you have better information?" There was irony in the question.

I said that I had.

"You want to make a statement?"

I said that I did.

"Good. It's about time." He flipped the switch on the

squawkbox on the corner of his desk, and summoned a stenographer.

My obligation to Peter Colton was growing too big for comfort. Apparently the conversation up to this point had been off the record. That suited me, because my performance had been painful. I'd bungled like an amateur when I found Dalling's body; gambled and lost on the chance that Miss Hammond or Joshua Severn might tell me something important if I got to them before policemen did. Gary had driven that home, in spite of my efforts to talk around the point. Vaudeville was dead as Dalling, and the Rover Boys were as out of date as the seven sleepers of Ephesus.

Gary gave up his chair to the young male stenographer.

"Do you want it in detail?" I asked him.

"Absolutely."

I gave the thing in detail from the beginning. The beginning was Dalling's visit to Mrs. Lawrence, which brought me into the case. The night died gradually, bleeding away in words. The police stenographer filled page after page of his notebook with penciled hieroglyphics. Gary paced from wall to wall, still looking for a way out. Occasionally he paused to ask me a question. When I told him that Tarantine had taken my gun, he interrupted to ask:

"Will Mrs. Tarantine corroborate that?"

"She already has."

"Not to us." He took a paper-bound typescript from his desk and riffled through it. "There's nothing in her statement about your gun. Incidentally, you didn't report the theft."

"Call her up and ask her."

He left the room. The stenographer lit a cigarette. We sat and looked at each other until Gary came back:

"I sent a car for her. I talked to her on the phone and she doesn't seem to object. She a friend of yours?"

"She won't be after this. She has a queer old-fashioned idea that a woman should stick by her husband."

"He hasn't done much of a job of sticking by her. What do you make of Mrs. Tarantine, anyway?"

"I think she made the mistake of her life when she married Tarantine. She has a lot of stuff, though."

"Yeah," he said dryly. "Is she trying to cover for him, that's what I want to know."

"She has been, I think." And I recited what she had told me about the early-morning visit to Dalling's apartment.

That stopped him in his tracks. "There's a discrepancy there, all right." He consulted her statement again. "According to what she said this afternoon, she drove him straight over from Palm Springs to Long Beach by the canyon route. The question is, which time was she telling the truth?"

"She told me the truth," I said. "She didn't know then that Dalling was dead. When she found out that he was, she switched her story to protect her husband."

"When did you talk to her?"

"Early this afternoon—yesterday afternoon." It was four o'clock by my wristwatch.

"You knew that Dalling was dead."

"I didn't tell her."

"Why? Could she have killed him herself, or set him up for her husband?"

"I entertained the possibility, but she's crazy if she did. She was half in love with Dalling."

"What about the other half?"

"Mother feeling or something. She couldn't take him seriously; he was alcoholic, for one thing."

"Yeah. Did she communicate all this, or you dream it up?"

"You wouldn't be interested in my dreams."

"Okay. Let's have the rest of the statement, eh?" And he went back to filling the room with his pacing.

It was ten to five when I finished my statement. The stenographer left the room with orders to have it typed as quickly as possible.

"If you've been leveling," Gary said to me, "it looks very much like Tarantine. Why would he do it?"

"Ask Mrs. Tarantine."

"I'm going to. Now."

"I'd like to sit in if possible."

"Uh-uh. Good night."

She met me in the corridor, walking in step with Sergeant Tolliver.

"We're always meeting in police stations," I said.

"As good a place as any, I guess." She looked exhausted, but she had enough energy left to smile with.

26

I woke up looking for the joker that would freeze the pile and win the hand for me. It wasn't under the pillow. It wasn't between the sheets. It wasn't on the floor beside the bed. I was climbing out of the bed to look underneath it when I realized that I had been dreaming.

It was exactly noon by my bedside alarm. A truck started up in the street outside with an impatient clash of gears, as if to remind me that the world was going on without me. I let it go. First I took a long hot shower and then a short cold one. The pressure of the water hurt the back of my head. I shaved and brushed my teeth for the first time in two days and felt unreasonably virtuous. My face looked the same as ever, as far as I could tell. It was wonderful how much a pair of eyes could see without being changed by what they saw. The human animal was almost too adaptable for its own good.

The kitchen was brimful of yellow sunlight that poured in through the window over the sink. I started a pot of coffee, fried some bacon, broke four eggs in the sizzling grease, toasted half a dozen slices of stale bread. After eating, I sat in the breakfast nook with a cigarette and a cup of black coffee, thinking of nothing. Silence and loneliness were nice for a change. The absence of dialogue was a positive pleasure that lasted through the second cup of coffee. But I noticed after a while that I was tapping one heel on the floor in staccato rhythm and beginning to bite my left thumbnail. A car passed in the street with the sound of a bus I was about to miss. The yellow sunlight was bleak on the linoleum. The third cup of coffee was too bitter to drink.

I went to the phone in the hall and dialed my answering service. A Mrs. Caroline Standish had phoned on Monday and again on Tuesday. No, she hadn't left her number; she said she would call again. A Mrs. Samuel Lawrence had phoned twice Tuesday morning. Tuesday afternoon a certain Lieutenant Gary had wanted to speak to me, very urgently. There had also been a call from Mr. Colton of the D.A.'s office. The only Wednesday call was long-distance from Palm Springs. A Mrs.

Marjorie Fellows wanted me to call her back at the Oasis Inn.

"When did you get that last one?"

"About two hours ago. Mrs. Fellows called about ten thirty."

I thanked the cool female voice, depressed the bar, and dialed Long Distance. They got me Marjorie Fellows person-to-person.

"This is Archer. You wanted to talk to me."

"I do, very much. So many things have been happening, I don't know which way to turn." She sounded rather beaten and bewildered.

"Give me an example."

"What did you say?"

"Give me an example, of the things that have been happening."

"Oh, so many things. The police and—other things. I don't like to speak of them over the telephone. You know these switchboard operators." She said it with direct malice, to a hypothetical operator listening on the line. "Could you possibly come out and talk to me here?"

"It might be more convenient if you came to town."

"I can't. I have no car. Besides, I'm quite disorganized. I've been so depending on you. I don't know anyone at all in southern California." A whine ran through the flat midwestern voice, in and out in a pattern of self-pity. "You *are* a private detective, as Lieutenant Gary said?"

"I am. What happened to your car?"

"Henry—is using it."

"You can fly in from Palm Springs in half an hour."

"No, I couldn't possibly fly. Don't you understand, I'm terribly upset. I need your help, Mr. Archer."

"Professionally speaking?"

"Yes, professionally speaking. Won't you come out and have lunch with me at the Inn?"

I said I would, if she was willing to wait for a late lunch. I put on a tie and jacket, and loaded a revolver.

By-passing Palm Springs, I reached Oasis shortly after two thirty. Its grid of roads lay on the flat desert, a blueprint for a boom hopefully waiting for the boom to happen. An escarpment of black stone overshadowed the unbuilt town, its steep sides creased and folded like a stiff black tarpaulin thrown carelessly on the horizon. Beyond it the desert stretched into rainbow distances. The bright new copper penny of the sun spun in its heat against a flat painted sky.

The stucco buildings of the Oasis Inn were dazzling white in the daytime. It was a pueblo hotel with the main building fronting the road and about twenty detached cottages scattered behind it. The watered lawn around them looked artificial and out of place, like a green broadloom carpet spread on the arid earth. I parked against the adobe wall beside the portico, and entered the lobby. Its air-conditioning chilled the sweat on my forehead. The big room was lined and furnished with light wood and leather, draped and upholstered with desert-colored cloth in Indian patterns. Whoever did it had both money and taste, an unusual combination anywhere.

The man behind the desk was expecting me. He called me by name and turned me over to a Filipino in a white-drill steward's jacket. I followed his thin impassive back down a concrete walk between spaced rows of cottages. Several half-naked bodies, male and female, were broiling in the sun or reclining on long chairs in the shadowed porches: castaways from Hollywood and Chicago and New York. More castaways were grouped around the pool that shimmered at the rear of the compound. *Dolce far niente* with a dollar sign.

My Filipino guide led me onto the porch of one of the smaller cottages and knocked discreetly on the screen door. When Marjorie Fellows appeared he said "Mr. Archer" and vanished.

She looked larger than life in a sleeveless linen dress that emphasized the width of her shoulders and hips. "I'm so glad you could come, I really am." She held the door for me and extended her hand at arm's length. It was large and cold and moist, and it held on for some time.

I murmured appropriate greetings as I disengaged myself. She led me into her sitting-room and seated me in an armchair.

"I took the liberty of ordering for you," she said. "They close the kitchens at three. I'm having shirred eggs with those cute little pork sausages they have. I ordered the same for you. Shirred eggs Bercy?"

I said that shirred eggs Bercy sounded delectable.

"Perhaps you'd like something to drink. You've had a long hot drive and all on my account. I *owe* you a nice cool drink." She was hovering around my chair. She wasn't built to hover, but she was hovering.

I said that I could do with a bottle of beer.

She went to the phone in a little skipping run that jolted the foundations of the building; turned with her hand on the receiver: "They have some very nice imported Loewenbrau, at least Henry likes it. Dark or light?"

"Dark will be fine." While she placed the order, I looked around the room for traces of Henry. There were no traces of Henry.

When she returned to her hovering, I asked her: "Where's your husband?"

Her face arranged itself in a meditative pout. Her large arms hung awkwardly at her sides. I felt a sudden sympathy for her, with a little insight mixed in. Her type had been invented to make men comfortable. Without a man to be nice to, she didn't know what to do with herself at all. And she was without a man.

I wished I could recall my brusque question and wrap it up in a prettier parcel for her.

She understood the look on my face and answered it along with the question: "I'm glad you brought it up, honestly. It's what I want to talk to you about, but I hated to broach the subject. I'm an awful dreamer, Mr. Archer. I live in a world of my own unless somebody snaps me out of it like you just did."

She flung herself on a bright-patterned sofa, which sagged and creaked under her weight. Curiously enough, her legs were good. She arranged them in such a way that I couldn't fail to notice the slimness of her ankles.

"The dirty bastard picked up and left me," she said in a deep harsh voice. Her eyes were round with anger, or surprise at her own language. "Good heavens," she said in her normal voice, "I never swear, honestly."

"Swear some more. It will probably do you good."

"Oh no, I couldn't." She had flushed to the ears. But she said: "I call him a dirty bastard because I believe he is one."

"You'd better go back and take it from the beginning."

"I hate to. I hate to talk about it, or even think about it. I've acted like a great fool. I let him take advantage of me all along the line."

"Where did you get on?"

"Get on?"

"How did you happen to meet him?"

"Oh," she said. "He was staying at the guest-ranch near Reno when I was waiting for my divorce. Everything was so romantic, and Henry could ride so well, and his conversation was so interesting. I sort of fell in love with him on the rebound.''

''Rebound?''

''From George, I mean. I was married to George for sixteen years and I guess I got bored with him, or we got bored with each other. It would have been seventeen years this coming June the 10th. We never went anywhere or did anything together any more. All George wanted to do was go out to the country club when he got finished at the office and try to break eighty. I always wanted to come out west but George never took me further than Minneapolis. The only reason we went to Minneapolis was because the business has a branch in Minneapolis. George is the secretary-treasurer of the Simplex Ball Bearing Company.'' Pride and resentment and nostalgia warred in her expression. Nostalgia won. ''I was a fool to leave him, a great fool, and now I'm having to take my medicine. I walked out on George, now Henry walks out on me. My second marriage lasted sixteen *days*.'' The contrast was too much for her. It brought tears to her eyes, still puffed and red from previous tears.

''Henry walked out on you?''

''Yes.'' The syllable lengthened shakily into a sob. ''He left this morning, with the car and the money and—everything.''

''After a quarrel?''

''We didn't even quarrel,'' as if Henry had denied her her rightful due. ''The police called from Los Angeles early this morning, and Henry answered the telephone, and afterwards he heard me talking to them over the phone. He started packing right away, before I put down the receiver, even. I begged him to tell me what was the matter. He wouldn't say a word, except that he had to go away on business. He checked out and drove away without even eating breakfast.''

''In your car?''

''I paid for it, only it's registered in his name. Henry wanted it that way, and he was so masterful, and besides we bought it for our honeymoon. It was really my idea to put it in his name, it made me feel more married.'' She hugged her large fine bosom, but there was cold comfort in that.

''You also mentioned money, Mrs. Fellows?''

''Yes.'' A nervous hurt plucked at her eyebrows, drawing

them closer together. "Please don't call me Mrs. Fellows, I hate it. Call me Marjorie, or Mrs. Barron."

"George's name?"

"Yes." She managed a weak smile, with tears still standing in her eyes. "George made me a very generous settlement, and I've thrown a lot of it away already. Great fool that I am."

"How much did Henry get into you for?"

"Thirty thousand dollars." The sound of the numbers seemed to appall her. Unconsciously, she reached for the alligator purse that was lying on the couch beside her, and pressed it to her girdled abdomen. "He said he had a wonderful chance to make a good investment for both of us: this apartment building in Hollywood. He showed me the apartment building, too. Now I guess it's gone with the wind."

There was a gentle tapping on the door behind me. She opened it, and an elderly waiter wheeled in our lunch on a cart. While he set the table, Marjorie left the room. She came back in time to tip him heavily, smiling with a washed and reconstructed face. At least Henry hadn't taken her for all she had, financially or otherwise.

She ate her lunch with appetite, and asked me how I liked mine. I said that the German beer was very good, and that the quality of the shirred eggs Bercy was not strained. I waited until we had lighted cigarettes, and asked her:

"What did you say to the police on the telephone this morning? Apparently that's what frightened Henry off."

"Do you think so? This Lieutenant Gary wanted to come and talk to me but I explained that I was on my honeymoon and he said he would get in touch with me again and arrange to have me make a deposition, or something of the sort. Then he asked me a lot of questions about Mr. Dalling's house: what I was doing there and if I found you unconscious, and of course I said I did—and what time it was. Finally he told me that Mr. Dalling was dead, isn't that dreadful?"

"Dreadful. Did Lieutenant Gary ask you what you were doing at the house when you found me?"

"Yes."

"What did you tell him?"

"The same as I told you." She dropped her eyes demurely, and tapped the ash from the end of her cigarette. "That I was just driving by, and saw you lying there on the porch."

"I think it's time you told somebody the truth about that."

She flared up feebly, like a moist firecracker. "How could I tell him the truth? Henry was standing right beside me at the phone, listening to everything I said. I didn't dare to say a word about my suspicions of him—"

"You'd been having suspicions, then."

"I was suspicious of Henry from the very beginning, if I'd admitted it to myself. Only he made me *feel* so good, I couldn't face up to the facts. I knew he hadn't much money, and he knew I had. I knew I was foolish to marry again so quickly before I checked his background. But I wanted so hard to believe that he loved me for myself, I deliberately blinded myself and rushed right in. I'd never have given him the thirty thousand if I hadn't wanted to blind myself. I'm stupid, but I'm not that stupid, Mr. Archer."

"I doubt that you're stupid at all," I said. "You're too darn emotional, is all. You probably made a mistake divorcing George, but a lot of women make the same mistake. Or else they make the mistake of not divorcing George."

"You're an awful cynic, aren't you? But what you say is perfectly true. I *am* too emotional. I'm a great emotional fool, and you've put your finger on my central weakness. It was my foolish emotions that made me give him the money. I trusted him because I wanted to so badly. I had to trust him to make the whole thing stay real for a little longer. I guess it was slipping already."

"When was this?"

"Last Thursday, the day after we came here. We were in Santa Barbara at the Biltmore before that. Our week there was a perfect idyll. They have a lovely big pool, and Henry actually taught me how to swim. Henry's a splendid athlete, and that's one of the things that appealed to me so much. I love to see a man be able to *do* things. He told me when he was younger, before he got his wound, that he was a boxing champion in the army." She noticed that she was softening towards Henry, and caught herself up short, the harsh disgusted note breaking out in her voice again: "I suppose that was a lie, like everything else."

"His wound?" I prompted her.

"His war wound. He was a colonel in the war, until he was

invalided out because of his wound. He was living on his disability pension.''

"Did he ever show you a government check?"

"No, but I know he wasn't lying about that. I saw the wound."

"Where was he wounded?"

"In Germany. He fought under General Patton."

"Not geographically. Physiologically."

"Oh." She blushed. "He had a dreadful scar on his abdomen. It still wasn't completely healed, after all these years."

"Too bad."

"That week in Santa Barbara he told me the whole story of his life. But even then I began to have my suspicions. There was this waiter at the Biltmore who knew him. The waiter called him by some other name: apparently he remembered Henry from when he worked at another hotel somewhere. Henry was quite put out. He explained to me that it was a nickname, but I knew waiters don't address hotel guests by their nicknames, and I wondered about it afterwards."

"What was the name?"

"It's queer, I don't remember. It'll probably come back, though. Anyway, that was when I started to have my real suspicions of him. Then when we came out here he was always going away, on business he said, and he wouldn't tell me where he went. On Sunday night we had a quarrel about it. He wanted to go out by himself and I wouldn't give him the keys to the car, so he had to take a taxi. When the taxi-driver got back to his stand, I tipped him to tell me where he had taken Henry, and he said it was this Mr. Dalling's house. I waited up for him, but he wouldn't tell me what he was doing there. The same thing happened Monday night. He went out and I waited and waited, and finally I drove out to the house to look for him."

"And found me instead."

"And found you instead." She smiled.

"But you didn't tell any of this to Lieutenant Gary."

"Not a smidgen. I couldn't, with Henry right there."

"Are you going to, when you give your evidence?"

"Do you think I should?"

"Definitely."

"I don't know." She pushed her chair back from the table,

marched up and down the length of the Indian-patterned rug, her plump hips teetering at the top of her long straight legs. "I don't know whether I will or whether I won't. He might have really gone on a business trip, and be coming back tomorrow like he said. Henry's a strange silent sort of man."

"He said that, did he, that he's coming back tomorrow?"

"Something like that. Do you think I should believe him? It would be terrible if this was all a mistake, and I had called the police in, and he really did come back." She stood facing the door, with a funny look of expectant remorse, as if Henry was there to upbraid her for having disloyal thoughts. "What shall I do, Mr. Archer? It's taken me a long time to get around to it, but that's really what I wanted to talk to you about."

"What do you want to do, get Henry back?"

"No, I don't think so, even if he would come. I don't trust him any more, I'm afraid of him. It isn't only his deception of me. I might be able to forgive that if he came back and proved that he loves me by turning over a new leaf. But I can't help feeling that he's mixed up in this terrible murder, that that's why he rushed away so unexpectedly. You see, I don't know who he is or what he is." She sat down on the edge of the couch, suddenly and weakly, as if her legs had given way.

"I have a good idea who and what he is. Did the waiter in Santa Barbara call him Speed?"

Her head jerked up: "Speed! That was it. I knew it would come back to me. How did you guess? Do you know him?"

"By reputation," I said. "His reputation is bad. He didn't get his abdominal wound in the war. He got it in a gang fight last fall."

"I knew it," she cried, and shook her head from side to side so the bright dyed hair swung forward and brushed her cheeks. "I want to go back to Toledo, where people are nice. I always wanted to live in California but now that I've seen it, it's a hellish place. I've fallen among thieves, that's what I've done. Thieves and murderers and confidence men. I want to go back to George."

"It sounds like a very good plan."

"I can't though, he'd never forgive me. I'd be a laughing-stock for the rest of my days. What could I tell him about the thirty thousand? It's nearer forty when you count the car and all the money I've spent." She kneaded her alligator bag with both clenched hands.

"There's a possibility you can get it back. You have no notion where Henry went, I don't suppose."

"He didn't tell me *anything*. He just went away. Now I know I'll never see him again. But if I ever do, I'll scratch his eyes out." Her eyes glared from the ambush of her hair. I didn't know whether to laugh at her or weep with her.

I looked out the window onto the lawn, where spray from a sprinkling system danced in the sun. "No letters? No telephone calls? No telegrams? No visitors?"

There was a long pause while I watched the dancing water.

"He had a person-to-person call from San Francisco yesterday. I answered the phone myself, then he made me go into the bedroom and close the door. Does that mean anything?"

"It may." I stood up. "I'll try it anyway. You got no hint of who was calling, no names given?"

"No."

"But you're positive it was a San Francisco call."

"Oh, yes. The operator said so." She had pushed back her hair from her face and was looking less upset. There was an ice-chip hardness in her eyes I hadn't noticed before.

"I ought to tell you, Mrs. Fellows—"

"Mrs. Barron," she said stubbornly. "I was never really married to him."

"Mrs. Barron, then. You might get better results if you took your story to the police."

"I can't. It would be in all the papers. I could never go home at all then. Don't you see?"

"If I recover your money, or any part of it, I'll take a percentage, fifteen percent. That would be forty-five hundred out of thirty thousand."

"All right."

"Otherwise I'll charge you for my expenses and nothing else. I usually work for a daily fee, but this case is different."

"Why is it so different?"

"I have my own reasons for wanting to talk to Henry. And if I find him, I'll do what I think best. I'm making you no promises."

27 _____

It was midnight when I parked my car under Union Square. A wet wind blew across the almost deserted square, blowing fogged breath from the sea on the dark pavements. Flashing neons on all four sides repudiated the night. I turned down a slanting street past a few late couples strolling and lingering on the sidewalk.

The Den's orange sign was one of a dozen bar signs on its block. I went down a dirty flight of stairs and looked into the place through a swinging glass door at the bottom. It was a large square room with rounded corners and a ceiling so low you could feel the weight of the city over it. A curved bar arched out from the left-hand wall, making space for a bartender and his array of bottles. The other walls were lined with booths and tables. In the cleared space in the middle of the room, a tired-looking man in a worn tuxedo was beating the life out of an exhausted grand piano. All the furniture, including the piano, was enameled a garish orange. A sequence of orange-haired nudes romped and languished along the walls under a glaze of grime. I went in.

There were several customers at the bar: a couple well-dressed and young and looking out of place, and a pair of lone-wolfing sailors. A few others, all of them men, were propped like dummies at the tables, waiting for something wonderful to happen, a new life to begin, in more delightful places, under different names. Five or six revelers, all of them women, and hard cases by their looks, were standing around the piano in a chorybantic circle, moving various members in approximate time to the music. One of them, a streaked blonde in a green dress with a drooping hemline, raised what passed for her voice in a banshee sort of singing. The whole thing had the general effect of a wake.

The pianist could have passed for a corpse in any mortuary if he had only stayed still, instead of tossing his fingers in bunches at the suffering keyboard. His batting average in hitting the notes was about .333, which would have been good enough for a Coast League ball-player. He was white and loaded to the gills, it was hard to tell with what. I sat down at a

136

table near the piano and watched him until he turned his face in my direction. He had the sad bad centerless eyes I expected, wormholes in a withered apple with a dark rotten core.

I ordered a beer from a sulky waitress in an orange apron. When I left her the change from a dollar, she hoisted a long-suffering smile from the depths of her despair and offered it to me: "Zizi's as high as a kite. They ought to make him shut up when he's so wild, instead of encouraging him."

"I'd like to buy him a drink."

"He doesn't drink." She corrected herself: "With the customers, I mean."

"Tell him I want to talk to him when he stops. If he can stop."

She gave me the twice-over then, and I tried to look as degenerate as hell. Maybe it came easier than I thought. I wanted to drink the beer, but I let it stand on the table, going flat, while Zizi battered his way through half a dozen requests. *Moonlight and Roses*, the girls wanted. *Stardust* and *Blue Moon* and other pieces that brought other times and places into the midnight basement at the bottom of the city. One of the sailors made up his mind and left the bar. Without preliminary, he attached himself to the blonde in the green dress and steered her out, lean-hipped and swaggering. The bartender's face watched them over the bar like a dead white moon. *Happy Days Are Here Again*, and *Stormy Weather*. One of the women tried to sing it and burst loosely into tears. The other comforted her. The pianist struck a plangent discord and gave up. A lone drunk sitting against the wall behind me was talking in a monotone to his absent mother, explaining very reasonably, in great detail, why he was a no-good son-of-a-gun and a disgrace to the family.

A stranger voice, husky and loose, wandering between the masculine and feminine registers, rustled like damp dead leaves in the corners of the room. It was Zizi announcing a break: "Excuse me folks my stint is done but I'll be back when the clock strikes one to bring you more hot music and fun." He pushed the mike away and rose unsteadily.

The waitress elbowed through the group of women around him and whispered in his ear, gesturing in my direction. He crossed to my table, a tall middle-aged man who had once been handsome, fixed by that fact in the mannerisms of a boy. Leaning with one hand spread on the table in an attitude of precarious grace, he inclined towards me. His jaw dropped lackadaisically, showing discolored teeth.

"You wanted to speak with me, boy friend? I am Zizi. You like my music?"

"I'm tone deaf."

"You are fortunate." He smiled sickly, revealing pale gums above the discolored teeth.

"It isn't music that's on my mind."

"Yes?" He leaned closer, his long frail body half-collapsed against the edge of the table.

I lowered my voice, and plucked at the sleeve of his greening tux in what I hoped was an appealing gesture. "I need a fix real bad," I said. "I'm going off my stick."

His thin weeded eyebrows rose towards his thinning hairline. "Why do you come to me?"

"I've been getting it from Ronnie in Pacific Point. He said you knew Mosquito."

He straightened slowly, swaying like a willow, and peered into my eyes. I let them gaze: "For God's sake, Zizi, give me a break."

"I don't know you," he said.

"Here's my card, then." I put a twenty on the table by his hand. "I got to have it. Where can I find Mosquito?"

The hand crawled over the bill. I noticed that its nails were broken and bleeding. "Okay, boy friend. He lives in the Grandview Hotel. It's just around the corner, a block above Market. Ask the night clerk for him." The hand closed over the bill and dove into his pocket. "Remember I haven't the faintest notion why you want to see him. Tee hee."

"Thank you," I said emotionally.

"Sweet dreams, boy friend."

The Grandview Hotel was an old four-story building of dirty brick squeezed between taller buildings. An electric sign over the entrance advertised SINGLE WITH BATH, $1.50. The brass fittings on the front door looked as if they went back to the earthquake. I pulled it open and entered the lobby, a deep narrow room poorly lit by a couple of ancient wallfixtures on each side. Two women and three men were playing draw poker at a table under one of the lights. The women were bulldog-faced, and wore coats trimmed with the fur of extinct animals. Two of the men were fat and old, bald probably under their hats. The third was young and hatless. They were using kitchen matches instead of chips.

I moved toward the lighted desk at the rear, and the hatless youth got up and followed me. "You want a room?" Apparently he was the curator. He suited the role. Bloodless and narrow, his face was set in a permanent sneer.

"I want to see Mosquito."

"Does he know you?"

"Not yet."

"Somebody send you?"

"Zizi."

"Wait a minute." He leaned across the desk and lifted a house-phone from a niche at one end, plugging it in to the old-fashioned switchboard above it. He spoke softly into the mouthpiece and glanced at me, with the receiver to his ear. He hung up and unplugged the connection: "He says you can go up."

"What room?"

He sneered at my ignorance of his mysteries. "307. Take the elevator if you want." His feet were soundless on the decayed rubber matting as he padded back to the poker game.

I piloted the ramshackle elevator cage to the third floor, and stepped out into an airless corridor. The brown numbered doors stood like upended coffins on each side, bathed in the static red flames of fire-exit bulbs that dotted the ceiling at intervals. 307 was halfway down the corridor to the left. Its door was open a crack, throwing a yellow ribbon of light across the threadbare carpeting of the hallway and up the opposite wall.

Then the light was half obscured by someone watching me from the other side of the door. I raised my hand to knock. The door swung inward sharply before I touched it. A young man stood in the doorway with his back to the light. He was middle-sized, but the great black bush of hair on top of his head made him seem almost tall. "Zizi's little friend, eh? Come on in." His voice was adenoidal.

One of his hands was on his hip, the other on the doorknob. I had to brush against him to enter the room. He wasn't heavy-looking but his flesh was soft and tremulous like a woman's. His movements seemed invertebrate as he closed the door and turned. He was wearing a soft green shirt, six-pleated high-rise trousers of dark green gabardine, a brilliant green and yellow tie held by a large gold clasp.

His other hand moved to his other hip. He cocked his head on one side, his face small and pointed under the top-heavy hair. "Carrying iron, old man?"

"I use it in my business." I patted my heavy jacket pocket.

"And what's your business, old man?"

"Whatever I can knock off. Do I need references?"

"Long as you don't try to knock off daddy." He smiled at the ridiculousness of the idea. His teeth were small and fine like a child's first set. "Where you from?"

"Pacific Point."

"I never see you in the Point."

"I work the whole coast," I said impatiently. "You want to know my history, send me a questionnaire."

"Hard up for it?"

"I wouldn't be here if I wasn't."

"All right, take it easy, I like to know who I'm dealing with, that's natural, isn't it? You want to use my needle or you snuff it?"

"The needle," I said.

He crossed the room to a chest of drawers in the corner, and opened the top drawer. Mosquito wasted no money on front. The room stood as he had found it: bare discolored walls, broken-backed iron bed, cracked green blind over the single window, the rug on the floor marked with a threadbare path from the bed to the door of the bathroom. He could move at a minute's notice into any one of ten thousand similar rooms in the city.

He set an alcohol lamp on top of the chest of drawers and lit it with a silver cigarette-lighter. A new-looking needle gleamed in his other hand. "You want the forty, or the sixty-five main-liner?" he asked me over his shoulder.

"Sixty-five. Your prices are high."

"Yeah, aren't they? I like to see the money first, old man."

I showed him money.

"Bring it over here."

He was melting some yellowish-white powder in a spoon. I counted sixty-five dollars down beside the hissing lamp.

Water began to run behind the bathroom door. Somebody coughed. "Who's in there?" I asked him.

"Only a friend of mine, don't get your wind up. Better take off your coat, or do you take it in the thigh?"

"I want to see who's in there. I'm loaded. I can't take chances."

"It's only a girl, old man." His voice soothing. "There ain't the teensiest danger. Take off your coat and lie down like a good boy now."

He dipped the needle in the spoon and charged it, turning to me. I slapped it out of his hand.

Mosquito's face turned purplish red. The loose flesh under his tiny chin shook like a turkey's wattles. His hand was in and out of the open drawer before I could hold him, and the blade of a spring-knife jumped up under my nose. "You dirty filthy beast, don't you dare touch me." He backed against the wall and crouched with the knife advanced, its double-edged blade pointing at the ceiling. "I'll cut you if you lay a finger on me."

I brought the revolver out of my jacket pocket. "Put it away, Mosquito."

His small black eyes watched me uncertainly, looked down at the knife and crossed slightly, focused on its point. I swung the gun on him, cutting the wrist of his knife hand with the muzzle. The knife dropped to the floor. I stepped on it and moved in closer to Mosquito. He tried to scratch my face. Since it was necessary to hit him, I hit him: a short right hook under the ear. He slid down the wall like a rag doll.

I crunched the hypodermic needle into the carpet with my heel, stooped for the knife, which I closed and dropped into my pocket. Mosquito was out, quick adenoidal breathing his only sign of life, his eyeballs under the heavy lids as blank-white as a statue's. His head was jammed against the wall, and I lifted him away from it so he wouldn't choke. His narrow black suède shoes pointed to opposite corners of the ceiling.

The bathroom door clicked behind me. I straightened up quickly and turned. The door creaked inward slowly, opening on darkness. It was the girl Ruth who emerged from the darkness, moving like a sleepwalker. She had on pajamas that were much too big for her, yellow nylon piped with red. Thin soft hanging folds obscured her lips and enhanced the dreaminess of her walk. Her eyes were dark craters in her smooth blanched face.

"Hello hello hello," she said. "Hello, hello." She noticed

the gun in my head, without fear or curiosity: "Don't shoot, cowboy, I give up." Her hands jerked upward in a token gesture of surrender, then hung limp from her wrists again. "I absolutely give up." She stood swaying.

I put the gun away and took her by the elbow. Her face didn't change. I identified its look of frozen expectancy. I had seen it on the face of a man who had just been struck by a bullet, mortally.

"Unhand me villain," she said without rancor; pulled away from me and crossed to the end of the bed where she sat down. She didn't notice Mosquito until then, though he was lying practically at her feet. She nudged his leg with a red-tipped toe: "What happened to the nasty little man?"

"He fell and hurt himself. Too bad."

"Too bad," she echoed. "Too bad he isn't dead. He's still breathing. Look, he bit me." She pulled the pajama collar to one side to show me the red tooth-marks on her shoulder. "He couldn't hurt me, though. I was a thousand miles away. Ten thousand miles away. A hundred thousand miles away." She was chanting.

I cut in: "Where were you, Ruth?"

"On my island, the island I go to. My little white island in the deep dark blue ocean."

"All alone?"

"All alone." She smiled. "I shut the door and lock it with a key and bar the door and fasten the chains and sit in my chair and no one can touch me. No one. I sit and listen to the water on the beach and never open the door until my father comes. Then we go down to the water and look for shells. We find the prettiest shells, pink and red and purple, great big ones. I keep them in my house, in a special room. Nobody knows where it is, I'm the only one that knows." Her voice trailed off. She drew her knees up to her chin and sat with her eyes closed, rocking gently back and forth on a remote inward surge.

The breathing of the man on the floor had changed for the better, easing and slowing down. His eyes were closed now. I went to the bathroom for a glass of water: Ruth's clothes were scattered on the bathroom floor: and poured the water over Mosquito's face. The little eyes snapped open. He gasped and sputtered.

"Upsadaisy," I said, and dragged him to a sitting position

against the wall. His head hung sideways but he was conscious, his eyes pointed with malice. "You won't get away with this, old man," he whispered.

I disregarded him, turned to the girl on the bed: "Have you seen Speed?"

"Speed?" she repeated from a great distance. Her face was closed and smooth as a shell listening to its own murmurings.

Mosquito struggled up onto his knees: "Don't tell him anything, he's a heister." Which told me that Mosquito had something to tell.

I bunched his tie and shirt-collar in both hands and lifted him against the wall. He hung limp, afraid to resist.

"You tell me where Speed is, then."

He twisted his wet head back against the plaster, his eyes watching me from their corners. "Never heard of him." His voice was thin, almost a rodent squeak. "Take your dirty hands—off me." His face was purpling again, and the breath piped in his throat.

"There's no way out of this one." I loosened the pressure of my fingers slightly. "I want Speed."

He tried to spit in my face. The bubbly white saliva ran down his chin. I tightened the pressure, carefully. He invited death, like a soft and loathsome insect.

He struggled feebly, gasping. "Turn me loose."

I released him. He dropped onto his hands and knees, coughing and shaking his head from side to side.

"Where is Speed?" I said.

"I don't know." He crouched like a dog at my feet.

"Listen to me, Mosquito. I don't like you. I don't like your business. Just give me a slight excuse, and I'll give you the beating of your life. Then I'll call the feds to cart you away. You won't be back for a long time if I do."

He looked up at me through a rat's-nest of hair. "You're talking big for a hood."

"No. It's what I'm going to do if you don't take me to Speed." I showed him my Special Deputy's badge to clinch it.

"I guess you win," he said to the threadbare carpet. Slowly he got to his feet.

I held my gun on him while he combed his hair and put on a green tweed coat. He blew out the alcohol lamp, replacing it in the drawer.

The girl was still balanced on the end of her spine, rocking blindly. I gave her a shove as I passed her. She tumbled sideways onto the bed and lay as she had fallen, with her knees up to her chin, waiting to be born into the world or out of it.

Mosquito locked the door. I took his key away before he could pocket it. He backed against the door, the malice on his face canceled by fear into a kind of stupidity. The red corridor light shone down on him like a dirty little sun, scaled to the world in his head. His outstretched hand was questioning.

"You won't speak to the night clerk, you won't even look at him. Is it far to Speed?"

"He's at Half Moon Bay, in a cabin. Don't take me there. He'll kill me."

"Worry about him," I said, "unless you're lying to me."

Behind one or another of the numbered doors, a woman cried out sorrowfully. A man laughed. Down the corridor, in the elevator, across the lobby, up the steep street to the empty square, I stuck to Mosquito like a brother. He walked as if every step he took had to be willed in advance.

28

There were clouds in the hills along the skyline route, obscuring the winding road and spraying my windshield with fine droplets of water. I used my yellow foglights and kept the wipers metronoming, but it was a long slow drive. Between the San Francisco limits and the bay, we passed no lighted houses and few cars. The city with all its lights had sunk behind us as if it had never existed.

The man beside me was quiet. Occasionally he uttered a little moan. Once he said: "He'll kill me. Speed will kill me."

"Small loss if he did," I said to cheer him up.

"He'll kill you too!" he cried. "I hope he does kill you."

"Naturally. Is he alone?"

"Far as I know he is."

"You'll go up to the door. You'll do the talking."

"I can't. I'm sick. You hurt me."

"Buck up. I hate a whiner."

He was quiet again, though he still moaned occasionally to himself. We crept on under the smothering gray sky, through the gray cloud-drowned hills. The sun and the other stars had burned out long ago, and Mosquito and I were journeying for our sins through a purgatory of gray space.

Eventually the road dipped below the cloudline. Below it to the right, a flat gray arm of the sea meandered among the hills like a slow river. The opposite bank was black with trees. I followed the shore for miles, losing it and coming back to it again as the road determined. In a narrow valley close by the forsaken shore, the road branched left and right.

I stopped the car. "Which way?"

"I don't know."

"Sure you do, Mosquito. Bear this in mind: you'll take your chance with Speed, or have the certainty of a Federal pen. Now which is it going to be? Which way?"

"To the right," he answered drearily. "It's only about a mile from here."

We crossed a long low bridge and followed a gravel road up the opposite bank of the bay. After a while we passed a dirt road that straggled downward towards the landlocked water. "That's it," he said.

I braked and backed, turning into the rutted lane. "How far down is it?"

"Just around the curve."

I cut my lights, stopped short of the curve and set my emergency brake. "Get out and walk ahead of me. If you give him warning, I'll drop you."

"Speed will kill me," he said slowly and distinctly, as if he was stating a theory I had failed to understand. In the dim light from the dashboard, I could see the water shining in his eyes. I took my flashlight out of the glove compartment, and tested it on his face. It looked sick.

"Get out." I leaned across him to open the door, and crowded out behind him. I closed the windows and locked both doors.

"I'm afraid," he said, "afraid of the dark. I never been out here at night."

"You'll never go back if you keep this up. Now walk ahead of me."

He was clinging to the door handle. I pushed him upright with the revolver muzzle, and prodded him into the road. He lurched ahead of me.

Below the curve the lane broadened into a small clearing. A cabin of rough-hewn logs sat in the clearing, one square lit window facing us. A man's shadow moved there, growing until it covered the whole window. Then the light died behind it. There was a long dark car parked beside the cabin.

"Call him," I said to the man at the end of my gun. The flashlight was in my left hand.

His first attempt was a dry gasp.

"Keep moving and call him. Tell him who you are. Tell him that I'm a friend."

"Mr. Speed," he cried thinly. "It's Mosquito."

We were halfway across the clearing. "Louder," I said in his ear, and jabbed him in the kidneys with the muzzle.

"Mr. Speed." His voice cracked.

I pushed him on ahead of me. The door opened inward as Mosquito set his feet on the plank stoop.

"Who is it?" a man's voice said from the deep inside shadow.

"Mosquito."

"What do you want? Who's with you?"

"A friend."

"What friend?" The hidden voice rose in pitch.

I'd got as far as I could with that approach. Even with tear gas, tommyguns and a police cordon, there is no way to take a desperate man without risking your life. I had an advantage over Speed, of course. I knew that he was still convalescing from Blaney's bullet, and was probably gun-shy.

I stepped around Mosquito. "The name is Archer. A Mrs. Henry Fellows"—I pronounced the name carefully—"hired me to look for you."

Before I finished speaking, I pressed my flashlight button. The white beam fanned the doorway. Speed crouched there, a massive figure with a black gun in his hand. We faced each other for a long tense instant. Either of us could have shot the other. I was so sharply aware of him, I felt his gun wound burning a hole in my own belly.

The starch went out of him suddenly. Without seeming to move, he shifted from the offensive to the defensive. "What do you want?" His pale bright eyes looked down at his gun, as if it was the gun that had somehow failed him.

"You might as well drop it," I said. "I have you covered."

He flung it down in a gesture of self-disgust. It skittered across the rough planks toward me. Instinctively, Mosquito moved to retrieve it. I set my foot on the gun and elbowed him back.

"Go away, Mosquito," I said, watching Speed. "I don't want to see you again."

"Where should I go?" He sounded both hurt and unbelieving.

"Anywhere but San Francisco. Start walking."

"All by myself? Out here?"

"Start walking."

He stepped off the porch into gray gloom. I didn't waste a backward glance on him. "We'll go into the house," I said to Speed. "You better hold your hands on top of your head."

"You're exceedingly masterful." He was recovering his style, or whatever it was that kept him upright and made him interesting to women. On the shooting level he was a bum, as useless as a cat in a dogfight. But he had his own feline dignity, even with his hands up.

I picked up his gun, a light automatic with the safety still on, and juggled it into my pocket, holding the flash under my arm. "About face, colonel. No false moves, unless you want a hole in the back to match the one in the front."

He turned in the doorway. I stayed close behind him as he crossed the room and relit the oil lamp. The flame steadied and brightened, casting a widening circle of light across the bare floor and up into the rafters. The room contained a built-in bunk, a cheap pine table, two kitchen chairs and a canvas deck-chair placed by the stone fireplace. A pair of new leather suitcases stood unopened at the end of the bunk. There was no fire in the fireplace, and the room was cold.

"Sit down." I waved my gun at the deck-chair.

"You're very kind." He sprawled in the chair with his long legs spraddled in front of him. "Is it necessary for me to retain the hands-on-head position? It makes me feel ridiculous."

"You can relax." I sat down facing him in one of the kitchen chairs.

"Thank you." He lowered his hands and clasped them in his lap, but he didn't relax. His entire body was taut. The attempt he made to smile was miserable, and he abandoned it. He raised one hand to shield his worried mouth. The hand stayed there of its own accord, brushing back and forth across his thin brown eyebrow of mustache. Its fingernails were bitten down to the quick. "I know you, don't I?" he said.

"We've seen each other. This is a comedown after the Oasis Inn."

"It is, rather. Are you a detective?"

I nodded.

"I'm surprised at Marjorie." But he showed no emotion of any kind. His face was unfocused, sagging wearily on its bones. Deep lines dragged from his nose to the corners of his mouth. His fingers began to explore them. "I didn't think she would go to such lengths."

"You hurt her feelings," I said. "It's never a good idea to hurt a woman's feelings. If you have to rob them, you should try to do it without hurting their feelings."

"Rob is a pretty strong word to use. She gave me the money to invest for her. She'll get it back, I promise you."

"And your word is as good as your bond, eh? How good is your bond?"

"One week," he said. "Give me one week. I'll pay it back with interest gladly."

"How about now?"

"That's impossible. I don't have the money now. It's already invested."

"In real estate?"

"In real estate, yes." The pale eyes flickered. The exploring hand climbed up to them and masked them for a moment.

"Don't rack your brain for a story, Speed. I know where the money went."

He peered at me, still hiding behind his fingers. "I suppose Mosquito told you?"

"Mosquito told me nothing."

"She tapped my phone at the Inn, then. The sweet sow." The hand slid down his face to his throat, where it pinched the loose skin between thumb and forefinger. "Oh, the sweet sow." But he couldn't work up any anger. The things that had been done to him looked worse and more important than the things he could do in return. He was sick of himself. "Well, what do you want with me? I guarantee she'll have her money back in a week."

"You can't see over the edge of the next five minutes, and you're talking about a week. In a week you may be dead."

A half-smile deepened the lines on one side of his face. "I may at that. And you may too. I certainly wish it for you."

"Who did you pay the money to?"

"Joe Tarantine. I wouldn't try to get it back from him if I were you."

"Where is he?"

He lifted his broad shoulders, and dropped them. "I don't know, and I haven't any desire to. Joe isn't one of my bosom pals, exactly."

"When did you see him last?"

"Two nights ago," he said, after some reflection.

"When you bought the heroin from him?"

"You seem to know my business better than I do." He leaned toward me, drawing his legs back. I moved the revolver to remind him of it.

"Put the gun away, please. What did you say your name was?"

"Archer." I kept the gun where it was, supported on my knee.

"How much is Marjorie paying you, Archer?"

"Enough."

"Whatever it is, I could pay you much better. If you'll give me a little leeway. A little time."

"I don't think so."

"I have two kilos of pure heroin. Do you know how much that's worth on the present market?"

"I haven't been following the quotations. Fill me in."

"A clean hundred thousand, if I have the time to make the necessary contacts. A hundred thousand, over and above my debt to the sweet sow." For the first time, he was showing a little animation. "I'm not even suggesting you double-cross her. All I ask is time. Four days should do it."

"While I sit holding a gun on you?"

"You can put it away."

"I think you're trying to con me the way you conned Marjorie. For all I know, you have the money on you."

He compressed the flesh around his eyes, trying to force them into an expression of earnest sincerity. Surrounded by puckered skin, they stayed pale and cold and shallow. "You're quite mistaken, old man." I'd wondered where Mosquito got the phrase. "You can take a look at my wallet if you like." His hand moved toward the inner pocket of his jacket.

"Keep your hands in sight. What about your suitcases?"

"Go right ahead and search them. They're not locked." Which probably meant there was nothing important in the suitcases.

He turned his head to look at the expensive luggage, and revealed a different face. Full-face, he looked enough like a gentleman to pass for one in southern California: his face was oval and soft, almost gentle around the mouth, with light hair waving back from a wide sunburned forehead. In profile, his saddle nose and lantern jaw gave him the look of an aging roughneck; the slack skin twisted into diagonal folds under his chin.

He had fooled me in a way: I hadn't been able to reach in behind the near-gentlemanly front. My acceptance of the front had even built it up for Speed a little. He was more at ease than he had been, in spite of the gun on my knee.

I spoke to the ravaged old man behind the front: "You're on your last legs, Speed. I guess you know that."

His head turned back to me, losing ten years. He said nothing, but there was a kind of questioning assent in the eyes.

"You can't buy me," I said. "The way things stand, you can't angle out of this rap. You've made your big try for a comeback, and it's failed."

"What is this leading up to? Or do you simply enjoy hearing yourself make speeches?"

"I have to take you back with me. There's the matter of Marjorie's money, for one thing—"

"She'll never get it if you take me back, not a red cent of it."

"Then she'll have the satisfaction of jailing you. She's in the mood to push it to the limit. Not to mention what the police will do. They'll have a lot of questions to ask you about this and that, particularly Dalling's murder."

"Dalling's murder?" His face thinned and turned sallow. "Who is Dalling?" But he knew who Dalling was, and knew I knew he knew.

"If they ever let you out, Dowser and Blaney will be waiting for you." I piled it on. "Last time they had no special grudge against you. All they wanted was your territory. This time they'll cut you to pieces, and you know it. I wouldn't insure your life for a dime if you paid me a hundred-dollar premium."

"You're one of Dowser's troopers." He looked at my gun and couldn't look away. I raised it so he could see the round hole in the barrel, the peephole into darkness.

"How about it, Speed? Do you come south with me, or settle with me here?"

"Settle?" he said, still with his eyes on the gun.

"I'm going back with you or the heroin, one or the other."

"To Dowser?"

"You're a good guesser. If Danny gets his shipment back, he won't care so much about you."

He said, with an effort: "I'll split with you. We can clear a hundred thousand between us. Fifty thousand for you. I have a contact in the east, he's flying out tomorrow." The effort left him breathless.

"You can't buy me," I repeated. "Hand it over."

"If I do, what happens to me?"

"It's up to you. Climb into your car and drive as fast as you can as far as you can. Or walk due west until you hit the ocean and keep on walking."

He raised his eyes to mine. His face was old and sick. "I should have shot you when I had the chance."

"You should have, but you didn't. You're washed up, as I said."

"Yes," he said to himself. "I am washed up." His voice was almost cheerful, in a wry thin way. I got the impression that he had never really expected to succeed, and was taking a bitter satisfaction from his own foresight.

"You're wasting my time. Where is it?"

"I'll give you a straight answer to that if you'll give me a straight answer to this. Who tipped my hand to you? I don't expect to do anything about it. I'd simply like to know."

"Nobody did."

"Nobody?"

"I put together a couple of hunches and a lot of legwork, and worked it out for myself. You won't believe that, naturally."

"Oh, I believe it. Anyway, what difference does it make?" He shook his head fretfully, bored by the answer to his own question. "The lousy stuff is in a tobacco can in the kitchen cupboard."

I found it there.

29

I had made up my mind about Ruth before I got back to the Grandview Hotel. I knew if I didn't go back for her I wouldn't be able to forget her. A teen-aged girl with heroin in her veins was the stuff bad dreams were made of.

The lobby was dark and deserted except where the night clerk sat behind his desk with a science-fiction magazine propped in front of him. He descended from inter-galactic space to give me a quick once-over. Neither of us spoke. I went up in the elevator and down the red-lit corridor again to 307.

The girl was sleeping as I had left her, on her side, her knees bent double and her long thighs clasped to her breast. She stirred and sighed when I closed the door and crossed the room to look at her. The short gold hair fallen across her face moved in and out with her breathing. I pushed it back and tucked it behind her ear. She raised her free arm as if to protect her head from attack, but she slept on. She was sunk deep in sleep, maybe beyond my reach.

I filled the bathroom glass with cold water again, straightened her out on the bed, and poured the water over her face. Her eyelids fluttered open, and she swore.

"Rise and shine, Ruth."

"Go away, you're rocking my dreamboat." She flipped over

onto her stomach, and buried her wet face in the soaking pillow.

I flipped her back. "Hey, kid! You've got to get up."

"No. Please," she whined, her eyes tight shut again.

I refilled the glass and brought it back from the bathroom. "More water?"

"No!" She sat up, calling me names.

"Get dressed. You're coming with me. You don't want to stay with Mosquito, do you?"

Her head lolled on her neck, to one side and then the other. "No. He's nasty." She spoke with childish earnestness, casting an orphaned look around the barren walls. "Where is Mosquito?"

"He's on his way. You've got to get out of here."

"Yes." She repeated after me like a lesson she had learned: "I've got to get out of here."

I gathered up her clothes from the bathroom floor and tossed them to her: sweater and skirt, shoes and stockings. But she was still far gone, unequal to the task of putting them on. I had to strip off the pajamas and dress her. Her entire body was cold to the touch. It was like dressing a doll.

Her polo coat was hanging on the bathroom door. I wrapped it around her and pulled her to her feet. She couldn't stand alone, or didn't choose to. Ruth had flown back to her island, leaving her vacant body for me to deal with. In one way and another I got her to the elevator and propped her in a corner while I ran it down to the lobby. I pushed back the metal door and lifted her in my arms. She was light enough.

The night clerk looked up as I passed the desk. He didn't say a word. No doubt he had seen more remarkable couples step out of that elevator.

My car was parked at the yellow curb in front of the hotel. I unlocked the door and deposited her on the seat with her head propped in the corner against a baseball cushion. She stayed in that position for the next six hours, though she had a tendency to slide toward the floor. Every hour or so, I had to stop the car in order to lift her back into her corner. Most of the rest of the time I kept the speedometer needle between seventy-five and eighty. She slept like the dead while I drove from foggy night to dawn and through the long bright morning, heading south.

She woke up finally when I braked for the stoplight at the Santa Barbara wye. The light changed suddenly, taking me by surprise, and I had to burn rubber. Ruth was flung from her seat. I held her back from the windshield with my right arm. She opened her eyes then, and looked around and wondered where she was.

"Santa Barbara." The light changed back to green, and I shifted gears.

She stretched and sat up straight, staring at the combed green lemon groves and the blue mountains in the near distance. "Where are we going?" she asked me, her voice still thickened by sleep.

"To see a friend of mine."

"In San Francisco?"

"Not in San Francisco."

"That's good." She yawned and stretched some more. "I don't really want to go there after all. I had an awful dream about San Francisco. An awful little man with bushy hair took me up to his room and made me do terrible things. I don't exactly remember what they were, though. God, I feel lousy. Was I on a jag last night?"

"A kind of one. Go to sleep again if you want to. Or how about something to eat?"

"I don't know if I can scarf anything, but maybe I better try. God knows how long since I have."

We were approaching the freeway, and there was a truckstop restaurant ahead. I pulled into the service station beside it and helped her out of the car. We were a very sorry couple. She still moved like a sleepwalker, and her pallor was ghastly under the noon sun. I had three hundred and forty brand-new miles on my gauge, and I felt as if I had walked them. I needed food, sleep, shave, and shower. Most of all I needed a talk with or even a look at somebody who was happy, prosperous, and virtuous, or any one of the three.

A steak and a pint of coffee did a lot for me. The girl nibbled halfheartedly at a piece of toast that she dipped in the yolk of one of her eggs. Heroin was her food and drink and sleep. It was going to be her death if she stayed with the kick to the end. The idea bothered me.

I said that to her, in slightly different words, when we were back in the car: "I've known weed- and opium-smokers, coke-sniffers, hemp-chewers, laudanum drinkers, plain and fancy drunks. Guys and girls who lived on canned heat and rubbing alcohol. There are even people in the world who can't leave arsenic alone, and other people who would sell themselves into slavery for a long cool drink of ether. But your habit is the worst habit there is."

"A lecture," she said, with adolescent boredom. I might have been a high-school teacher objecting to bubble-gum. "What do you know about my habits, Mr. Drag?"

"Plenty."

"Who are you?"

"I'm a private detective. I told you that before, but you've forgotten it."

"Yeah, I suppose I did. Was I in San Francisco last night? I think I remember, I rode up there on a bus."

"You were there. I don't know how you got there."

"What happened to my shoulder? I noticed in the rest room, it looks like somebody bit me."

"You were bitten by a mosquito."

I turned from the road to look at her, and our eyes met for a moment. Hers were uncomprehending.

"That isn't funny," she said icily.

I was angry and amused at the same time. "Hell, I didn't bite you." But not angry enough to remind her unnecessarily of the night she had forgotten. Even to me, Mosquito seemed unreal, the figment of a red-lit dream.

I glanced at the girl's face, and saw that she was remembering: the shadow of the memory shaded her eyes. "It's true," she said, "what you said about the habit. It's terrible. I started out trying it for kicks, with Ronnie. The first few times he gave it to me free. Now it's the only thing that makes me feel good. In between, I feel awful. How do you think I feel now?"

"Half dead, the way you look."

"Completely dead, and I don't even care. I don't even care."

After a while she dropped off to sleep again. She slept through the heavy truck-traffic on 101 Alternate and the even heavier traffic on the boulevard. It took Main Street to wake her finally.

I found a parking place near the Hall of Justice. It was nearly two o'clock, a good time to catch Peter Colton in his office. She came along quietly enough, still walking as if the sidewalk were foam rubber, until she saw the building. Then she jerked to a stop:

"You're going to turn me in!"

"Don't be silly," I said, but I was lying. A couple of sidewalk loungers were drifting toward us, prepared to witness anything we cared to do. "Come along with me now, or I'll bite your other shoulder."

She glared at me, but she came, on stiff unwilling legs. Our short black shadows stumped up the steps together.

Colton was in his office, a big jut-nosed man in his fifties, full of quiet energy. When I opened the door, his head was bowed over papers on his desk, and he stayed in that position for a measurable time. His light brown hair, cut *en brosse*, gave him a bearish look that went with his disposition. I pushed the girl ahead of me into the room, and shut the door rather sharply. She moved sideways along the wall, away from me.

Colton looked up with calculated effect, his powerful nose pointed accusingly at me. "Well. The prodigal son. You look terrible."

"That comes of living on the husks that the swine did eat."

"A Biblical scholar yet, and I wasn't even certain you could read." Before I cold answer, he aimed his face at the girl, who was trembling against the wall: "Who's this, the prodigal daughter?"

"This is Ruth," I said. "What's your last name, Ruth?"

She stammered: "I won't tell you."

Colton regarded her with cold blue interest. "What's the girl been taking?"

"Heroin."

"It's a lie," she said woodenly.

Colton shrugged his shoulders. "You're in the wrong department, aren't you? I'm busy. Why bring her to me?"

"Busy on the Dalling case?"

"You've got nerve, Lew, even to bring up the name. Lucky for you the Tarantine woman backed up your story about the gun. The Assistant D.A. wanted to clap you in one of the nice new cells till I talked him out of it. Stick around and waste my time and I'll talk him right back into it. And it won't be hard to do. We've had a lot of trouble with private operators the last couple of years."

"Yeah," I said. "Like when I took Dwight Troy for you."

"Don't brag, I know you're hot. Now why don't you take all that Fahrenheit and peddle it someplace else? You can't polish apples with us by bringing in a little old junkie. They're two for a nickel. I could round up fifty any time between here and Union Station." Colton was angry. He had kept me out of a cell, but he hadn't forgiven me for what I had done to the law.

The girl looked at me sideways, smiling slightly. It gave her pleasure to see me taking it. She sat down in a straightbacked chair against the wall and crossed her legs.

"Go ahead and ride me," I said. "It's the old Army play, when somebody's riding you."

"Nobody's riding me. I'll tell you frankly, though, this Hammond woman has been ugly to deal with. And all day yesterday she was after us to release the body to her. Why in God's name did you have to go and stir up Jane Starr Hammond?"

"It seemed like a promising lead at the time. I'm not infallible."

"Don't act as if you thought you were, then. Next time the wolves can have you." He rose and moved to the window, his back to the room.

"All right," I said. "I apologize. Now if your wounded feelings have had enough of a therapeutic workout, let's get back to business."

He growled something unintelligible.

"You haven't found Tarantine, have you?"

That brought him back from the window. "We have not." He added with heavy irony: "No doubt he gave you his forwarding address."

"I think I know where to look for him. In the sea."

"You're a little late. The Sheriff's Aero Squadron in Pacific Point has been working on that for two days. The Coast Guard's carrying on dragging operations."

"Any trace of his companion?"

"None. They're not even sure he had a companion. The only witness they have won't swear there were two in the skiff. It was just an impression he had."

"Ruth is a witness. She saw him swim ashore."

"I heard something about that." He turned on the girl: "Where have you been?"

"Around." She drew herself together, shrinking in his shadow.

"What about this man you saw?"

She told her story, haltingly.

He considered it. "Are you sure it wasn't a dream? You junkies have funny dreams, I hear."

"I'm no junkie." Her voice was strained thin by fright. "I saw the man come out of the water, just like I said."

"Was it Tarantine? Do you know Tarantine?"

"It wasn't Joe. The man on the beach was bigger than Joe. He had a smooth shape." She giggled unexpectedly.

Colton looked at me: "She know Tarantine?"

"He sold her heroin."

The giggle ceased. "It's a lie."

"Show her a picture of Dalling," I said. "It's what I brought her here for."

He leaned across his desk and took some blown-up photographs out of a drawer. I looked at them over his shoulder as he shuffled them. Dalling lying full-length in his blood, his face like plaster in the magnesium light. Dalling close up and full face. Dalling right profile, with the black leaking hole in the side of his neck. Dalling left profile, looking as handsome as ever, and very dead.

One at a time, he handed them to the girl. She gasped when she saw the first one. "I think it's him." And when she had looked at them all: "It's him all right. He was a neat-looking fellow. What happened to him?"

Colton scowled down at her. He hated questions that he couldn't answer. After a pause he said more or less to himself: "We've practically assumed that Tarantine killed Dalling. If it was the other way around, wouldn't that be a boff?" He gave no sign of laughing, though.

"If Dalling killed Tarantine, who killed Dalling?" I said.

He looked at me quizzically. "Maybe you shot him yourself, after all."

Though Colton didn't mean it seriously, the warmed-over accusation irritated me. "If you can take time off from making funny remarks, I want you to do something for me." I emphasized the "me."

"Well?"

"Call up the head of the ~Narcotics Bureau and ask him nicely to come over here."

The girl looked up at me sharply, her mouth working. I was

threatening her food and drink and sleep, threatening to sink her island in the sea.

"For her?" Colton snorted. "Maybe you need a rest, Lew. I'll get a matron for her."

The girl had shrunk up small again, her thin shoulders curved forward like folded wings to nullify her chest. Matron was another word she feared. Her mouth worked miserably, but no words came. She gazed dully toward the open casement window as if she might be contemplating a running jump. I moved between her and the window. We were several floors from the street.

"Yeah, send for a matron. Ruth doesn't want to take a cure, but she needs it."

Colton lifted the receiver of his phone. The girl collapsed on herself, her head bent forward into her lap. The back of her neck was white and thin, feathered with a light soft fuzz of hair.

When Colton had given his order and hung up, I said: "Now call Narcotics."

"Why?"

"Because I've got a hundred thousand dollars' worth of heroin in my car. Maybe you want me to peddle that elsewhere along with my Fahrenheit, you lousy phrasemonger."

For the first time in my experience, Colton blushed. It wasn't a pretty sight.

30

It was late afternoon when I drove up the hill to Dowser's house for the third and last time. The guard at the gate had changed, but it was the same shotgun, its double muzzle watching me like a pair of binoculars. After the usual palaver and frisking, I was admitted to the sacred portals. My gun was locked in the glove compartment of the car, along with the can of heroin and Speed's automatic and Mosquito's knife.

Sullivan, the curly-headed Irishman, met me at the door. His face was sunburned fiery red.

"Have a nice time in Mexico?" I asked him.

"Rotten. I can't eat their rotten food." He looked at me sullenly, as if he could smell policeman on my clothes. "What do you want?"

"The boss. I phoned him, he knows I'm coming."

"He didn't say nothing to me." Sullivan was jealous.

"Maybe he doesn't trust you."

He gazed at me blankly, his slow brain taken by the plausibility of my suggestion.

"Let's get in to the boss," I said. "He's very eager to see me. I think he wants to offer me your job."

Dowser and his blonde were playing two-handed canasta in the patio. They were in the middle of a hand when I stepped out through the French doors, and Dowser was losing. The woman had half a dozen melds on the table; Dowser had nothing down. He was so intent on the cards in his hand that he didn't look up.

She did, though. "Why, hello, there," she said to me. She was looking very pleased with herself in a strapless white bathing suit that justified her pleasure.

"Hello."

Dowser grunted. With infinite reluctance, he disengaged a king of hearts from the fan of cards in his hand and tossed it onto the pile.

"Ha!" she cried. "I was holding out a pair." And she reached for the pile of discards.

Dowser was quicker. He snatched up the king of hearts and tucked it back in his hand: "I didn't mean to give you a king. I thought it was a jack."

"The hell you thought it was a jack," she said. "Give me back my king." She grabbed for his hand across the table, and missed.

"Settle down, Irene. I made a mistake. You wouldn't want to take advantage of me because my eyes are bothering me, would you now?"

"Take advantage of him, he says!" She slapped her cards on the table, faces up, and rose from her chair. "Why should I try to play cards with a damn cheat? It should happen to you what happened to Rothstein.''

He crouched forward, heavy arms on the table: "Take that back.''

The righteous indignation drained out of her suddenly. "I didn't mean it the way it sounded, Danny. I was only talking, that's all.''

"You talk too friggin' much. You get your mouth washed out with something stronger than soap.''

"I'm sorry," she said meekly. "You want to finish the game?''

"Nah!'' He stood up, wide and pudgy in his bathrobe. "Why should I play you for it when I can take it any time I want? Beat it, Irene.''

"If you say so.'' She transported her physical equipment through the French doors and out of sight.

Dowser threw down his cards and turned to me. "Psychiatry! That's what you got to use on them. Psychiatry! Sullivan, you can beat it too.''

Sullivan departed with a backward unwanted glance. I sat down across the table from Dowser and looked him over. He took a few strutting paces on the patio tiles, his arms folded across his chest. With his swollen body wrapped in a white beach robe, he reminded me a little of a Roman emperor sawed off and hammered down. It was strange that men like Dowser could gain the power they had. No doubt they got the power because they wanted it so badly, and were willing to take any responsibility, run any risk, for the sake of seizing power and holding on. They would bribe public officials, kill off rivals, peddle women and drugs; and they were somehow tolerated because they did these things for money and success, not for the things themselves.

I looked at the bold eyes bulging in the greased face and felt no compunction at all for what I was going to do to him.

"Well, baby?'' When he smiled, his thick lower lip protruded. "You said you got something for me?'' He sat down.

"I couldn't be very definite over the phone. It might be tapped.''

"Uh-uh. Not any more. But that's showing good sense.''

"Speaking of your phone, I've been intending to ask you:

you said a woman called you on Tuesday morning, and told you that Galley Tarantine was home at her mother's.''

"That's right. I talked to her myself, but she wouldn't say who she was.''

"And you haven't any idea?''

"No.''

"How would she know your number?''

"You've got me. She may have been a friend of Irene's, or one of the women the boys have on the string.'' He moved restlessly, brushing his rosebud ear with the tips of his fingers. "You said you had something for me, baby. You didn't say you wanted to come up and ask me a slew of questions.''

"That was the only question.—You offered me ten grand for Tarantine.''

"I did. You're not going to try and tell me you got him stashed someplace.'' He gathered up the cards and began to shuffle them absently. In spite of the swollen displaced bones in the knuckles, his touch was delicate.

"Not Tarantine,'' I said. "But it wasn't really Tarantine you wanted.''

"Is that so? Maybe you can tell me what I really wanted.''

"Maybe I can. Joe was carrying a tobacco can. It didn't have much tobacco in it, though.''

His gaze was sticky on my face. "If I thought you heisted it from Joe,'' he said, "you know what I'd do to you, baby?'' He picked up one card and tore it neatly in half.

"I know it, and I didn't. Joe sold it to a third party.''

"Who?''

"I couldn't say.''

"Where is it now?''

"I have it. Joe got thirty thousand for it. I'm not so greedy.''

"How much?''

"Make a bid. You offered ten for Joe. He's in the deep freeze somewhere, out of my reach. But the heroin is worth more.''

"Fifteen,'' he said. "I've already paid for it once.''

"I'll take it. Now.''

"Don't rush me. Fifteen grand is a lot of green. I got to be sure you've giving me the McCoy. Where's the stuff?''

"The money first,'' I said.

He half-lowered the thick eyelids over his bulging eyeballs, and the sharp pink point of his tongue did several laps around his mouth. "Whatever you say, baby. Wait here for a minute. And I mean in this chair."

I sat there for ten minutes, keenly aware that my skin was in one piece and might not be for long. I dealt myself a few poker hands, and got nothing worth betting on. When Dowser returned, he had changed to soft flannels. Blaney and Sullivan were with him, one at either elbow. The three made a curious picture as they advanced across the patio, like a fat powerful shark attended by a pair of oversize scavenger fish. Dowser had money in his hand, but it gave off a fishy smell. I saw when he came up to me that the money consisted of thousand-dollar bills.

He tossed them on the table: "Fifteen, count 'em."

Blaney and Sullivan watched me count the money as if it were edible and they were starving. I put it in my wallet.

"Not so fast," Dowser said. "I want a look at the stuff, that's natural."

"You can roll in the stuff. It's in the glove compartment of my car. Shall I go and get it?"

"I'll do that." He held out his hand for my keys.

I sat some more, with Blaney and Sullivan looking down at me. To indicate my general carefreeness, I laid out a hand of solitaire on the tabletop. When I tried to play it, though, the numbers on the cards didn't make sense. Blaney and Sullivan were perfectly silent. I could hear the tiny lapping of the swimming pool, then Dowser's footsteps coming back through the house. The wallet in my hip pocket felt heavy as lead.

Dowser was smiling his canine smile. Gold-capped molars gleamed in the corners of his mouth. Blaney and Sullivan stepped apart so that he could come between and ahead of them.

"It's the McCoy," he said. "Now tell us where you got it. That's included."

"I don't think so."

"Think again." His voice had softened, and he was still smiling. His lower lip stuck out far enough to stand on. "You got about ten seconds."

"Then what?"

He clicked his teeth with a sound like a pistol hammer. "Then we start over again. Only this time you got nothing to sell me. Just information is all. You were up in Frisco last night. There's a tag from the Union Square parking lot on your windshield. Who did you meet in Frisco?"

"I'm the detective, Danny. You're stealing my stuff."

"I'll tell you who it was," he said. "Gilbert the Mosquito, am I right?"

"Gilbert the who?"

"Brighten up. You're dumb, but not that dumb. Mosquito worked for me till he set up for himself. He was peddling in Frisco."

"Was?" I said.

"I said *was*. They found him on the road near Half Moon Bay this morning. Killed. A hit-run ran him down."

"It couldn't have happened to a nicer fellow."

"And what do you know, I find his knife in your car." He brought the spring-knife out of his jacket pocket. "Recognize it? It's got his initials on the handle." He handed it to Blaney, who nodded his head.

"I took it away from him when he tried to knife me."

Dowser grinned. "Sure, it was self-defense. You laid him out in the road and ran over him in self-defense. Don't get me wrong, he got what was coming to him, and you did me a favor when you did it. But I'm in business, baby, you got to realize that."

"Selling old knives?" I said.

"Maybe you're not so dumb. You catch on pretty fast." He dropped his voice to a whisper. "Pass the lettuce, huh?"

Blaney and Sullivan showed their guns. I stood up, raising my hands. This was the moment I had been living over and over for the past half-hour. Now that it was happening, it seemed hackneyed.

"You dirty double-crossers," I said from the script I had written in my head.

"Come on now, don't be like that. You sold me something valuable of mine, I sell you something valuable of yours. It's just that I'm smarter than you are." He said it with deep sincerity. "I'll mail you the knife some time, if you're sweet about things. Make trouble, though, and I'll deliver it in person." He dropped it back in his pocket, and reached around me. My wallet was lighter when he replaced it on my hip.

"Double-crossing dip." I counterfeited anger, but I was

inwardly relieved. If Dowser hadn't dreamed up something to pin on me, he might have thought it necessary to kill me. It was the chance I had to face from the beginning.

Dowser's pleasure was more obvious than mine. His face was shining with it. "Where would Mosquito get thirty grand? The sprout was strictly small-time for my money. Or maybe that was just part of the spiel. Maybe he used the knife on Joe, huh, and didn't need thirty grand?"

"That would be nice," I said.

"You still around?" He pantomimed surprise, and his gunmen smiled dutifully over their guns. "You can go now. Remember, you go quiet and stay sweet. I'm holding on to the knife for you."

Blaney and Sullivan escorted me to the car. In order to keep their minds occupied, I swore continuously without repeating myself. The guns were missing from the glove compartment. The guard at the gate held his shotgun on me until I was out of sight. Dowser was careful.

A quarter mile south of the private road, two black sedans, unmarked, were parked on the left side of the highway. Peter Colton was beside the driver of the lead car. The other eleven men were strangers to me.

I U-turned illegally under the eyes of twelve policemen, local and Federal, and stopped by the lead car.

"He has the can," I told Colton, "probably in his safe. Do you want me to go in with you?"

"Dangerous and unnecessary," he snapped. "By the way, they found Tarantine's body. He was drowned all right."

I wanted to ask him questions, but the black cars started to roll. Two cars coming from the other direction joined them at the entrance to the private road. All four turned up toward the hilltop where Dowser lived, not forever.

31

The Pacific Point morgue was in the rear of the mortuary two blocks from the courthouse. I avoided the front entrance— white pseudo-Colonial columns lit by a pink neon sign—and went up the driveway at the side. It curved around the back, past the closed doors of the garage, and led me to the rear door. Callahan was smoking a cigarette just outside the door, his big hat brushing the edge of the brown canvas canopy. A pungent odor drifted through the open door and disinfected the twilight.

He showed me the palm of his hand in salutation. "Well, we found your man. He's not much good to anybody, in his condition."

"Drowned?"

"Sure looks like it. Doc McCutcheon's coming over to do an autopsy on him soon as he can. Right now he's delivering a baby. So we don't lose any population after all." A smile cracked his weathered face as dry heat cracks the earth. "Want to take a look at the corpus?"

"I might as well. Where did you find him?"

"On the beach, down south of Sanctuary. There's a southerly current along here, about a mile an hour. The wind blew the boat in fast, but Tarantine was floating low in the water and the current drifted him further south before the tide brought him in. That's how I figure it." His butt pinwheeled into the gathering darkness, and he turned toward the door.

I followed him into a low deep room walled with bare concrete blocks. Five or six wheeled tables with old-fashioned marble tops stood against the walls. All but one were empty. Callahan switched on a green-shaded lamp that hung above the occupied table. A pair of men's feet, one of them shoeless, protruded from under the white cotton cover. Callahan pulled the cover off with a sweeping showman's gesture.

Joe Tarantine had been roughly used by the sea. It was hard to believe that the battered, swollen face had once been handsome, as people said. There was white sand in the curled black hair and white sand on the eyeballs. I peered into the gaping mouth. It was packed with wet brown sand.

166

"No foam," I said to Callahan. "Are you sure he drowned?"

"You can't go by that. And those marks on his face and head are probably posthumous. The stiffs all get 'em when the surf rolls 'em in on the rocks."

"You have a lot of them?"

"One or two a month along here. Drownings, suicides. This is a plain ordinary drowning in my book."

"In spite of what the girl said, about the man swimming ashore?"

"I wouldn't worry about that if I was you. Even if the girl was telling the truth, which I doubt—some of these biddies will say anything to get their picture in the paper—even if she was, it was probably one of these midnight bathers or something. We have a lot of nuts in this town."

I leaned closer to the dead man to examine his clothing. He had on worn blue Levi's and a work-shirt, still dark with sea-stain and smelling of the sea. There was sand in the pockets and nothing else.

I glanced at Callahan. "You're certain this is Tarantine?"

"Him or his brother. I knew the guy."

"Did he usually wear dungarees? I understood he was a flashy dresser."

"Nobody wears good clothes on a boat."

"I suppose not. Speaking of his brother, where is his brother?"

"Mario should be on his way now. Him and the old lady were out all afternoon; we finally got in touch with them. They're coming in for a formal identification."

"What about Mrs. Tarantine? The wife?"

"She's coming, too. We notified her soon as we found the body. Seems to be taking her time about it, doesn't she?"

"I'll stick around, if you don't mind."

"It's all right with me," he said, "if you like the scenery. It suits me better outside." Raising his arm in an exaggerated movement, he squeezed his veined nose between thumb and forefinger.

The dead man lay under the light, battered and befouled and awesome. Callahan turned the switch and we went outside.

Leaning against the wall with a cigarette, I told him about Dalling's early morning swim and Dalling's early morning death. I didn't expect the information to do him any good. I was talking against the stillness that circled outward from the dead man as sound waves spread from their source. The late green twilight faded from the sky as I talked, and darkness rolled in a slow surge over the rooftops. All I could see of Callahan was his dark hulk like a buttress against the wall, and the orange eye of the cigarette glowing periodically under his hatbrim.

A pair of bright headlights swept into the driveway and froze in the massive stillness.

"Bet that's the patrol car," he said, and moved to the corner of the building.

Over his shoulder, I saw Mario step out of the sheriff's car. He came into the glare of the headlights, towing his mother like a captive balloon. I stepped back into the shadow to let them pass, and followed them to the door.

Callahan switched on the lamp above the dead man's face. Mario stood looking down, his mother leaning heavily on his shoulder. The bruise marks on his face were turning yellowish and greenish. Other men had been as rough on him as the sea had been on his brother. He might have been thinking that, from the look in his eyes. They were mocking and grim.

"That's Joe," he said finally. "Was there any doubt about it?"

"We like to have a relative, just to make it legal." Callahan had removed his hat and assumed an expression of solemnity.

Mrs. Tarantine had been silent, her broad face almost impassive. She cried out now, as if the fact had sunk through layers of flesh to her quick: "Yes! It is my son, my Guiseppe. Dead in his sins. Yes!" Her great dark eyes were focused for distance. She saw the dead man lying far down in hell.

Mario glanced at Callahan in embarrassment, and jerked at his mother's arm. "Be quiet, Mama."

"Look at him!" she cried out scornfully. "Too smart to go to Mass. For many years no confession. Now look at my boy, my Guiseppe. Look at him, Mario."

"I already did," he said between his teeth. He pulled at her roughly. "Come away now."

She laid one arm across the dead man's waist to anchor herself. "I will stay here, with Guiseppe. Poor baby." She spoke in Italian to the dead man, and he answered her with silence.

"You can't do that, Mrs. Tarantine." Callahan rocked in pain from one foot to the other. "The doctor's going to perform an autopsy, you wouldn't want to see it. You don't object, do you?"

"Naw, she don't object. Come on, Mama, you get yourself all dirty."

She allowed herself to be drawn towards the door. Mario paused in front of me: "What do you want?"

"I'll driver you home if you like."

"We're riding with the chief deputy. He wants to ask me some questions, he says."

The mother looked at me as if I was a shadow on the wall. There was a stillness in her to match the stillness of the dead.

"Answer a couple for me."

"Why should I?"

I moved up close to him: "You want me to tell you in Mexican?"

His attempt to smile when he got it was grotesque. He shot a nervous glance at Callahan, who was crossing the room toward us. "Okay, Mr. Archer. Shoot."

"When did you see your brother last?"

"Friday night, like I told you."

"Are those the clothes he was wearing?"

"Friday night, you mean? Yeah, those are the same clothes. I wouldn't be sure it was him if it wasn't for the clothes."

Callahan spoke up behind him: "There's no question of identification. You recognize your son, don't you, Mrs. Tarantine?"

"Yes," she said in a deep voice. "I know him. I ought to know him, the boy I nursed from a little baby." Her hands moved on her black silk expanse of bosom.

"That's fine—I mean, thank you very much. We appreciate you coming down here and all." With a disapproving glance at me, Callahan ushered them out.

He turned to me when they were out of earshot: "What's eating you? *I* knew the guy, knew him well enough not to grieve over him. His mother and his brother certainly knew him."

"Just an idea I had. I like to be sure."

"Trouble with you private dicks," he grumbled, "you're always looking for an angle, trying to find a twist in a perfectly straight case."

32

An inner door opened, and a plump coatless man in a striped shirt appeared in the opening. "Telephone for you," he said to Callahan. "It's your office calling." He had an undertaker's soft omniscient smile.

"Thanks," Callahan said as he passed him in the doorway.

The man in the striped shirt moved like a wingless moth toward the lighted table. His bright black boots hissed on the concrete floor.

"Well," he said to the dead man, "you aren't as pretty as you might be, are you? When doctor's through with you, you won't be pretty in the least. However, we'll fix you up, I give you my word." His voice dripped in the stillness like syrup made from highly refined sugar.

I stepped outside and closed the door and lit a cigarette. It was half burned down when Callahan reappeared. He was bright-eyed, and his cheeks had a rosy shine.

"What have you been doing, drinking embalming fluid?"

"Teletype from Los Angeles. Keep it to yourself, and I'll let you in on it." I couldn't have prevented him from telling me. "They raided the Dowser mob—Treasury agents and D.A.'s men. Caught them with enough heroin to give the whole city a jag."

"Any casualties?" I was thinking of Colton.

"Not a one. They came in quiet as lambs. And get this: Tarantine worked for the corporation, he fronted for Dowser down at the Arena right here in town. You were looking for an angle, weren't you? There it is."

"Fascinating," I said.

A car came up the driveway, turned the corner of the building and parked beyond the canopy. A slope-shouldered man with a medical bag climbed out.

"Sorry I'm so late," he said to Callahan. "It was a slow delivery, and then I snatched some supper."

"The customer's still waiting." He turned to me. "This is Dr. McCutcheon. Mr. Archer."

"How long will it take?" I asked the doctor.

"For what?"

"To determine cause of death."

"An hour or two. Depends on the indications." He glanced inquiringly at Callahan: "I understood he was drowned."

"Yah, we thought so. Could be a gang murder, though," Callahan added knowingly. "He ran with the Dowser gang."

"Take a good look for anything else that might have caused his death," I said. "If you don't mind my shoving an oar in."

He shook his tousled gray head impatiently. "Such as?"

"I wouldn't know. Blunt instrument, hypo, even a bullet wound."

"I always make a thorough examination," McCutcheon stated. That ended the conversation.

I left my car parked in front of the mortuary and walked the two blocks to the main street. I was hungry in spite of the odors that seemed to have soaked into my clothes, of fish and kelp and disinfected death. In spite of the questions asking themselves like a quiz program tuned in to my back fillings, with personal comments on the side.

Callahan had recommended a place called George's Café. It turned out to be a restaurant-bar, lower-middle-class and middle-aged. A bar ran down one side, with a white-capped short-order cook at a gas grill that crowded the front window. There were booths along the other side, and a row of tables covered with red-checked tablecloths down the center. Three or four ceiling fans turned languidly, mixing the smoky air into a uniform blue-gray blur. Everything in the place, including the customers phalanxed at the bar, had the air of having been there for a long time.

As soon as I sat down in one of the empty booths, I felt that way myself. The place had a cozy subterranean quality, like a time capsule buried deep beyond the reach of change and violence. The fairly white-coated waiters, old and young, had a quick slack economy of movement surviving from a dead regretted decade. The potato chips that came with my sizzling steak tasted exactly the same as the chips I ate out of greasy newspaper wrappings when I was in grade school in Oakland in 1920. The scenic photographs that decorated the walls—Route of the Union Pacific—reminded me of a stereopticon I had found in my mother's great-aunt's attic. The rush and whirl of bar conversation sounded like history.

I was finishing my second bottle of beer when I caught sight of Galley through the foam-etched side of the glass. She was standing just inside the door, poised on high heels. She had on a black coat, a black hat, black gloves. For an instant she looked unreal, a ghost from the present. Then she saw me and moved toward me, and it was everything else that seemed unreal. Her vitality blew her along like a strong wind. Yet her face was haggard, as if her vitality was something separate from her, feeding on her body.

"Archer!" The ghastly face smiled at me, and the smile came off. "I'm so glad I found you."

I pulled a chair out for her. "How did you?"

"The deputy sheriff said you were here. Callahan?"

"You've seen the body, then."

"Yes. I saw—him." Her eyes were as dark as a night without stars. "The doctor was cutting him up."

"They shouldn't have let you in."

"Oh, I wanted to. I had to know. But it's queer to see a man in pieces after you've lived with him. Even if I am a nurse."

"Have a drink."

"I will. Thanks. Straight whisky." She was breathing quickly and shallowly, like a dog on a warm day.

I let her down the drink before I asked her: "What did the doctor say?"

"He thinks it's drowning."

"He does, eh?"

"Don't you?"

"I'm just a floating question-mark, waiting for an answer to hook onto me. Have another drink."

"I guess I will. They got Dowser, did you hear? Mr. Callahan told me."

"That's fine." I didn't feel like bragging about my part in it. Dowser had friends, and the friends had guns. "Tell me, Galley."

"Yes?" There were stars in her eyes again, and no whisky in her shot-glass.

"I'd like a better picture of that week-end you spent with Joe in the desert."

"It was a lost one, believe me. Joe was wild. It was like being shut up in four rooms with a sick mountain-lion. I was pretty wild myself. He wouldn't tell me what it was all about, and it drove me crazy."

"Facts, please. A few objective facts."

"Those are facts."

"Not the kind that help much. I want details. What was he wearing, for example?"

"Joe was in his underwear most of the time. Is that important? It was hot out there, in spite of the airconditioning—"

"Didn't he have any clothes with him?"

"Of course."

"Where are they now?"

"I wouldn't know. He had them in a club-bag when I drove him down here."

"What was he wearing?"

"Blue work-clothes."

"The same as he has on now?"

"He hadn't anything on when I saw him. I suppose they're the same. Why?"

"His brother said he was wearing those clothes Friday night. Was he?"

Her curved brows knitted in concentration. "Yes. He didn't change when he got home Friday night."

"And he wore them, when he wasn't in his underwear, right through to Tuesday morning. It doesn't fit in with what I've heard about Joe."

"I know. He wasn't himself. He was in a sort of frenzy. I had dinner waiting for him when he got home—he phoned that he was coming—but he wouldn't even stop to eat it. I barely had time to pack anything, he was in such a hurry. We rushed out to Oasis, and then we sat and looked at each other for three days."

"No explanations?"

"He said he was getting out, that we were waiting for money. I thought he had broken with the gang, as I'd been urging him to. I knew he was afraid, and I thought they were hunting him. If I hadn't believed that, I wouldn't have gone with him, or stayed. Then when he did go, he went by himself."

"You wouldn't want to have gone along, not where he's gone."

"Maybe I would at that." She raised the empty shot-glass in her fist and stared down into its thick bottom like a crystal-gazer rapt in tragic visions.

The waiter, a fat old Greek who moved on casters, appeared beside our booth. "Another drink?"

Galley came out of her trance. "I think I should eat something. I don't know whether I can."

"A steak like the gentleman's?" The waiter molded an imaginary steak with his hands. She nodded absently.

"A beer for me." When he had gone: "Another detail, Galley." Her head came up. "You didn't say a word about Herman Speed."

"Speed?" Her fine white teeth closed over her lower lip. "I told you I nursed him."

"That's the point. You must have recognized him."

"I don't know what you mean. When should I have recognized him?"

"Sunday night, when he came to your house in Oasis. You must have known he bought the heroin from Joe."

"I don't believe it."

"Didn't you see him?"

"I wasn't there Sunday night. I haven't seen Mr. Speed since he got out of the hospital. I heard he left the country."

"You heard wrong. Where were you?"

"Sunday? About eight o'clock, Joe told me to get out, not to come back for a couple of hours. He let me take the car. How do you know Speed was there?"

"It's beside the point. He was there, and he did buy the heroin—"

"This heroin you've been talking about, did Joe steal it from Dowser?" Her face was intent on mine.

"Apparently."

"And sold it to Speed?"

"For thirty thousand dollars."

"Thirty thousand dollars," she repeated slowly. "Where is it now?"

"It could be in Joe's club-bag at the bottom of the sea, or making a fat roll in somebody's pocket."

"Whose?"

"Possibly Speed's." It seemed in retrospect that he'd handed over the heroin to me much too easily. "He might have known Joe's plans, and been waiting for him on the boat Tuesday morning. He had a motive, in addition to the money. Your sainted husband fingered him for the mob last fall."

Her eyes dilated. "I thought they were friends."

"Speed thought so, too. Perhaps he found out different, and decided to do something about it. I say perhaps. There's another possibility I like better."

"Yes," she said softly. "Keith Dalling."

"You're a quick girl."

"Not really." Her smile was one-sided. "I've been thinking about him for days, trying to understand why he acted as he did, and why he was killed. He was spying on us in Oasis, you know. I thought he was carrying a torch for me. I didn't suspect it was money he was after, though God knows he needed it."

"You saw him Sunday night, I believe."

"Yes. Did he tell you? He was waiting up the road when I left the house. He pretended to be worried about me. We went to a little place in Palm Springs, and he drank too much and tried to persuade me to run away with him."

"Did he know what Joe was carrying?"

"If he did, he didn't tell me. Frankly, I thought he was naïve, quite a bit of a fool. A nice fool, even."

"So did I. But it's pretty clear that he was on the boat, Tuesday morning. He was seen swimming ashore."

"No!" She leaned forward across the red-checked tablecloth. "That would seem to make it definite, wouldn't it?"

"Except for a couple of things that bother me. One is the fact that he was shot himself within an hour or two."

"With your gun."

"With my gun. It would be a nice irony if Dowser's men shot him because they thought he was Joe's partner. But how would they get hold of my gun? You said Joe took it. Are you sure of that?"

"I saw him. He put it in the club-bag along with his own."

"There is a way it could have happened," I said. "If Dalling took my gun when he took the money and brought it ashore with him, then Dowser's men took it away from him in his apartment. It's an old gang trick, shooting a man with his own iron."

"Is it? I wouldn't know." Her head was sagging again, under the weight of too much information at once.

"It would be a nice irony," I said, "but a little too neat for real life. And it doesn't begin to cover the second thing that bothers me. Why did Dalling go to the trouble of talking your mother into hiring me? It doesn't make sense. Unless he was really schizo?"

"No. I think I know the answer to that one. One possible answer, anyway."

"If you can figure it out, I'll give you a job."

"I could use one. The point is that Keith was deathly afraid of Joe. He wanted you to come out there and make trouble, the worse the better. If both of you got killed, that would be perfect. I'd be there in his house, unencumbered, complete with dowry. He wouldn't even have to carry me across the threshold. Does it make sense? He'd be afraid to hire you personally for a job like that—too many things to go wrong."

The waiter set a steak in front of her, and poured beer for me.

"The job is yours," I said. "The steak is an advance on your first week's salary."

She paid no attention to the food, or to me. "It didn't work out the way Keith wanted it to. Joe survived, and so did you. What did happen was, Joe thought that the gang was closing in, and he had to run for it. Maybe that's all Keith counted on. Anyway, he was there at the dock, or on the boat, when Joe got there. And he did his own dirty work after all."

"Very fine," I said. "But how did he know where Joe was heading? You didn't tell him?"

"I didn't know. He might have followed us down here."

"He might have. Or he might have had an accomplice."

"Who?" Her eyes burned black.

"We'll discuss that later. Eat your steak now, before it gets cold. I'll be back shortly." I slid out of my seat.

"Where are you going?"

"I want to catch the doctor before he leaves. Guard my beer, will you?"

"With my life."

33

McCutcheon, assisted by the man in the striped shirt, was sewing up an incision that ran from the base of the dead man's throat to his lower abdomen. The doctor was wearing rubber gloves, a white coverall, and a hat that gave him an oddly casual appearance. A dead cigar projected from his mouth.

It didn't turn in my direction till the sewing job was finished. Then McCutcheon straightened, using his forearm to push the hat back on his head. "Rotten sort of task," he said. "I shouldn't kick, I guess. He's fresher than some."

"Exactly how fresh, can you tell?"

"It's a hard question, with bodies found in water. Rate of deterioration depends on water temperature and other factors. We happen to know that this laddie's been in the water between fifty and sixty hours. If I didn't know that, I'd say he'd been in longer. Decomposition's rather far advanced for this time of year." He started to reach for a pocket under the coverall, then remembered his gloved hands: "Light my cigar for me, will you?"

I gave him a light. "What about cause of death?"

He dragged deep, regarding me through a cloud of blue smoke. "It isn't definite yet. I need some work from the pathology lab before I stick my neck out." He pointed a thumb at a row of jars the undertaker was labeling on the adjacent table. "Stomach contents, blood, lung tissue, neck structures. You a reporter?"

"Detective. Private, more or less. I've been working on this case from the beginning. And I simply want to know if he was drowned."

"It's not impossible," he said around the cigar. "Some of the indications are consistent with drowning. The lungs are water-logged, for one thing. The right side of the heart is dilated. Trouble is, those conditions are equally consistent with asphyxia. There are chemical tests we can use on the blood to determine which it is, but I won't have a report on them before tomorrow."

"In your opinion, though, he was drowned or smothered?"

"I don't have an opinion until the facts are in."

"No signs of violence?"

"None that I can ascertain. I'll tell you this: if he was drowned, it was an unusual drowning; he must have died as soon as he hit the water."

The mortician glanced up brightly from his jars. "I've seen it happen, doctor. Sometimes they die *before* they strike the water. Shock. Their poor hearts just stop ticking." He coughed delicately.

McCutcheon ignored him. "If you don't mind, I'd like to get out of here."

"Sorry. But would you call it murder?"

"That depends on a lot of things. Frankly, there's something a little peculiar about the tissues. If it weren't a patent impossibility, I'd say he might have frozen to death. Anyway, I'm making a couple of microscopic sections. So there you have three alternatives. See what you can make of them." He turned back to the table where Tarantine lay.

I drove to the sheriff's office and found Callahan. He was huddled over a typewriter that looked too small for his hands, filling out an official form of some kind. He looked pleased when I walked in, providing him with an excuse to leave off typing.

"How was George's?"

"Fine. I left Mrs. Tarantine there."

"Did her brother-in-law find you all right?"

"Mario? I didn't see him."

"He left here a few minutes ago. He wanted to invite her for overnight—you wouldn't think a dame with her class would want to stay with them guineas, though. Hell, I wanted to hold him in a cell but the Chief says no. We need the Italian vote in the election. Matter of fact, the Chief is one himself, shut my big mouth."

"If the vote depends on Mario, you'll probably lose it. I've just been talking to McCutcheon."

"What did he say?"

"A lot of things. Which boil down to three possibilities: drowning, suffocation, freezing."

"Freezing?"

"That's what he said. He also said that it was impossible, but I don't know. Maybe you can tell me if Mario's boat had a freezer."

"I doubt it. The big commercial boats have. You don't see

them on a sport boat that size. There's an ice plant down near the dock, though. Maybe we better take a look at it."

"Later. Right now I want to see Mario."

I was frustrated. When we reached George's Café, the booth I had occupied was empty.

The old Greek waiter hustled across the room. "I'm sorry, sir, I poured out your beer after the lady left. I thought—"

"When did she leave?"

"Five minutes, ten minutes, hard to tell. When her friend came in—"

"The man with the bandaged head?"

"That's him. He sat down with her for a minute, then they got up and left." He twisted his head towards Callahan. "Is something the matter, sheriff?"

"Huh. Did he threaten her? Show any kind of a weapon?"

"Oh, no, nothing like that." The old man's face had turned a dull white, like bread dough. "I see any trouble, I call you on the telephone, you know that. They just walked out like anybody else."

"No argument?"

"Maybe they argued a little. How can I tell? I was busy."

I drew Callahan to one side.

"Did she have her car?"

He nodded. "They're probably in it, eh?"

"It looks to me like a general alarm, with road-blocks. The quicker the better."

But the alarm and the road-blocks were too late. I waited in the sheriff's office for an hour, and nobody was brought in. By ten o'clock I was ready to try a long shot in the dark.

34

For two hours I drove down the white rushing tunnel carved by my headlights in the solid night. At the end of the run the unbuilt town lay dark around me, its corners desolate under the sparse streetlights. When I stepped out of my car the night shot up like a tree and branched wide into blossoming masses of stars. Under their far cold lights I felt weak and little. if a fruit fly lived for one day instead of two, it hardly seemed to matter. Except to another fruit fly.

There was light behind the Venetian blinds of the house that Dalling built, the kind of warm and homey light a lonely man might envy as he passed the house. The same light that murderers worked in when they killed their wives or husbands or lovers or best friends. The house was as quiet as a burial vault.

The light was in the living-room. I mounted the low veranda and looked in between the slats of the blind. Galley lay prone on the tan rug, one arm supporting her head, the other outstretched. The visible side of her face was smeared darkly with something that looked like blood. Her visible eye was closed. There was a heavy automatic gun in her outstretched hand. The too-late feeling that had driven me across the desert went to my knees and loosened them.

The front door was standing open and I went in, letting the screen door close itself behind me. From the hall I heard her breathing and sighing in slow alternation. She sounded like a runner who has run a fast race and fallen and broken his heart.

I was halfway across the room toward the prostrate girl when she became aware of me. She rose on her knees and elbows, her breasts sharp-pointed at the floor, the blunt gun in her right hand pointed at me. Behind the tangled black hair that hung down over her face, her eyes gleamed like an animal's. I froze.

She straightened gradually, rocking back on her heels and rising to her feet; stood swaying a little with her legs apart, both hands holding the gun up. She tossed her hair back. Her eyes were wide and fixed.

"What happened to you?"

She answered me in a small tired voice: "I don't know. I must have passed out for a while."

"Give me the gun." I took a step toward her. Another step would put me within kicking distance, but my feet stuck to the floor.

"Stand back. Back to where you were." Her voice had

changed. It cracked like an animal trainer's whip. And her hands were steady as stone.

The soles of my feet came unstuck and slid away from her. Her eyes were blank and ominous, like the gun's round eye:

"Where's Mario?"

She shrugged impatiently. "How should I know?"

"You left the café together."

Her mouth twisted. "God, I despise you, Archer! You're a dirty little sees-all hears-all tells-all monkey, aren't you? What difference does it make to you what people do?"

"I like to pretend I'm God. But I don't really fool myself. It takes a murderer to believe it about himself. Personally, I'm just another fruit fly. If I don't care what happens to fruit flies, what is there to care about? And if I don't care, who will? It makes no difference to the stars." My talk was postponing the gun's roaring period, but I couldn't talk it out of her hands and out the window.

"You're talking nonsense, chattering like a monkey." Her foot felt for the armchair behind her, and she sat down carefully, cradling the gun on her knee. "If you must talk, we'll talk seriously. You sit down, too."

I squatted uncomfortably on a leatherette hassock by the fireplace. Yellow light fell like an ugly truth from the bulbs in the ceiling fixture. Galley was bleeding from a wide cut on one cheekbone.

I said: "There's blood on your face."

"It doesn't matter."

"Blood on your hands, too."

"Not yours. Not yet." She smiled her bitter smile. "I want to explain to you why I killed Keith Dalling. Then we'll decide what to do."

"You have the gun."

"I know. I'm going to keep it. I didn't have the gun when I shot Keith. I had to fight him for it."

"I see. Self-defense. Neat. Only, can you get away with it?"

"I'm telling you the truth," she said.

"It's the first time if you are."

"Yes, the first time."

She spoke rapidly and low. "When I drove Joe to the Point Tuesday morning, I saw Keith's car at the docks. He knew Joe would turn up there: I told him myself. I didn't realize what

Keith was planning. I went back to Los Angeles, to Keith's apartment, and waited for him there. When he came home I asked him what he had done, and he confessed to me. He'd fought with Joe on the boat and pushed him into the ocean. He thought the way was clear now for us to marry. I couldn't conceal what I thought of him, I didn't try. He was a murderer, and I told him so. Then he pulled a gun on me, the gun he'd taken from Joe, your gun, as you guessed he did. I pretended to be convinced—I had to save my life—and I made up to him and got the gun away from him. I shot him. I had to. Then I panicked and ran out and threw the gun in the drain, and when the police questioned me I lied about everything. I was afraid. I knew that Joe was dead, and it made no difference to him if I blamed Keith's death on him. I know now I made a mistake. I should have called the police when it happened, and told them the truth."

Her breast rose and fell irregularly. Like any pretty woman with mussed hair, blood on her face, she had a waiflike appeal, which the steady gun destroyed. I thought of Speed, and saw how easy it was to wilt in a gun's shadow. Though I had faced them before, single and multiple, each time was a fresh new experience. And a single gun in the hands of a woman like Galley was the most dangerous weapon. Only the female sex was human in her eyes, and she was its only really important member.

"What truth?" I said. "You've changed your story so often I doubt if you know what really happened."

"Don't you believe me?" Her face seemed to narrow and lengthen. I had never seen her look ugly before. An ugly woman with a gun is a terrible thing.

"I believe you partly. No doubt you shot Dalling. The circumstances sound a bit artificial."

The blood from her cut cheek wriggled like a black worm at the corner of her mouth. "The police will believe me, if you're not there to deny it. I can turn Gary round my little finger." It was a forlorn boast.

"You're losing your looks," I said. "Murders take it out of a woman. You pay so much for them that they're never the bargain they seem to be." I had heard a noise from the back of the house, and was talking to cover it. It sounded like a drunk man floundering in the dark.

She glanced at the gun in her hands and back to my face, imagining the flight of the bullet. I saw her knuckles tense around the butt.

And I leaned forward a little without rising, shifting my weight to the balls of my feet, still talking: "If you shoot me, I'll get to you before I die, I promise. You'll have no looks left, even if you survive. Even if you survive, the police will finish the job. You're vulnerable as hell." The back door creaked. "Vulnerable as hell," I repeated loudly. "Two murders, or three, already, and more coming up. You can't kill everybody. We're too many for one crazy girl with a gun."

The floundering footsteps moved on the kitchen floor. She heard them. Her eyes shifted from me to the door on her right, came back to me before I could stir. She stepped sideways out of the chair, retreating with her back to the window, so that her gun commanded my side of the room and the kitchen doorway.

Mario came into the doorway and leaned there for an instant with one raised hand gripping the frame. His chin had been smashed by something heavier than a fist. Blood coursed down his neck into the black hair that curled over his open shirt-collar. There was death in his face. I wasn't sure he could see until he advanced on Galley. His smashed mouth blew a bubble in which the room hung upside down, tiny and blood-colored.

She yelped once like a dog and fired point-blank. The slug spun Mario on his heels and flung him bodily against the wall. He pushed himself away from the wall with his hands and turned to face her. She fired again, the black gun jumping like a toad. Still her white hands held it firm, and her white devoted face was watching us both.

Mario doubled forward and sank to his knees. The indestructible man crawled toward the woman, leaking blood like black oil on her rug. Her third shot drilled the bandaged top of his head, and finished Mario. Still she was not content. Standing over him, she pumped three bullets into his back as fast as she could fire.

I counted them, and when the gun was empty I took it away from her. She didn't resist.

35 _____

When I set the telephone down, she was sitting in the chair I had pushed her into, her closed eyelids tremorless as carved ivory, her passionate mouth closed and still. From where I stood on the other side of the room, she seemed tiny and strange like a figurine, or an actress sitting on a distant stage. Mario lay face down between us.

A shudder ran through her body and her eyes came open. "I'm glad I didn't kill you, Archer. I didn't want to kill you, honestly." Her voice had the inhuman quality of an echo.

"That was nice of you." I stepped over the prone body and sat down facing her. "You didn't want to kill Mario, either. Like Dalling, you killed him in self-defense." I sounded strange to myself. The fear of death had made a cold lump in my throat which I was still trying to swallow.

"You're a witness to that. He attacked me with a deadly weapon." She glanced at the metal knuckles on the dead man's fist, and touched her cheek. "He struck me with it."

"When?"

"In the garage a few minutes ago."

"How did you get there?"

"He came into George's Café and forced me to leave with him. I had no gun. He'd got the idea that I knew where his brother had left the money. I knew there was a gun out here, in the garage where Joe had hidden it. I told Mario the money was here, and he made me drive him out." Her voice was clear and steady, though the words came out with difficulty. "He was almost crazy, threatening to kill me, with that awful thing on his hand. I got hold of Joe's gun and shot him with it, once. I thought he was dead. I managed to get into the house before I fainted." She sighed. With the emotional versatility of a good actress, she was slipping back into the brave-little-woman role that had taken me in before, and wouldn't again.

"You might get by with a self-defense plea if you'd only killed one man. Two in a week is too many. Three is mass murder."

184

"Three?"

"Dalling and Mario and Joe."

"I didn't kill Joe. How could I? I can't even swim."

"You're a good liar, Galley. You have the art of mixing fact with your fantasy, and it's kept you going for a week. But you've run out of lies now."

"I didn't kill him," she repeated. Her body was stiff in the chair, her hands clenched tight on the arms. "Why should I kill my own husband?"

"Spare me the little-wife routine. It worked for a while, I admit. You had me and the cops convinced that you were shielding Joe. Now it turns my stomach. You had plenty of reasons to kill him, including thirty thousand dollars. It must have looked like a lot of money after years of nurse's work on nurse's pay. You probably married Joe with the sole intention of killing him as soon as he was loaded."

"What kind of a woman do you think I am?" Her face had lost its impassivity and was groping for an expression that might move me.

I touched the dead man with the toe of my shoe. "I just saw you pump six .45 slugs into a man who was dying on his feet. Does that answer your question?"

"I had to. I was terrified."

"Yeah. You have the delicate sensitivity of a frightened rattlesnake, and you react like one. You killed Mario because he figured out that you murdered his brother. Joe probably warned him about you."

"You'd have a hard time proving that." Her eyes were like black charred holes in her white mask.

"I don't have to. Wait until the police lab men have a look at the deep-freeze unit in your kitchen."

"How—?" Her mouth closed tight, an instant too late. She had confirmed my guess.

"Go on. How did I know that you kept Joe in cold storage for three days?"

"I'm not talking."

"I didn't know it until now. Not for certain. It clears up a lot of things."

"You're talking nonsense again. Do I have to listen to you?"

"Until the sheriff's car gets here from Palm Springs, yes. There's a lot of truth to be told, after all the lies, and if you won't tell it I will. It might give you a little insight into yourself."

"What do you think you are, a psychoanalyst?"

"Thank God I'm not yours. I wouldn't want to have to explain what made you do what you did. Unless you were in love with Herman Speed?"

She laughed. "That old stallion? Don't be a silly boy. He was my patient."

"You used him then. You got the lowdown on Joe's dope-smuggling from him. I take it he was glad enough to spoil the game for the man who fingered him and stole his business. Perhaps Speed was using you, at that. After talking to both of you, I imagine it was his idea in the first place. He was the brains—"

"Speed?" I had touched a nerve. So it had been her idea.

"Anyway, you went to San Francisco with him when he got out of the hospital. You sent your mother a Christmas card from there, and that was your first mistake—mixing sentiment with business. After you'd worked out the plan, you let your mother sweat out the next two months without hearing from you, because you intended to use her. You came back to Pacific Point and married Joe: no doubt he'd asked you before and was waiting for your answer. Speed went to Reno to try and raise the necessary money. Unfortunately he succeeded. Which brings us down to last Friday night—"

"You," she said, "not us. You lost me long ago. You're all by yourself."

"Maybe some of the details are wrong or missing: they'll be straightened out in court. I don't know, for example, what you put in Joe's food or drink Friday night when he came home from his last boat-trip. Chloral hydrate, or something that leaves no trace? You know more about things like that than I do."

"I thought you were omniscient."

"Hardly. I don't know whether Dalling pushed in on your project, or was it invited. Or was it a combination of both? In any case, you needed the use of this house of his, and you needed help. Speed was busy holding up his end of a phony honeymoon. Dalling was the best you could get in the clutch. When Joe went to sleep, Dalling helped you carry him out through his apartment and down the back way to the car. At this end, you hoisted him into the freezer and let him smother. So far it had been simple. Joe was dead, and you had the heroin. Speed had the money and the contacts. But your biggest problem still faced you. You knew if Dowser caught on to you, you wouldn't live to enjoy your money. Perhaps you heard what his gorillas did to Mario Friday night, just on the off chance that he knew something about it. You had to clear yourself with Dowser. That's where I came in, and that's where you made your big mistake.''

"Anything with you in it is a mistake. I only hope you repeat this fable in public, to the police. I'll put you out of business." But she couldn't muster enough conviction to support the words. They sounded desperately thin.

"I'll be in business when you're in Tehachapi, or in the gas chamber. You thought you could call me in to take a fall, then turn me off like a tap, or kiss me off with a little casual sex. It was a tricky idea, a little too tricky to work. You and your radio actor persuaded your mother to hire me to look for you: you probably wrote the script. Then you arranged for me to find you and be convinced that Joe was alive and kicking. Dalling sneaked up on the porch behind me and sandbagged me. You even faked a warning that came too late, to demonstrate good faith. You removed my gun and filed it for future reference. I don't know whether you were already planning to kill your partner. You must have seen that he was going to pieces. But you kept him alive as long as possible, because you still needed his help.

"Joe went back into the trunk of your car. In his condition, he must have made an awkward piece of luggage. You and Keith drove separately to Pacific Point. He got the body aboard the *Aztec Queen*, took it to sea, dumped it into the water, and swam ashore to your headlights. You took him back to the dock, where his car was, and the two of you drove to Los Angeles. That took care of the body, and more important, it took care of Dowser. It would be obvious, if and when the body was found, that Joe had drowned in a getaway attempt.

"That left just one fly in your ointment, your partner. He was useful for physical work that you couldn't do, like rowing dead bodies around harbors and starting boat-engines, but he was a moral weakling. You knew he couldn't stand the pressure that was coming. Besides, he'd be wanting his share of the cash. So you went up to his apartment with him and paid him off with a bullet. A bullet from my gun. Hid my gun where the cops would be sure to find it. Went home to bed and, if I know your type, slept like a baby.''

"Did I?"

"Why not? You'd killed two men and kept yourself in the clear. I have an idea that you like killing men. The real payoff for you wasn't the thirty thousand. It was smothering Joe, and shooting Keith and Mario. The money was just a respectable excuse, like the fifty dollars to a call-girl who happens to be a nymphomaniac. You see, Galley, you're a murderer. You're different from ordinary people. You like different things. Ordinary people don't throw slugs into a dead man's back for the hell of it. They don't arrange their lives so they have to spend a week-end with a corpse. Did it give you a thrill, cooking your meals in the same room with him?''

I had finally got to her. She leaned out of the chair towards me and spoke between bared teeth: "You're a dirty liar! I couldn't eat. I hated it. I had to get out of the house. By Sunday night I was going crazy with it—Joe crouched in there with frost on him—" A dry sob racked her. She covered her face with her hands.

Somewhere in the distance a siren whined.

"That's right," I said. "Sunday night Speed came to babysit for you. Later, when I talked to him, he covered for you. It will convict him along with you."

She mastered her sobbing, and spoke behind her hands: "I should have saved a bullet for you."

"I served your purpose, didn't I? I couldn't have done it better if you had briefed me. Of course you set it up for me rather nicely, phoning Dowser Tuesday morning to let him know you were available. You must have trusted me pretty far at that. I know three or four private operators who wouldn't have followed you up to Dowser's house. Ironic, isn't it? I thought I was rescuing a maiden from a tower. Fall guys usually do, I guess. And the women who use them often make the mistake you did. They forget that even fall guys have minds of their own, until they fall for keeps." I looked down at Mario, and her gaze followed mine. Her fingers were still spread across her face, as if she needed them to hold it together.

The siren rose nearer and higher, building a thin arch of sound across the desert.

"It's sort of sad about you," I said. "All that energy and ingenuity wasted, because you had to tie it in with murder. Now before the police get here, do you want to tell me where the money is? I need it for a client, and if I get it I'll give you the best break I can."

"Go to hell." Her eyes burned furiously between her fingers. "They won't be able to hold me, you know that. They can't prove anything, not a thing. I'm innocent, do you hear me?"

I heard her.

The siren whooped like a wolf in the street. Headlights swept the window.

36

After Galley was taken away, a deputy named Runceyvall and I spent an hour or so going over the house. Mario had left a trail of blood across the kitchen floor and out the back door to the attached garage. We followed it and found the place where the gun had been cached, behind a loose board in the wall between the garage and the house. It contained a box of .45 cartridges, but no money. We found only one other thing of any significance: a couple of black hairs stuck to the interior wall of the deep-freeze. I told Runceyvall to seal it shut, and explained why. Runceyvall thought the whole thing was delightful.

Shortly after two I checked in at the Oasis Inn for the rest of the night. The clerk informed me that Mrs. Fellows was still registered. I asked to be called at eight.

I was. When I had showered and looked at my beard in the bathroom mirror and put on the same dirty clothes, I strolled across the lawn to Marjorie's bungalow. It was a dazzling morning. The grass looked as fresh as paint. Beyond a palm-leaf fence at the rear of the enclosure, a red tractor was pulling a cultivator up and down through a grove of date-palms that stood squat against the sky. High above them in ultramarine space, too high to be identified, a single bird circled on still wings. I thought it was an eagle or a hawk, and I thought of Galley.

Marjorie was breakfasting alfresco under a striped orange beach umbrella. She had on a Japanese kimono that harmonized with the umbrella, if nothing else. At the table with her a gray-headed man in shorts was munching diligently on a piece of toast.

She glanced up brightly when I approached, her round face glowing with sunburn and *Gemütlichkeit*: "Why, Mr. Archer, what a nice surprise! We were just talking about you, and wondering where you were."

"I slept here last night. Checked in late, and thought I wouldn't disturb you."

"Now wasn't that thoughtful," she said to the gray-headed man. "George, this is Mr. Archer. My husband, Mr. Archer— my ex, I guess I should say." Surprisingly, the large kimonoed body produced a girlish titter.

George stood up and gave me a brisk hand-shake. "Glad to know you, Archer. I've heard a lot about you." He had a thin flat chest, a sedentary stomach, a kind bewildered face.

"I've heard a lot about you. From Marjorie."

"You have?" He bestowed a loving look on the top of her head. "I feel darn silly in these shorts. She made me wear 'em. Oh well, as long as there's nobody here from Toledo—" He gazed short-sightedly around him, seeking spies.

"You look handsome in them, George. Pull in your stomach now. I love you in them." She turned to me with a queenly graciousness: "Please sit down, Mr. Archer. Have you had your breakfast? Let me order you some. George, bring Mr. Archer a chair from the porch and order more ham and eggs." George marched away with his stomach held tautly in, his head held high.

"I didn't expect to find him here."

"Neither did I. Isn't it wonderful? He saw my name in the papers and flew right down from Toledo on the first plane, just like a movie hero. I almost fainted yesterday when he walked in. To think that he really cares! Of course it was somewhat embarrassing last night. He had to sleep in a separate bungalow because we're not legally married yet.''

"Yet? Don't you mean 'any more'?''

"Yet.'' She blushed rosier. "We're flying to San Francisco at noon to pick up the car there, and then we'll drive over to Reno and be married. They don't make you wait in Reno and George says he won't wait a single minute longer than necessary.''

"Congratulations, but won't there be legal difficulties? You can have your marriage to Speed annulled, of course, since he married you under a false name. Only that will take time, even in Nevada.''

"Haven't you heard?'' Her face, blank and unsmiling now, showed the strain she was under. "The San Francisco police recovered my Cadillac last night. He left it in the middle of the Golden Gate Bridge.''

"No.''

"Yes, he's dead. Several persons saw him jump.''

It hit me hard, though Speed meant nothing to me. Now there were four men violently dead, five if I counted Mosquito. Galley and I between us had swept the board clean.

"You didn't find him, did you?'' she was saying. "You didn't reach him?''

"I beg your pardon?''

"I mean, you had nothing to do with his suicide? If I thought he did it because I hunted him down—it would be dreadful, wouldn't it? I couldn't face it.'' She shut her eyes and looked like a well-fed baby blown up huge.

There was only one possible answer: "I didn't find him.''

She breathed out. "I'm so relieved, so glad. I don't give a hang for the money, now that I've got George back. I suppose it was swept out to sea with his body. George says we can probably deduct it from our income tax anyway.''

George stepped off the porch with a deck-chair. "Is somebody using my name in vain?'' he called out cheerfully.

She smiled in response: "I was just telling Mr. Archer how wonderful it is to have you back, darling. It's like waking up from a nightmare. Did you order the food?''

"Coming right up.''

"I'm afraid I can't stay,'' I said.

They were nice people, hospitable and rich. I couldn't stand their company for some reason, or eat their food. My mind was still fixed on death, caught deep in its shadow. If I stayed I'd have to tell them things that they wouldn't like. Things that would spoil their fun, if anything could spoil their fun.

"Must you go? I'm so sorry." She was already reaching for her bag. "Anyway, you must let me pay you for your time and trouble."

"Fine. A hundred dollars will do it."

"I'm sorry it turned out the way it did. It's hardly fair to you." She rose and pressed the money into my hand.

"Marjorie's taken quite a shine to you, Archer. She's actually a very remarkable woman. I never realized before what a very remarkable woman Marjorie is."

"Go on with you." She pushed George playfully.

"You are. You know you are." He pushed her back.

"I'm the silliest fat old woman in the world." She tried to push him again but he clung to her hand.

"Good-bye. Good luck. Give my regards to Toledo."

I left them playing and laughing like happy children. Above the date-palms, half-hidden in space, the unknown bird described its dark circles.

The case ended where it began, among the furniture in Mrs. Lawrence's sitting room. It was noon by then. The dim little room was pleasant after the heat of the desert. Mrs. Lawrence herself was pleasant enough, though she looked haggard. The police had come and gone.

We sat together like strangers mourning at the funeral of a common friend. She was wearing a rusty black dress. Even her stockings were black. Her drawn and sallow cheeks were spottily coated with white powder. She offered me tea which I refused because I had just eaten. Her speech and movements were slower but she hadn't changed. Nothing would change her. She sat like a monument with her fists clenched on her knees:

"My daughter is perfectly innocent, of course. As I told Lieutenant Gary this morning, she wouldn't hurt a hair of anyone's head. When she was a child, I couldn't even force her to swat a fly, not if her life depended on it." Her eyes were sunk deep in her head, under brows like stony caverns. "You believe her innocent." It was a statement.

"I hope she is."

"Of course. She's never been well-liked. Girls who are

pretty *and* clever are never well-liked. After her father died and our money went, she withdrew more and more into herself. She lived a dream-life all through high school and that didn't help to make her popular. It earned her enemies, in fact. More than once they tried to get her into trouble. Even in the hospital it happened. There were unfounded accusations from various people who resented Galley's having had a distinguished father—"

"What sort of accusations?"

"I wouldn't taint my tongue with them, or offend your ears, Mr. Archer. I know that Galley is inherently good, and that's enough. She always has been good, and she is now. I learned many years ago to close my ears to the base lying chatter of the world." Her mouth was like iron.

"I'm afraid your conviction isn't enough. Your daughter is in a cell with a great deal of firm evidence against her."

"Evidence! A wild fabrication the police made up to conceal their own incompetence. They shan't use my daughter for a scapegoat."

"Your daughter murdered her husband," I said. It was the hardest speech I ever uttered. "The only question is, what are you going to do about it? Do you have any money?"

"A little. About two hundred dollars. You are quite mistaken about Galley's guilt, however. I realize that things look black for my girl. But as her mother I know that she is absolutely incapable of murder."

"We won't argue. Two hundred dollars isn't enough. Even with twenty thousand, and the best defenders in southern California, she wouldn't get off with less than second-degree murder. She's going to spend years in prison anyway. Whether she spends the rest of her life there depends on just one thing: her defense in Superior Court."

"I can raise some money on this house, I believe."

"It's mortgaged, isn't it?"

"Yes, but I do have an equity—"

"I have some money here." I took Dowser's folded bill from my watch pocket and scaled it into her lap. "It's money I have no use for."

Her mouth opened and shut. "Why?"

"She needs a break. I'm going to have to testify against her."

"You are kind. You can't afford this." Tears came into her

eyes like water wrung from stone. "You must believe that Galatea is innocent, to do this."

"No. I was police-trained and the harness left its marks on me. I know she's guilty, and I can't pretend I don't. But I feel responsible in a way. For you, if not for her."

She understood me. The tears made tracks on her cheeks. "If only you'd believe she's innocent. If only someone would believe me."

"She'll need twelve and she won't get them. Did you see the papers this morning?"

"Yes. I saw them." She leaned forward, crumpling the bill in her lap. "Mr. Archer."

"Is there something I can do?"

"No, nothing more. You are being so good, I really feel I can trust you. I must tell you—" She rose abruptly and went to the sewing machine beside the window. Raising the lid, she reached far inside and brought out an oblong packet wrapped in brown paper. "Galley gave me this to keep for her, Tuesday morning. She made me promise not to tell anyone, but things are different now, aren't they? It may be evidence in her favor. I haven't opened it."

I broke the tape that sealed one end, and saw the hundred-dollar bills. It was Galley's thirty thousand. Speed's thirty thousand. Marjorie's thirty thousand. Thirty thousand dollars that had lain hidden in an old lady's sewing machine while men were dying for it.

I handed it back to her. "It's evidence, all right: the money she killed her husband for."

"That's impossible."

"Impossible things are happening all the time."

She looked down at the money in her hand. "Galley really killed him?" she whispered. "What shall I do with this?"

"Burn it."

"When we need the money so badly?"

"Either burn it, or take it to a lawyer and let him contact the police. You may be able to make a deal of some kind. It's worth trying."

"No," she said. "I will not. My girl is innocent, and Providence is watching over her. I know that now. God has provided for her in her hour of greatest need."

I stood up and moved to the door. "Do as you like. If the

police discover the source of the money, it will wreck your daughter's defense."

She followed me down the hallway. "They shan't know a thing about it. And you won't tell them, Mr. Archer. You believe that my daughter is innocent, even though you won't admit it."

I knew that Galley Lawrence was guilty as hell.

The colored fanlight over the door washed her mother in sorrowful purple. She opened the door, and noon glared in on her face. The tear-tracks resembled the marks of sparse rain on a dusty road.

"You won't tell them?" Her voice was broken.

"No."

I looked back from the sidewalk. She was standing on the steps, using the brown paper package to shield her eyes from the cruel light. Her other hand rose in farewell, and dropped to her side.

ABOUT THE AUTHOR

"ROSS MACDONALD" was the pseudonym of Kenneth Millar. Born outside San Francisco in 1915, he grew up in Vancouver, British Columbia. He returned to the U.S. in 1938, earned a Ph.D. at the University of Michigan, served in the Navy during World War II and published his first novel in 1944. He served as president of the Mystery Writers of America and was awarded both the Silver Dagger award by the Crime Writers' Association of Great Britain and the Grand Master Award by the Mystery Writers of America. He was married to the novelist Margaret Millar. He died in 1983.